Asylum

by

Tamera Lawrence

Asylum

Cover Art by *The Wild Rose Press, Inc.*

The Wild Rose Press, Inc.
PO Box 708
Adams Basin, NY 14410-0708
Visit us at www.thewildrosepress.com

Publishing History
First Edition, 2021
Trade Paperback ISBN 978-1-5092-3522-3
Digital ISBN 978-1-5092-3523-0

Published in the United States of America

"Five more minutes, please…"

The bully punched Kyle's foot as it neared him. "Get off that swing!"

Thankfully, Kyle's sneaker absorbed the blow. Still, he continued to pump his legs. He went higher. "Just four more minutes," Kyle yelled. But the bully had moved his position, now behind the swing set.

Real fear hit home. Kyle dragged his sneakers in the dirt, trying to stop the swing. But then the bully's hands slammed into his back, forcing the swing upward.

"I'm getting off!" Kyle yelled, twisting around. "I'm stopping the swing."

"No," the bully said. "Keep swinging. I'll push you."

Another blow to the back. Now the swing shifted sideways. Kyle grabbed tightly onto the chain. Again, another attack. The swing went higher. After the fifth blow to his spine, Kyle jumped from the swing. For a second, he flew into the air and then, smash. He hit the ground. Something sharp ripped into his knee. He rolled over, crying out.

Blood soaked through his jeans. He held his knee, staring at the damage.

"Looks like someone got a boo boo," the bully said, nudging Kyle with his foot. He leaned closer and pointed at the wound. "Poor baby. Maybe, next time you'll get off when I tell you to."

Dedication

This book is dedicated to my son, Tim, who brought home a pair of boots from the original Pennhurst State School & Hospital and ignited this creepy tale. Thanks, Tim, for giving me insight into urban exploring and sharing some of your adventures.

Prelude

Rose Hill Asylum, Pennsylvania, 1984

Beneath the cover of darkness, Kyle Hampton dove behind a wooden crate. The nine-year-old huddled against the barrier, bracing himself against the balls of his feet. The crate was just high enough to block him from view. He peeked around the box, fingers gripping the slats, waiting for the inevitable. Time ticked away.

Someone moved into the cellar, footsteps heavy and deliberate. Kyle panicked, pressing his palm against his mouth to still his breath. Hot tears scaled his eyes, but he dared not cry.

"Kyle?"

Kyle pressed his body closer to the crate. His mind screamed, *don't see, don't see*. His clogged nose stifled his breathing. Above him, the ceiling light flickered to life. The illumination pierced the gloomy cellar, casting his shadow against the wall.

"I know you're in here," the teenager whispered. "Come out, come out, wherever you are."

Soft laughter rolled from his seeker's throat.

Snot dripped onto Kyle's top lip. Salty moisture gnawed his broken skin. He felt Benny's gaze upon him, or at least in his general direction.

"If you twitch, you'll get stitched." The taunt came in a slow, steady draw. Benny creeped around the room, looking behind boxes and crates. "Come out, boy. Don't be such a baby. If you keep me waiting, I'll lock you up in the hidey hole."

The "hole" was a closet with nothing in it but an old chair. It was the darkness and isolation Kyle feared the most. He had spent hours in the hole. At one point, a full day before he was rescued by one of the janitors. It was alleged the hole was haunted by a dead boy who had jumped out of a third floor window. The specter would stand behind you and poke your spine with a razor-tipped fingernail. Some of the kids claimed they had the marks to prove it, scars and holes in their skin. It was a terrifying prospect.

He shouldn't have taken the soda cans. Kyle's chin dropped to his chest. Whatever had possessed him to steal from Benny in the first place? The bully coveted his treats. Benny hid snacks under his cot, mostly stolen from Rose Hill residents. Kyle had taken a chance, grabbed the two sodas, and had raced off, hoping somebody else would get the blame. Obviously, he'd been seen. Someone had squealed on him, and now Benny was seeking retribution.

"I'm waiting, Kyle."

He was just fooling himself. Benny would find him. The elder boy knew every crook and cranny, every hiding spot. The waiting was worse than the pummeling he'd surely receive. He hated to beg, but it was his only defense. On shaky knees, Kyle stood and stepped out of the shadows.

His tormentor grinned, rubbing his hands together. A glint lay in his green eyes.

"I'm here," Kyle said, hands held out in a plea. "Please, don't put me in the hole."

"Are you telling me what to do, boy?"

"No," Kyle said without conviction. He hated being called boy but when the aides weren't around, Benny liked to play he was in charge. No one knew the true extent of his bullying.

"I'll do whatever I want to you," Benny said. "Do you think you can stop me?"

"It was just one soda."

"One?" Benny's mouth twisted into a smirk. "It was two. Do you think I don't know my own stuff? Where's Roy? I know he drank a can. I want him."

Kyle shuddered, swallowing hard. When he fled into the asylum's tunnels, he had assumed Roy had run off in another direction and escaped. It was hard enough worrying about himself, let alone Roy. Could his brother have followed him?

"Roy didn't take your soda," Kyle said, lifting his chin. "He was just my lookout. I drank both of them. He didn't even know they were yours."

"Liar," Benny said. "I don't care if he did drink it. He was your lookout, so that makes him just as guilty."

Hatred filled Kyle's heart, overrunning his fear. Roy was only seven years old, two years younger than he. The boy still sucked his thumb and wet the bed. But Benny wouldn't care. He liked tormenting anyone smaller than himself.

"Roy's not with me," Kyle said. "I don't know where he is."

"Liar," the teen said, pointing a finger into Kyle's face. "I want Roy now, or so help me God, you'll spend a week in the hole."

Another tear slipped down Kyle's cheek as he tried to think of a solution.

Benny's face darkened into a scowl. His eyebrows dipped low.

"I'll tell on you if you hurt us," Kyle said. His fear for Roy surpassed his own.

Shocked, Benny's eyes morphed into saucers. His eyes glowed in rage as his mouth twisted into a sneer. Two seconds later, Kyle yelped as Benny's fingers bit into his arm, dragging him along the floor, then dropped him face-first. His chin hit the cold floor, jarring his teeth.

"Tell who?" Benny shoved his foot into his back, digging in his heel. "Who you gonna tell?"

Kyle begged him to stop, the pain unbearable.

"I do what I want around here. You don't know who you're messing with. You know what happens to tattlers?"

"No, please. I won't say anything. I swear!" Kyle cried out as the boot tip jabbed his spine.

"Now I want Roy," the teen said. "And I want him now."

"Please. Just leave him alone. It's my fault. I made him be the lookout."

"Roy?" Ignoring Kyle's plea, Benny's voice boomed across the room. "It's going to go worse for you if you don't make an appearance. I know you're in here."

A muffled sob came from the distant side of the room.

"See that?" the teen said, shoving Kyle one last time with his boot. "Roy was here all along."

There was movement in the shadows. Kyle lifted his head, staring at Roy, who appeared from behind a chair, moving into the light. Blotchy-faced, the boy's freckles stood out against his pale skin. Dirty cobwebs clung to his blond head.

"Very wise, Roy." A grin slowly curved Benny's mouth. "Now we'll work this out, boys. Just the three of us. Stealing is a harsh offense. I know treats can be hard to come by around here." The teen's eyes glued onto Roy. Then with a jerk of his thumb, he glanced down at Kyle. "Get off your knees, boy. I'll deal with you later. You can go."

"But what about Roy?"

"Me and Roy are going to have a little talk. Now move it. Go upstairs. And don't look back."

Helplessly, Kyle observed Roy. The boy's thin shoulders shook in fear.

"Let him come with me," Kyle said. He rose to his feet, panic for Roy rooting him to the spot. "He's just a little kid."

For speaking out, he was slapped. Face stinging, Kyle yelped as he was flung onto the hard floor. Blood filled his mouth. He rolled over and sat up.

"It's okay, Kyle." Roy's voice sounded oddly flat. "Just go."

Stunned, Kyle gaped at him. So did Benny, who seemed pleased by the turn of events.

But then Roy's jaw stiffened, mouth set into an angry line. His clouded eyes cleared, replaced by defiance. "Go, Kyle. I'll be fine."

"You heard him. Now get." Benny reached down, hauling Kyle to his feet. He shoved him toward the door. "And keep going."

Dodging another blow, Kyle found himself forced into the corridor. He turned, helplessly staring at Roy.

Now Benny had one hand gripped around Roy's

arm, forcing him toward Kyle and the doorway. But then he was reaching for the door, slamming it shut in Kyle's face.

Kyle stood by the metal barrier, listening. Nothing.

"Leave him alone!" he yelled, kicking the door. His toe stung from the abuse. "He didn't take the soda. I did. I did." Softly, he exhaled. "I took it."

Then he was running through the endless corridor, moving as fast as he could. Tears streamed down his face as his hands balled into fists.

He'd tell. Faces swam in his mind. But who'd listen?

He stopped running.

No one. That's who.

Chapter One

Twenty-eight years later, Rose Hill

In its deplorable condition, Rose Hill Asylum was shocking. The campus was overgrown, appearing desolate and forsaken. Inside most of the brick buildings, it was worse. Mold and decay lingered in the air, eerily familiar and still just as gross.

Kyle Hampton braced himself against the tunnel wall, gathering what little courage he could muster. Rose Hill had been a bad mistake. He didn't even know where he was. The corridor beneath the catwalk was like an endless maze, and he was stuck within its core. He had plunged into the ordeal without giving it much thought. Now he was stuck finishing what he and Randy had started or at least until he found his way out. His headlamp barely made a dent in the darkness.

He closed his eyes. Damn it. Why the heck did he ever let Randy talk him into this trip down memory lane? There was a reason he'd forgotten this hell hole.

The obscurity of the tunnel encroached on both sides of him, teasing his eyesight with what lay beyond. Memories came in sordid waves, his imagination on overdrive. At any moment, he expected a whisper, "If you twitch, you'll get stitched."

His headlamp dimmed and thrust him into the inky gloom. His stomach turned into slush. The endless tunnel system had been designed with an underground entrance to each of the buildings on the campus. Each structure had a basement with an access door to the tunnel. It was those doorways he sought.

Reaching an adjacent tunnel, he rounded a corner. His light penetrated the shadows. An old, corroded bed lit up beneath his beam. A naked porcelain doll lay on a moldy mattress; one remaining eye gawked at him. Its broken body held fractured lines.

An odd noise sounded farther away, just out view. His stomach lurched, bile nuzzling his throat.

"Kyle," a voice shouted from the dark.

Kyle jumped, lost his footing and fell, hard. Cursing, he stared up at a human being – one with a smirk on his face. "You scared the hell out of me. Where'd you come from?"

"Searching the next tunnel," Randy said. His face was smudged with dirt, dark hair in disarray. "I couldn't find you. Where the heck did you go?"

"Exploring, remember?" Kyle held back that he'd been lost and was hoping Randy would find him. He'd never hear the end of it. "Were you here a minute ago?"

"No. Why?"

He stared hard at Randy's lean mug. It wouldn't be the first time he screwed with him. Randy would never grow up; it was a fact he'd come to accept. "Just hearing things."

"Ghosts?" Randy's laughter boomed along the corridor. "I told you this place was haunted."

"Whatever," Kyle said, ignoring his smug grin. He rose to his feet, rubbing his back. "That's what everyone says when they can't explain something. Your spooks can stay the hell away from me."

Kyle hated the paranormal crap, but he supposed if a place was going to be haunted, Rose Hill would fit the bill. Over its eighty-year reign, hundreds of people had died at the asylum, mostly from their diseases or handicaps. Botched operations or wrong medication also gave a helping hand to a person's demise.

Over the years, he had lied to himself, allowing himself to believe Rose Hill wasn't really as bad as it was. He had a few good memories, but he realized they were distorted, maybe his way of coping.

"Which way?" Kyle mumbled.

"There," Randy said, flashing his light down an adjacent hallway.

Kyle followed him, already on edge. It was hard enough dwelling in the darkness with every morbid thought coming back to haunt him. He didn't want to dwell on the past, at least not at the moment.

Kyle adjusted the weight of his backpack. This was Randy's second or third trip to Rose Hill. His stories had enticed Kyle into coming to take a look himself. It had been years since he'd been at the compound. He'd been a teenager. Now that he was older, he thought he could handle it. He shook his head in disgust, the truth like a dagger. There was a reason he had let his childhood go. Rose Hill held a crappy legacy. Over the years, the state had failed to upgrade the massive buildings or tend to its disabled residents. People were rotting away in their beds, basically fending for themselves. Instead of improving lives, Rose Hill stole their souls. It was disheartening not to be able to do anything about it and now it was too late.

"I know living here sucked." Randy leaned a rugged shoulder against the damp wall, whistling between his teeth as he exhaled. "You got out so what's the big deal?"

"The big deal is that this place should've never have existed in the first place," Kyle said. "No child should've been forced to live here."

"It was a place to get rid of a responsibility." Randy's words were softly spoken, but straight to the point. "The unwanted."

Kyle's jaw clenched, a bitter retort on the edge of his tongue. He and his brother, Roy, were born at Rose Hill. It wasn't an easy life for a kid, lost in a sea of many. His mother was a ward of the state. Her mental status would not allow her to care for her sons. For the first few years, they lived in the same cottage, but after her death, Kyle had been moved into another section. He and Roy had grown distant. Kyle began spending weekends with the Hampton family, who later adopted him. It was that situation that tore the brothers apart. When Roy found out Kyle was moving away, his brother's jealousy turned to hatred. Before the final departure, Roy had shared the sentiment on numerous occasions. Their relationship had ended, and they had not seen each other since.

Who was he fooling? If Roy wanted to find him, he'd have done it by now. Still, he was puzzled as to what happened to his brother and how his life had turned out.

Kyle shook his head, hating his errant thoughts. He hadn't thought about Roy for a few years, or at least for more than a few seconds at a time. His brother wasn't part of his everyday life. Truthfully, he wasn't sure if he even wanted him to be. But now touring Rose Hill, he expected to see Roy's face around every corner. Would he even recognize him? Roy was a man, not a kid.

It had taken years for Rose Hill to close down. The asylum began to dismantle, lawsuits on the rise. The children were the first to go. They were either sent back to their families or to other state-run facilities. Roy had been taken away; to where, he hadn't a clue. At the time of closure, he was already settled into his new life with the Hampton family.

Kyle lowered his head, throat convulsing. He supposed in some way he considered Randy as his brother. They'd been friends for years. Randy had been dumped at Rose Hill as an orphan. Randy's father had been in jail, and his mother had run off with another man. Although their situations were a bit different, Rose Hill life had bound them together.

"You were lucky to get out of here when you did," Randy said. "I wasn't so lucky."

"Don't think I'm not grateful," Kyle said, leveling his gaze. "I am. I wish I could've taken you with me. There wasn't anything I could do about it. You seemed to have adjusted despite it all."

Randy shrugged, glancing away.

Kyle drew in a ragged breath. "Just forget it for now. I want to get done with this."

They trudged through the tunnel. Articles of clothing, broken furniture and trash littered the floors. Fetid air teased Kyle's lungs as he moved. His light shined upon a broken doorway, a metal door hanging precariously from rusted hinges. Inside, a huge basement greeted them, the rooms broken into sections.

"I forgot how huge this place is," Randy said. "We could explore here all week and not see everything."

Kyle grimaced. He'd seen enough of everything. It

was all beginning to look the same. Randy led the way to a rear staircase that led to the first floor. The muted daylight was a welcomed sight, even though it displayed the building's demise.

On the first floor, they stopped at the first room on the right. It was once an office. Kyle stood in the doorway, absorbing the room. A large stained desk sat against the wall. Old papers were thrown all over the floor, as if a mini tornado had descended upon the chamber.

Impulsively, he yanked open the top desk drawer. A red rubber ball rolled across the cracked wood, hit the corner, and spun in a circle.

His heart hammered as he picked up the ball, clenching it in his palm. His mind dimmed into the past.

"Let's play Jacks," Louie said, grabbing Kyle's arm. The boy held a bag filled with jacks and a rubber ball. They ran over to the sidewalk and plopped down across from one another.

"You first," Louie said, dumping out the bag. He quickly spread the jacks out evenly.

Kyle grabbed the rubber ball and gave it a bounce. The game began.

After several minutes, two teenage girls began watching them. Kyle began getting bolder with bouncing the ball while scooping up the jacks with lightning fingers. Suddenly, the ball hit against his knee, bounced against the concrete and then rolled under the sidewalk railing. It disappeared into the thick grass. Before he could blink, the two girls scrambled after it.

Kyle ducked between the railing; his eyes glued

onto the older teens. The one had her back to him, a suspicious bulge in her pocket. She nudged the other girl with her elbow, dipped her head to one side and pierced Kyle with her blue eyes. "Guess it's gone."

"What's that in your pocket?" Kyle said as Louie joined him.

"Nothing," the girl said. She linked arms with the other girl, tugging her along.

"Let me see your pocket," Kyle said, following their quickened steps.

The braided teenager turned with a flounce, lifting her chin. She dipped her hand into her now flat pocket, yanking out the inside. "See, nothing's there."

"You took it out," Kyle said. He moved to her other side. Her other pocket was flat, but her hand was curved into a fist "Give me our ball."

"I don't have your ball, weirdo," she said. She giggled with her comrade and the two raced off.

For a moment, Kyle almost ran after them, but what was the use. They were bigger, stronger, and faster. He wouldn't have a prayer getting it back now.

"Sorry," Kyle mumbled to Louie, who looked about to cry. "I'll try to find you another ball."

Kyle blinked, shaking the bitter memory. Gingerly he squeezed the rubber ball between his thumb and forefinger. He dropped it onto the desk where it bounced and rolled off the edge. It continued across the floor, disappearing into a pile of crud.

"What are you doing?" Randy said, breaking into his thoughts.

"Nothing." They continued exploring the huge building. Most of the rooms held old furniture, shelving, and more garbage. The graffiti continued throughout the tour. They moved up to the second and third floor before descending back into the tunnels to look for more doorways to the other buildings.

"Look at that," Randy's flashlight lit upon a wheelchair, tucked into a darkened corner. Thick with dust, its rusted wheels had seen better days. "Check me out." He sat on the seat. Immediately, it collapsed, spilling him onto the damp floor. He broke out in laughter.

"Serves you right," Kyle said, moving past him. "Ass."

They entered another doorway, which led to another basement, divided into numerous areas. Toys, clothes, and dust littered the floors. Wooden desks and rubber chairs were sporadically positioned.

Randy flashed his light across the main corridor. "Is this the Kellogg building?"

"Yes," Kyle said. "I was put in here with the nonverbals for a few days as a punishment."

"Same," Randy said. "It wasn't so bad though; peace and quiet. I stole stuff they couldn't use."

"Like what?"

"Stuff their families left, food, comics and other odds and ends."

"That's pretty low," Kyle said, gritting his teeth.

"Oh, like you never stole anything." Randy laughed, slapping his knee.

Kyle pushed by him, holding back a bitter retort. Nothing he'd say would matter anyway. Yes, he stole, but only from those who deserved it, not from helpless people. It made a difference in his book. With burning thoughts, he entered a rear room. A ping pong table sat against the wall, littered with clothing. He fingered the pile, picked up several shirts and threw them aside. A box of shoes sat beneath the table, catching his eye. He dug through the items and a boot stood out. He sat it on the ping pong table and shined his light over it. Not too bad. It appeared a man's eleven. He shook it, checked the soles. A few scattered stones fell out. With a rapid heart, he searched the bin, finding the other boot.

"What's that?

Kyle jumped, twisting around. "Will you stop creeping up on me? It's not funny." He ignored the innocent shrug Randy gave him. "It's a pair of boots. I'm taking them home."

"What for?"

"They're in decent shape." Kyle tied the laces together and slung them over his shoulder. "I'll use them for work."

"No, you won't." Randy moved closer, sizing them up. "Give them to me. I will actually use them."

"No." Kyle tightened his grip on his prize. Randy was always collecting junk, hoarding it. He doubted Randy even wanted the boots. It was all about getting one up on someone else. He supposed it was an asylum trait that'd stuck with Randy. Always preparing for that unexpected emergency.

They left the building, walked through the tunnels and entered another basement. Similar in proportion to the other buildings, this cellar was also cut up into various rooms. In the last room, the limited sunlight filtered in through the windows. Colorful artwork was displayed on all four walls, childish in style. Using an old crate, they stood on the box and climbed out the way they had come in, through the jimmied window.

Outside, the wind tore through the trees in the courtyard, scattering auburn leaves. As they moved into the center of the campus, Kyle looked over his shoulder and paused. Out of a third floor window, a cluster of bats burst into freedom. Their bodies spread out in a black wave, lifted, and then hovered in a circle around the Kellogg building.

Brow furrowed, Kyle watched as they dispersed into the horizon.

"Did you see all those bats?"

Randy turned around, scoping the landscape. "No."

"There had to be a dozen of them."

"I'm sure there's plenty more," Randy replied. "They got access to all these buildings."

Kyle didn't answer. He held tighter to the boots slung over his shoulder. His stomach clenched as a biting chill skimmed his spine. Yes. He should never have returned to Rose Hill.

Chapter Two

As soon as Kyle entered the kitchen, the grim lines of Beth's mouth warned of her mood; angry. His wife moved past him, clutching their infant daughter. She balanced the baby in her arms as she stirred a spoon inside a steaming pot of scented chicken soup.

"I'm sorry, I lost track of time." Kyle hunched against the door jamb, aware of his filthy appearance. Her stark expression never changed, busy in her task.

A stretch of silence followed.

Just when he thought she was going to ignore him, hoping that she would, she said, "Don't bother with your apology."

She dropped the spoon, put the baby into her infant swing and pressed the on button. The seat began to rock as Samantha squirmed.

"I couldn't call." Defeated, he lifted his hands. "My phone couldn't get a signal in the tunnels. I didn't know what time it was."

"Forget it." She stood; arms crossed against her ample breasts. A lock of auburn hair hung over her right eye. She shoved it behind her ear. "I've had a rotten day. I'm tired, and the baby fussed all afternoon. Not that you care."

"I do care…"

"I had to cancel my hairdresser appointment."

He rubbed his jaw, considering her as she tucked a

blanket around the baby. Damn. He'd forgotten. She had reminded him twice about it yesterday. He had gotten caught up in the asylum.

"Couldn't your mom do it?"

"She's sick," she replied, obviously annoyed. "Besides, you were the one that said you'd do it. It's not her responsibility."

"Sorry."

Beth rolled her eyes and sat on a kitchen chair. She scanned him critically, like someone dissecting an insect. After a moment, she said, "My hairdresser can take me tomorrow morning. Do you think you can remember that?"

"Sure." Her sarcasm almost unleashed his rising temper. Better to leave her alone. He turned, one foot through the threshold.

"Aren't you going to tell me about your trip to Rose Hill?"

"What's to tell?" He paused, shrugging. "It's overgrown. Trash and graffiti is everywhere. Everything is wet, some of it moldy."

"That's it?" Her eyes morphed into saucers. "You left early this morning. You've been over there all day, and that's all there is to tell?"

"Pretty much," he said. "Most of the buildings are boarded up. It's dark in the tunnels. It takes a while to get your bearings."

"Well, I suppose I should be glad you weren't arrested for trespassing, and I didn't have to pick you up from jail." Her brows lifted, arms pressed under her breasts.

"That would've have gotten you out of the house." He grinned in an effort to break her mood.

"For real?" Her mouth dropped. "You're not funny."

"Okay, truthfully." He reconsidered his words. "Rose Hill was depressing. I barely recognized it. No one has touched it all these years. It's falling apart, a total mess. I can't believe I lived there. I went to see the Maxwell building, the area where I lived. The ceiling's partially caved in. There's broken furniture, old beds. Everything is morbid. I'm sorry I went. Happy?"

"No, not if it upsets you," she said, relaxing her shoulders.

"The worst part is Roy," he said. "I can't stop thinking about him."

"That's to be expected, I suppose." Her eyes turned softer. "You never talk about him."

"It's been so many years. I supposed I've moved on, but now it's bothering me. He is my brother. It's not right how things were left between us." He ran his hand over his jaw. "I need to know what happened to him. If he doesn't want anything to do with me, then at least I know I tried. What do you think?"

"I think it's a good idea, she replied. "I'd like to meet him. Of course, we have to find him first. I can check around for you."

"That would be great." Concealing his frayed emotions, Kyle's gaze slid over his daughter, who sucked noisily on her fist. "How's my sweetie?"

"She's fine now." She grabbed several envelopes, sliding them across the table. "I picked up your father's mail. There are a lot of bills. There has to be a solution."

"My boss recommended a realtor," he replied. "The house will be listed in the next week or so. I'm pricing it to sell. It's just hard to let it go."

"There's nothing you can do about it," she said. "Even if Pop recovers from the stroke, he can't afford the mounting bills, and neither can we."

"I know," he said, slouching against the wall. He had been trying to think of a way of keeping his dad's house, but it was a lost cause. There was no way he could continue to pay for two properties. In a way, it was letting go of hope, something he'd been clinging to.

"It's a nice house, a bit dated, but solid." Beth stretched out her arms, yawning. "Someone will buy it. Did you know there's dry blood on the back of your shirt?"

"No." He twisted and pulled his flannel toward his chest. Blood splattered the bottom hem. He removed his shirt, turned and showed her his chilled skin. "Do I have a cut?"

"A long scratch," she said. "It doesn't look too deep."

He shrugged, throwing the shirt over his shoulder. "I must've caught it on a nail."

Five minutes later, he paused by the bathroom mirror, staring at his grimy features. His blond hair appeared gray from the added layer of grunge. Stepping into the shower, the hot water cascaded over him, washing off his troubles. Beth had a right to be mad at him, but he'd promised Randy weeks ago that he'd go to Rose Hill. She hated when he hung out with Randy. It was a problem with no solution. He was stuck in the middle of two people who hated one another. Lord knew, he'd tried to soothe things over, without any success.

He soaped up a washcloth, plying away at his skin. *Cleanliness is next to godliness.* Before he could catch it, the words slipped through his mind. How many times had he heard that phrase at Rose Hill? He supposed it was a way to make a kid want to bathe, but bath time was hardly a fun affair. It was embarrassing. Modesty wasn't protected. Fights broke out.

Rose Hill had taken its toll. He knew it would, yet still he'd gone. Some of the things Randy alleged pissed him off. So what if he'd been adopted? That didn't mean his life had been easy. It had been rough being uprooted, even from a place like Rose Hill. Living with a new family wasn't all a fairytale. He'd spent a lot of time worrying that they'd return him to Rose Hill. It was stressful trying to be a perfect kid. He closed his eyes, allowing the memories to flow.

Like a new puppy, his newly acquired relatives had to come take a peek. A party had been planned; his name sprawled across a cake. The Hamptons had a large family, aunts, uncles and cousins. There was a new grandmother, who was very frail, but she had a hearty laugh. They brought him gifts, patted his head, smiled at him. At first, he'd liked the attention, but then he overheard their questions, concerns.

"Is there anything you should be worried about?" an elderly woman asked his pop. "You know you never can tell if there's been damage." She nodded knowingly. "We don't need any more family issues."

"There's no concerns," Pop replied, mouth grimacing. "He's been screened."

Kyle sat in the recliner as the conversations continued around him. He began rocking the chair, blocking out their voices. Faster he went.

"Hey," a boy said, nudging his knee against the chair.

Kyle stopped the chair, staring at an older boy. Through a pair of thick glasses, the kid's squinty eyes assessed him. With a pudgy finger, the boy shoved the frame up the bridge of his nose.

Kyle didn't reply. He waited.

"Are you retarded?"

"What?" Shocked, Kyle's stomach lurched. He stared across the room, searching out Pop, but everyone was busy talking.

"I said are you retarded?" The boy's nose crinkled as his head lowered slightly, studying Kyle's features. "You don't look retarded."

"I'm not," Kyle said in a small voice.

"Would you know if you were?"

Kyle's mouth dropped, the nasty words hitting home. All of his life, as young as it was, he feared there was something wrong with him. Could there be? Would he even know it if there was?

"Go away." Kyle began rocking the chair. The motion pushed the boy's body away. He rocked harder; cheeks flamed. Still, the other child continued to stay put and gawk. Face frozen, eyes staring straight ahead, Kyle rocked faster. Now the chair's wooden base began to lift, causing a thumping noise. He didn't care.

"Kyle," Pop said, rushing over to him. "Stop that at once."

Kyle halted his movements. The room fell silent. Now they all stared at him. The dark-haired boy had retreated to a spot near the window, satisfaction in his features.

*"Would you like to go outside for some fresh air?"
Pop asked. "I think you need a breather." He smiled,
patting Kyle's hand. "Come on, we can have a catch."*

*The kindness of Pop's touch and the warmth of his
smile soothed his soul. Tears gathered in the corner of
his eyes. Hastily, he blinked them away.*

"I'd like that."

"Good," Pop said. "Let's go."

Rocking on the balls of his feet, Kyle opened his
eyes, staring at the water running over his toes. He
braced his right hand against the shower wall, ceasing
his movements, a source of solace in his youth. Thanks
to his new cousin Bradley, his self-esteem had taken a
major nose-dive. Living under the guise of normality
was excruciating—until he'd found sports. Baseball had
become his passion, his outlet. His adopted parents
were proud, which felt good. It also helped that Bradley
sucked at everything. Kyle let the past go, and no one
outside of his adoptive family or Randy knew of his
Rose Hill ties. It had been hard enough telling Beth,
although he'd given her a water-downed version. Being
a charity case was nothing to brag about.

Deliberately, he stood beneath the spray until the
water grew cold. When he exited the bathroom, he
paused by the nursery. Beth was sitting in the rocker,
breastfeeding. He paused in the doorway, face flushing.
He averted his gaze, swallowing the dry lump in his
throat.

"If you pump me a bottle, I'll get up with the baby
tonight," he said softly.

"Are you sure you can handle her?" Her chin lifted;
eyes full of doubt. "She's colicky."

"Of course." He moved away, bothered by her fears. Even if he couldn't handle Samantha, he'd tell her he could. Sleep deprivation definitely affected her. Like the weather, her mood swings were up and down. All the anticipation over Samantha's birth had faded. Now it was sleepless nights, poopy diapers, and engorged breasts. Their sex life was nonexistent. He missed being intimate. He wasn't sure how much more he could take.

Tiredly, Kyle went down to the living room, flicked on the television and fell asleep in the recliner. Sometime in the middle of the night, the baby's wails stirred through his dreams. He struggled to wake, but her persistence propelled him off the chair. Upstairs in the nursery, he picked up his squirmy daughter. Blonde and blue-eyed, she reminded him of his brother, Roy. Love swelled his heart. Samantha was a piece of his family, a part of them all, something good and untouched.

He sat in the recliner and fed the baby. He paced the room, rocking her in his arms. After a while, she quieted. Walking to the bassinet, he tucked her inside.

Kyle yawned and stretched. The hall clock chimed but sleep eluded him. Rose Hill lurked in his thoughts. Roy. Now that he had reconnected with his past, the asylum brandished its hold over him. Familiar dread had rooted deep; a painful reminder of his youth.

Moving into the foyer, he opened the closet door and grabbed the boots from Rose Hill. He spread a newspaper over the kitchen table and got to work. The scent of leather cleaner filled the room as he scrubbed the boots. They were aged, a deep, dark green. Stains marked the right boot. He worked at the spots, making little progress. He slid on the boots and strolled around the kitchen. They'd do. He needed another pair of boots, might as well use them for work.

He moved into the living room, peering down at the slumbering infant. Kissing his fingertip, he pressed it against her warm cheek. He settled into the recliner, admiring his boots from his vantage point.

It was only when Kyle heard his name that he cracked open an eye. Sunlight streamed in through the front blinds. Beth stood over him, hands on hips. A troubled line burrowed between her brows. At this rate, she'd make it permanent if she kept it up.

"What were you thinking?"

He opened both eyes and shifted in the chair. "About what?"

"Samantha."

"What about her?"

She pointed toward his chest. Samantha lay snuggled beneath his chin. She was asleep, fist partially tucked into her mouth.

"It's dangerous to sleep with a baby," Beth said. "She could've rolled off."

"That wouldn't have happened." He considered his daughter, touching her downy head. "I knew where she was the whole time. She's fine."

Beth lifted the baby, who woke abruptly. "There've been cases of babies suffocating. You don't take chances."

"I wasn't really sleeping…"

"Just stop already," she said. "If you hadn't been late to the hospital the day we were discharged, you'd have heard the nurse explicitly tell me not to sleep in bed with Samantha. But typical you had to be late, a no-show for over an hour."

"I had trouble with the car seat."

She slowly exhaled. "Your father told me you overslept."

"Not true." He shrugged. "I was in our bedroom. How could he know what I was doing?"

"Because he said he had to pound on the bedroom door." She soothed Samantha, who began to fuss. She paused, tilting her head. "Honestly, I don't know why you have such trouble owning up to the truth."

She had him. As she walked away, he thought about her words. Lying did come easy for him. It wasn't one of his finest traits. As a boy he'd learned how to skirt the truth. It was a protective measure. There were times at Rose Hill he'd had little choice but to lie. At times it meant survival.

"Honey," he yelled. "I still have trouble with the car seat."

Chapter Three

Stitches picked up his coffee cup and drained the contents. Spread out on the kitchen table, a current newspaper lay open. An image of an elderly woman standing by a gloomy building filled half the page. Rose Hill Asylum was for sale. Prime opportunity for a land developer, or so it said.

He nibbled his bottom lip; blood flowed as he licked it away.

Well, now that was unwelcome news. The place had been closed for over twenty-eight years. Why would someone want to buy such a liability? His long fingers tapped the tabletop. But then again there were a few habitable buildings. Salvageable. Someone with the funds could make it work.

Alarmed, he peered closer at the image. The woman's beady eyes bore into his. In a flash, he remembered her sour breath, breathing on him, her cold hands impacting his cheek.

"That old hag," he said, emotions hot. "She's still alive?"

He stood, turned on the kitchen faucet and dipped his hands in the water, rubbing at his bloody mouth. Get a grip. So, they interviewed Doris Goodwin, a former doctor at Rose Hill. The paper wanted her opinion on the controversy of selling the historical landmark. It figured she'd get her face on the front page. Who'd listen to her? She was a nobody. They'd have to get township approval for whatever zoning they wanted for the property. All of that would take time. There would be testing for ground contamination. There were so many buildings. To tear it all down would be costly.

Uncontrollably, his right eye twitched.

A train whistle spliced the room. His thoughts scattered. But no, there were no trains running in this area, not anymore. Again, the blast. This time, he knew; a car honking its horn. He looked out the window at the parking lot below his apartment. A boy and girl were riding bikes in the lot. A car had pulled in, driver's head out the window, shouting for them to move.

He studied the little girl, so beautiful in her braids, so perfect in her youth. Leaning against the windowsill, he pressed his head against the cool pane. A shock of adrenaline hit his belly, traveling to his loins.

"No," he whispered. "You're trying to be good."

A delicious chill shook his reserve. Perhaps just this day he'd allow his mind to roam free. But that would lead to the itch. And the itching needed to be scratched.

Still…

The itch felt good at times. It gave his fingers something to do. Feed the needy.

Walking into his bedroom he opened the closet door. High up on a shelf was a metal box. He reached for it and with a twist of the lock, he hit the numbers and unlocked it. A variety of contents were exposed. Finally, he took out a pack of pictures and stared at the first one. He sat down on the bed, placing them in a neat order. He pulled out a pack of balloons. A large bowtie. His breath stilled. With a trembling hand, he pulled out a red rubber nose.

"Hello, old friend." His breath drew in as memories cascaded over him. Gently, he caressed the nose and put it over his own. It still fit but lacked adhesive. He shoved it tighter onto his crooked beak. The smell of aged rubber filled his nostrils. He smiled, threw his head back and chuckled heartily. It wasn't his real laugh, but the one he had learned to master over the years.

Walking over to the mirror, he paused and moved closer to the glass. His dark eyes bore into his reflection. Unfiltered exhilaration hit him, strangely uplifting. He stuck out his tongue, rolling it around his lips. He smacked his lips together. But still he wasn't satisfied. He couldn't reconnect. It was his hair. It had been months since he colored it. He should've treated himself to a new wig, something crazy and wild.

He grabbed another box from the closet and sat it on the bed. Reverently, he placed it on the bed and opened it. His eyes lit in excitement when he spied the handmade jester's cap. Gently, he caressed it, touching the bells. A soft clank rang out.

His breath caught. He'd been avoiding the cap. It was a trigger. Gently, he eased it out of its wrappings. He slid it over his head, leaving his ears sticking out. His heart leaped in joy. Better. Now positively giddy, he ran down the hallway, opened another closet door.

"Yes!" he cried. A tall stack of labeled totes filled all the available space.

He grabbed the top plastic container of accessories, rummaging through them. He'd been collecting various pieces of costumes from a dumpster behind Pete's costume shop, once his place of employment. It was an easy way to get bits and pieces of disguises. After a minute, he stopped. Same old crap. He shoved the tote against the wall.

Back in the bedroom, he tucked his ears beneath the cap. The material stretched but didn't quite cover his bottom lobes. Over the years it had aged, shrunk a bit. He'd have to work with the material, perhaps do a bit of sewing. He twisted and turned his face, making kissy faces. He stopped, frowning. Still no good.

What he needed was makeup. Lipstick, the darker the better. But he didn't have any. He'd thrown it away, thinking it would aid in his bid to behave.

"You're a failure," he said, laughing. He no longer cared. Tomorrow he'd shop. Plan. He hadn't felt this good in months.

Entering the bathroom, he pulled open the medicine cabinet. He grabbed a tube of toothpaste and opened the cap. He dabbed a bit on his finger. White. It would do. He squirted a large dose into his palm, rubbed his hands together and began dabbing his face. The scent of toothpaste filled his nostrils. He added more paste to his face, repeating the process.

"Yes," he said to his reflection. "I see you now."

He opened the medicine cabinet, rummaging for something else of use.

"Ah ha!" He grabbed the bottle of cough syrup. It was thick and red. A Q-tip made a great dipping stick. He smeared it across his forehead, cheeks. "What a bloody mess." Once again, his reflection met with his approval. If only he had black eyeliner.

"Hmmm. What else do I have?"

He opened the sink cabinet, finding black shoe polish. Once again, he used a Q-tip to draw on brows and a sinister grin.

He stood back, staring at his reflection. Carousel music filled his mind and he hummed along to it. Abruptly it stopped, but he didn't care. He was making music in his heart, and he could sing, sing, and sing.

Smiling, he lay back on the queen-sized bed, stretching his arms above his head. He reached his hand across the blanket, searching for one of the pictures. He didn't care which one. They were all precious to him. He picked one up: ah. Karen. So beautiful. So…special. He pressed his lips to the image, allowing himself to absorb the memory. His breathing grew erratic. A delicious chill shook him to his core.

He began to giggle, filling the room with his voice. Louder, he shrilled. He could make bird calls. Oh, how could he have forgotten? He began chirping, then whistling. His voice rose excitedly. A bang on the wall stopped him in his tracks. A man yelled through the wall of the adjoining apartment.

"Knock it off!"

"Shut the hell up!" he yelled in response.

His fervor died, replaced by anger. Standing, he walked into the bathroom, staring at his reflection. Taking his hands, he smeared his face art into a messy gore of colors. His features changed from happy, to crappy. He liked the motto, repeating it over and over in his mind.

He slapped himself.

"Get a grip."

He needed to tie up loose ends. He'd put it off long enough, but now he had no choice. Perhaps, he would even enjoy the journey. Or make a final curtain call.

Yes, it was time. Stitches wanted to play.

Chapter Four

The banquet hall was filled with wedding guests. Kyle and Beth sat with several other family members, watching the couples dance beneath shimmering lights.

Beth leaned in toward Kyle. "I'm going to go outside so I can call my mom and check on the baby. I can't hear with all this noise."

"You did that an hour ago," he replied. "Samantha's fine. Your mother will call if there's a problem. Besides, the wedding's almost over."

Beth glowered at him, crossed her arms and leaned back in her chair.

Stunned she'd conceded, Kyle relaxed, enjoying the moment. The bride and groom sashayed on the dance floor. His thoughts traveled to his own wedding, three years earlier. Now it seemed like a lifetime ago.

Beth had been working at a pharmacy. Over a period of two years he'd visited the drugstore, attracted to the brunette and her sea-green eyes. Then by chance, they crossed paths in the mall and had lunch. It was a whirlwind courtship. On a whim, he proposed. At thirty-two, Beth couldn't wait to marry him. At thirty-five, he wasn't eager to take the plunge, but he wanted to make her happy.

He guessed the problems began when Beth wanted a baby. He hadn't and arguments ensued. Then Beth gave him the news. She was pregnant. His resentment subsided when his daughter took her first breath.

But Beth was having trouble with motherhood. She'd been an independent woman, working a full-time job giving orders to the staff. But now she was taking orders from an infant. He smiled at his musings. The apple never fell far from the tree.

Sighing, he shook off his negative thoughts. Who was he fooling? He loved Beth. Her mood swings had him on edge.

"Hey," he said, impulsively grabbing her hand. For a moment, he thought she'd pull away, but then she allowed him to hold her stiff fingers. "Dance with me."

"I don't want to," she said, shaking her head.

"Why not?" Still, she hesitated. It was enough for him to press on. "You love to dance."

"You know why."

His gaze skimmed over her form. Beth wore black slacks with a beige top. Her breasts size had increased due to milk production and her belly was slightly protruding. She'd always prided herself on her slender figure, but she hated the extra baby weight. Still, he found her incredibly attractive.

"No, I don't. Everyone is jealous of your voluptuous assets." His gaze swept over her breasts, followed by a mischievous grin.

Her eyes lit up, a bit of gratitude in her face.

"That's not it and you know it," she admitted. She looked away, a pained expression on her face. "I had to buy a larger blouse."

"Beth," he said, rubbing her hand. "You are beautiful just the way you are. You just had a baby. Go easy on yourself. Dance with me, honey."

The music changed to a slower pace. The

boisterous dancers were forced to exit the floor or grab a partner. Beth nodded, and they moved onto the dance floor, blending in with various couples.

The music concluded, and they returned to the table. People began to disperse. After hugs and goodbyes, the bride and groom exited. The DJ played a final farewell and the lights came on.

A dozen or so people stayed behind to clean up the banquet hall. Kyle began helping, despite Beth's reluctance.

"It will only be a few minutes," he said. "Sammy's asleep. What's the problem?"

"Nothing," she murmured, tight-lipped.

The warmth of their dance faded within seconds. He shook it off and began stacking chairs with a few family members while Beth gathered decorations with the ladies. He spied his uncle in the rear of the room. Uncle Bill looked so much like his pop, it hurt; however, that was where the similarities ended. He didn't like Bill that much. But the man had played a role in his adoption. Of that, he was grateful.

He swallowed, thoughts plummeting into the past.

At eight years old, Kyle was skinny and pale. He was always hungry but not just for food. He wanted attention. On Sunday, parents arrived for their weekly visits. Rose Hill became active with visitors. Kyle would pretend someone was coming to visit him. It was a lie, but hope was a hard thing to deny. He had no father. His mother lived at Rose Hill, but he wasn't allowed to see her unaccompanied. Now that he was older, it was rare anyone took him to visit her. He didn't much care. The visits were always the same. He was curious but afraid of his mother. She was childlike and yet an adult. She tugged and pulled on his arms, grabbed at his face. He often ran away.

Sunday afternoons were the best. It was the best time to play on the playground. With visitors about, there were less kids or adults in the area. And today, Kyle managed to grab an empty swing, proud of his feat. He shoved off, pumping his legs. Higher he went, staring up into the cloudless sky. It was his favorite thing to do.

"Get off," a voice said from below.

Jolted out of his reverie, Kyle stared at the keeper of the voice. A burly teenager stood in front of the swing. The red-headed kid was new at Rose Hill, and he liked lording it over anyone weaker than himself. The teenager's feet were braced apart, hands on his stout hips. Kyle's sneakers barely missed hitting his freckled face.

"Are you talking to me?" Kyle asked, pretending not to understand. On the swings beside him, two girls stared at the bully in fear. They continued pumping their legs, worry in their features.

"I'm talking to you, blondie," the bully said. "I said get off. It's my turn."

"Just give me five minutes more," Kyle said, heart racing. Here it was, the perfect day. He was doing what he liked to do, and this guy was going to wreck his good time. If only an aide would appear, but there wasn't anyone to help him.

"Now!" The bully's voice meant business.

"Five more minutes, please…"

The bully punched Kyle's foot as it neared him. "Get off that swing!"

Thankfully, Kyle's sneaker absorbed the blow. Still, he continued to pump his legs. He went higher. "Just four more minutes," Kyle yelled. But the bully had moved his position, now behind the swing set.

Real fear hit home. Kyle dragged his sneakers in the dirt, trying to stop the swing. But then the bully's hands slammed into his back, forcing the swing upward.

"I'm getting off!" Kyle yelled, twisting around. "I'm stopping the swing."

"No," the bully said. "Keep swinging. I'll push you."

Another blow to the back. Now the swing shifted sideways. Kyle grabbed tightly onto the chain. Again, another attack. The swing went higher. After the fifth blow to his spine, Kyle jumped from the swing. For a second, he flew into the air and then, smash. He hit the ground. Something sharp ripped into his knee. He rolled over, crying out.

Blood soaked through his jeans. He held his knee, staring at the damage.

"Looks like someone got a boo boo," the bully said, nudging Kyle with his foot. He leaned closer and pointed at the wound. "Poor baby. Maybe next time you'll get off when I tell you to."

Kyle held back tears. His face burned. He got to his feet and walked to the gate. As he approached, a man stood watching them, eyes narrowing in on Kyle's face.

"You're bleeding," the man said. He frowned, glaring at the bully, who was now on the swing. "You need to go over to the hospital and have it checked."

"I'm okay," Kyle replied. The hospital was scary.

No way was he going there.

"I'll take you." And with that, the man grabbed Kyle's upper arm and forced him along. Kyle stared at man's name tag, Bill Hampton. With little compassion, Bill handed Kyle's care over to a nurse, and he received seven stiches.

In time he discovered Benny was the name of the bully, and Bill Hampton was a recent employee of Rose Hill. The orderly had a way of making you squirm if he looked in your direction. Bill was quick to discipline and take away privileges. Kyle avoided him.

There came a day when another man was with Bill. The pair looked almost identical. But unlike Bill's rigid stance, the newcomer boasted a warm smile. To Kyle's shock, the man approached him during recess and asked him how he was doing. A friendship ensued. Eventually, Scott Hampton became more than just a visitor, donating his time, becoming the mentor Kyle never had. Ultimately, opportunity knocked, and he became Scott Hampton's adoptive son.

Shaking out of his memories, Kyle focused on Bill's hooded eyes and aged features.

"Hey, Bill," he said, approaching his uncle. "How've you been?"

"Good," Bill replied, tugging at his tie. "Where's your suit?"

"I forgot to get it dry cleaned." Kyle shrugged, shoving his hands deep into his pant pockets. Being around Bill, he hated feeling like a kid again, an all too common reaction.

"That doesn't sound like something Beth would let you forget."

Kyle ignored the reproach. Wearing a suit wasn't his style, but Bill knew that. Over the years nothing had changed in Bill's disposition, the man was still a cold fish.

"She feels bad about it." Kyle winked, shrugging off his annoyance. "She blamed me, I blamed her."

Bill frowned, mouth tightening. "So how is Scott?"

Kyle straightened his shoulders, never flinching as Bill referenced Scott by name, instead of 'your father'. Like all the Hampton family, Bill never let Kyle forget that he was adopted. Not so much in words, but in his offhanded remarks. It had been a source of discourse when Pop took offense on Kyle's behalf and tried to correct it.

"There hasn't been much difference in my father's condition."

"Any change in the prognosis?"

"Still unknown, but hopeful. He's getting daily therapy. In time, his brain function could improve, and he could gain some normalcy."

"Scott would hate being kept in his kind of state," Bill said. "He has a living will."

"I know my father's wishes," Kyle said, jaw clenched. "But Pop will come back to us. I know he's still in there. I'm not giving up hope. Neither should you."

Bill's stare was unnerving. Kyle cleared his throat, changing the topic. "I recently visited Rose Hill."

"Rose Hill?" Bill scowled. "How did you get inside?"

"It's not hard. You remember Randy. He goes urban exploring, and he invited me to go."

"Randy." His lip curled. "That troublemaker.

Urban explorers are people breaking into abandoned places. It's just a fancy word they use."

"He doesn't see it that way."

"Not surprising." Bill replied. "You should've dropped that dead weight a long time ago. You're lucky you both didn't get arrested. I heard the fines are pretty steep."

"Whatever," Kyle said, ignoring Bill's scowl. He regretted seeking out the man. He should've just left. "The state abandoned the property so as far as I'm concerned, they have no business saying anything, especially to me."

"It's hazardous," Bill said. "Asbestos. Lead paint. Who knows what other contaminates are in the grounds. It should be torn down. It's disgraceful."

"'I won't disagree. A lot of windows are boarded up. The tunnels are the worst, my flashlight barely made a dent in the dark. You'd never recognize the place."

Kyle was met with stony silence. Obviously, he'd tripped upon a bitter subject, but he didn't care. He wasn't a kid anymore who needed reprimanding. He ached to tell Bill so.

"The state is selling it," Bill said. "I saw it on the news. Maybe they'll get a buyer and find a use for the buildings. Do something good for the community. Build a park or something."

"Selling it?" Kyle repeated. "I didn't know." Mixed emotions filled him. "I guess it can't sit like that forever."

"It's about time."

"I suppose." Kyle shook his head. "It certainly was a shock to see."

"Just stay away from there, Kyle." Bill leaned closer, his eyes flashing. "Let the past go. Move on with your life and forget about Rose Hill."

That was easy for Bill to say, he wasn't born at Rose Hill. It had only been a job to the man, and obviously one Bill detested. But to him, it was once a place he called home, or something like that. He wanted to ask about Roy but bit his tongue.

"Let me know when you're going to see your Pop," Bill said. "Depending on the day, I might be able to meet you."

"Sure thing," Kyle replied, lying through his teeth. "I'll give you a call."

As the conversation transitioned to shop talk, Kyle noticed that almost everyone had left. Beth stood by the exit, giving him the once-over. When she caught his gaze, she motioned with her hand.

"Looks like I'm being summoned," Kyle said beneath his breath.

On the way home, Beth shared the gossip she'd heard during the wedding. Kyle listened wearily but it was good to hear her chatting about something rather than motherhood. He slid his gaze sideways. Beth's hair was disheveled. Her eyes were bright, cheeks rosy. His gaze slid to her cleavage, which due to a twist in her blouse, was hard to avoid. He swallowed hard, inwardly stirred. He slid his hand over the console, grabbing hers in a warm embrace. Beth paused in her ramblings, fingers stiffening.

"It was nice dancing with you," he said. "Almost like old times." He raised her hand, kissing her cool skin.

"I still think we could've brought the baby," she

said, disengaging her hand. She leaned in the seat, staring out the window. "She would've slept the whole time. I'd have liked showing her off."

Kyle's gaze narrowed on the road ahead. The car fell silent. They had almost had a real conversation. Almost.

Chapter Five

Stitches inhaled, beat his chest with his gloved hands, and flung them into the air. He picked up the cane by his left foot, threw it above his head and caught it, twirling it around. Humming, he moved his shoes. Tap. Tap. He lifted his gaze to the high chipped ceiling. His humming crested as he danced. Tap. Tap. Tap. He held the cane, spinning in an elaborate prance. A silly song sprang from his mouth, the words a cross between gibberish and a ditty.

Across the stage, he gave his all to his performance. Dust swirled around his feet. Three times he rotated, threw the cane in the air, and caught it. After a flourishing bow, he stood at attention. Eyes straight ahead.

"Bravo. Bravo." A single handclap echoed in the still room.

Stitches grinned and for good measure, did a quick spin, bowing low.

"Woo-hoo," the young woman said. She sat in the front row of the Assembly Hall, the only guest in attendance. "Spectacular."

"Thank you, beautiful miss," Stitches said. He jumped off the stage, landing on his feet. He leaned low, gawking into Donna's blue eyes. "It was my pleasure to entertain you."

"And it was my pleasure to watch." She wiggled

against the hard bench. "So now what?"

"Now it's your turn to entertain me." His brow lifted, eyes leering.

"Here?" Donna laughed. "No offense, Stitches, but this place is kinda dirty and gross."

"Maybe I like dirty and gross," Stitches said. He touched the right side of her face. Her makeup was ugly, he decided. She wasn't a true artist. Her lipstick was too amber, her eyeshadow barely noticeable. For a private escort, she could've done a better job for his buck. And she was a bit too big in the gut. Muffin top. She had squeezed herself into a tight red dress at least two sizes too small. Not that he minded, but he didn't approve of her lying. Her online photo was clearly taken at least ten pounds earlier. Dimples appeared by her mouth whenever she smiled, which was often forced.

He grabbed her hand, helping her up. She barely reached his shoulder.

"I want to show you something," he said. "Ready for a surprise?"

"Is it a pleasant surprise?"

"Yes."

"Bring it on."

Stitches took her hand, led her up to the stage and into an adjoining dressing room. Sunlight filtered in through the windows, revealing the dust lingering in the air. He grabbed one of the two chairs against the wall, placing it in the middle of the expanse.

"Sit."

Donna did as he asked, crossing her legs. One heel dangled off her right foot.

Stitches stepped into the closet, reappearing with a

wooden box.

"What's that?"

"You'll see." He put the box on the floor and opened it. "I want to make you beautiful, like me."

"But you kind of look like a vampire without the teeth."

"Vampire," he repeated. "I'm a jester. Right now, my face is in baseline paint. I'm not wearing my specialty cap. It takes me hours to get the effect I crave. I've got many talents. Art is my passion. I want to share this passion with you. Please be my student. My queen. My masterpiece."

Donna's smile iced; eyes wary. "No offense, Stitches, but that wasn't part of the date. I don't know if I like someone messing with my face. Some of the things you say are off the wall. Even scary."

He considered her features. She really did have nice bone structure. High cheekbones, a slight cleft in her chin. Her ears stuck out, but she'd curled her bleached shoulder-length hair just enough to hide the flaw.

"You want more money?" His words were barely audible as he absorbed her image. She should've plucked her bushy eyebrows. Dark in color, they clashed with her hair.

"You paid me for three hours," she replied. "And it's been interesting. In fact, the most interesting experience I've ever had. I love this creepy old place."

"As do I." He knelt by her chair. He pressed his gloved hands together, prayer-like. "Please, Donna. Do me this honor. I picked out your online photo because I just know you will look incredible when I'm through with my creation."

"So I'm guessing you want to get kinky?"

His nostrils flared at her words. The audacity.

"You mock my sincerity?"

"No." She laughed, drawing his eyes toward her mouth.

"How many fillings do you have?"

Her laughter stopped short. She gawked at him. "Are you serious? Who'd want to know that?"

"I saw a flash of silver."

"Geeze," she said, squirming. She tried to stand, but he pressed her back into her seat. Stunned, her face blanched. "Look. It's almost time for me to leave. If we're going to get it on, let's get going."

Rude. He was beginning to not like her. His palms began to sweat as he held his temper in check. He'd given her three hundred dollars for three hours. He just wanted to have some fun, but here she was judging him like some high and mighty princess. He'd intended to let her go after a while. But now...

"I'll give you another two hundred for two more hours. Five hundred bucks just for a bit of pretend. What do you say?"

"This is getting too weird," she replied. She fussed with her dress, tugging it over her bare thigh. "I think I'd just like to get going. It took forever getting into this place. And we had to walk over those train tracks. I shouldn't have worn heels."

"Five hundred more for three hours," he said cutting into her words. "Please. It will be fun. I'll even take your picture to show the girls. That's eight hundred bucks. Pretty good pay for six hours of time."

Her eyes brightened as she considered his offer. Finally, she relaxed, leaning into the chair. "You're only putting makeup on my face."

"Of course," he assured her. He picked up a pallet of base color. He began to hum, dipping his fingers into the various hues. Minutes ticked away.

"You know this is kind of fun," she said as he carefully crafted her face. "Am I going to get to see the finished product when you're through?"

"Of course," he assured her. "I told you I want a picture. And there's a mirror in the closet."

"Cool. You certainly are a perfectionist. I've never worked on my face longer than five minutes. It's been close to an hour."

"It'll be worth it," he replied. "Think of it as a day at the spa."

"I didn't think of it that way." She tilted up her chin as he added definition to her cheekbone. "So why do you come here to do this?"

"Because it's my home, or was."

"Home?" She blinked. "You mean you lived at this place? Wasn't this a nuthouse?"

"No. It was for people with physical issues. Some mental."

"And so what were you?"

"What do you think?"

"I would guess physical since you're wearing heavy makeup, maybe to hide a flaw?" She paused, studying him. "Am I right?"

"No."

"Oh." Her gaze wavered as she slowly swallowed. "Are you a crazy person?"

This time he laughed. After a moment, he stilled. "You really are delightful, Donna. I've never had so much fun with a playdate."

"Playdate. That's a funny way of putting it."

"Well, what would you call it?"

"A date," she replied. "A paid date. But still, a date."

"No more talking," he said. "I need to get your mouth just right. I'm almost done."

She did as she was instructed, pursing her lips. Ten minutes later, he put all his instruments into the box. He picked up a red rose and slid it behind her ear. "Beautiful. Ready to see yourself in the mirror."

"Yes."

"First, a picture." He went into the closet, came back with a camera and snapped several photos. He put the camera away and came over to her, grabbing her hand. "This way."

Donna followed Stitches into the closet. A propane lantern lit up the small room. She went toward the rear, moving past the various junk on the floor. She pivoted around.

"Where is the mirror?"

"I have to close the door. It's on the other side of the panel."

Stitches shut the door behind him. His form blocked the mirror. Then he moved away.

Donna stepped up to the mirror. "I look like a porcelain doll. What's that written on my forehead?" She stepped closer, squinting. She backed up, bumping into Stitches' chest. She pivoted, backing into the mirror. Her voice crested into a cry. "Is this a joke? What's that mean? 'Don't twitch.'"

"Exactly what it says."

"I'm leaving." Donna turned around and fumbled for the doorknob.

Stitches slid up against her, whispering in her ear. "Not a joke. A game. If you twitch, you'll get stitched." His laughter mingled with her pleas.

Chapter Six

The face of an angel hovered over Kyle. Her blue orbs were brilliant, mouth puckered in a soft smile. Blonde tresses caressed his skin as she leaned inward, her hand cupping his face. He reached out to touch her beauty, but suddenly she was gone. In a field of wildflowers, he found her again. Against the horizon, others stood with her, indistinguishable and just out of focus. The woman's nightgown stirred in the silent breeze. Lifting her finger, she pressed her lips.

"Shush," she whispered. "I have a secret."

Crying out, Kyle jumped upright in bed, startling Beth. Over the monitor, the baby cried.

"What's the matter with you?" Beth rose on her elbow, staring at him like he'd grown two heads. "You scared the heck out of me."

"I...I had a dream." He hung his legs over the bed, head in hands, barely able to catch his breath. Perspiration beaded his brow.

"Well, you woke up the baby screaming like that."

"I didn't scream."

"Yes, you did." She belted her robe. "What were you dreaming about?"

"I don't remember," he lied.

Beth moved from the room. Over the monitor, he heard her quiet the baby. His heart racing, he glanced at the clock. The dream had been so real. Too real. He groaned, his feet hitting the floor with a jarring thud. After showering, he put on his work clothes.

Cold air filtered up the staircase as he descended into the foyer. In the kitchen, Beth was just shutting the back door. Confusion filled her features as a few scattered leaves rustled across the tiles.

"The door was open," she said. "Look at this mess. It must've been open for hours. You never shut it last night." She hugged herself, trembling from the chilly air. "How could you forget to lock the door? I hope the baby doesn't get sick. It's freezing."

He was at a loss. He clearly remembered closing and locking it.

"And what's this?" She pointed to the newspaper-draped table. "You're cleaning your boots again?"

"So what? I put them in the laundry room to dry. Not a big deal."

"Not a big deal?" She rotated on her heels. "Why are you cleaning them again? Do you have any idea how unsanitary it is to use the table where we eat?"

"Nothing got on the table. I covered it." Brushing her off, he walked toward the back door. "I forgot to throw out the trash."

"You're so odd with those boots." She pointed toward his retreating feet. "They're old. Stained. I can't tell if they're green or brown. Why do you keep cleaning them? You drive a backhoe and work in dirt, why bother?"

Kyle opened the door, studying the door jamb, looking for an issue. He checked the lock mechanism, which appeared fine. "I was bored," he said beneath his breath.

"Bored?" Her hands flew in the air. "And that's

what you do for fun? Think about where you found them, that dirty asylum. It's absurd! Buy yourself a new pair. In fact, I'll buy you two, if you just get rid of those."

"No," he said. "You're being dramatic. I won't use the table again."

Anger burned in his throat. He wasn't letting Beth get him into an argument.

He opened the screen door and stepped onto the porch. Crisp air rolled across his exposed skin. At the porch edge, he paused. Their property spread out before him, a half-acre, buffered by a privacy fence. In the windy grove, trees swayed in vibrant colors against the cobalt sky. He breathed in the scents of autumn, his favorite time of year.

Serenity slipped over him. He ran his hand over his jaw, sighing. After a moment, he turned around. By the porch window, he paused, brow lifting. Well that was new. A huge eyeball glared at him. A soapy decoration had been drawn on the windowpane. Pranks already? Halloween was still a couple of weeks away. They'd had mischief-makers in the past, but not this early. Last year, it'd been toilet paper on a tree.

"Someone soaped our house," he said, walking through the kitchen door. "Mischief prank."

"For real?" Beth put down her coffee mug. "Where?"

"There." Kyle moved to the window and pulled open the curtain. The eye stared at them.

"What!" Beth moved to the other window by the kitchen sink. She pulled open the curtain and gasped. Another eye, this time with fringed eyelashes.

"Someone has a weird sense of humor," she said.

"Ugh. Just what I want to do, wash windows today!"

On a mission, she went into the dining room, yanked open the curtains and found another eye with a questioning brow.

"How absurd," Beth exclaimed, storming out of the room. "They must've soaped every window." She moved into the living room, drawing open the drapery. Normally lit in the morning light, the bay window was darker than usual. She recoiled, gasping.

Kyle hurried into the room. "What's the matter?"

Beth stepped aside, dragging the curtain with her.

An elaborate portrait of a woman's face was painted on the pane, well drawn in various hues. It was ghastly. Hollow eyes appeared soulless against a sunken skull. The mouth was opened in muted horror. Tuffs of blonde hair spiked from the scalp. One side of the head sported a large crack from which butterflies emerged. It appeared three-dimensional, created with lumpy, tissue-like material. Whoever had drawn the picture had artistic talent and a gruesome imagination.

"Oh, my God!" Beth turned to Kyle. Her eyes were huge, face pale. "That's paint, not soap. I'll never get it off. How horrible! Who would do such a thing?"

The image snared his mind. He moved closer to it. In a way, it really was stunning, but he reserved that sentiment. "It's almost Halloween." He shrugged. "Kids are going to prank people. I did it."

"Vandalism is a crime," Beth said, tight-lipped. "And no child can draw that good." Then a thought dawned. "Oh, my God! I think they were in the house. The door was open. Maybe they stole something. Quick, Kyle. Go see if anything is missing while I check on Samantha."

Alarmed, they parted ways. Kyle began upstairs, moving from room to room, checking windows, doors and for any missing property. He passed Samantha's bedroom. Protectively, Beth guarded the sleeping baby.

Kyle searched the first floor. After a while, Beth followed him, the baby on her shoulder as he retreated to the kitchen.

"Should I call the police?"

"Just wait," Kyle said. "Let me check the basement."

"Hurry up. I'm freaking out." She put the baby into her infant carrier, pulled out the glass coffee pot and filled it with water.

Kyle entered the basement. The windows were closed and locked. The basement door was secure, lock firmly in place.

"Kyle, what are you doing?" Beth yelled to him. "See anything?"

"Everything's fine. Just calm down."

The basement lay in shadows, a cold reminder of the asylum. Apprehension washed over him, his breath unsteady. Having been a victim of a prank messed with his head; he couldn't shake a sense of doom. Maybe Rose Hill had taken more of a toll on him than he realized, emotionally and now physically. The asylum had crept back into his life and was slowly encasing him with his old childhood fear. Slowly, he walked back upstairs.

"Nothing's been taken," he said. "I'll check outside. I'm sure it was just some teens getting off on a prank. I don't think they came inside. Kids don't have that much nerve."

Beth's face revealed her doubt as she pointed out,

"The windows are pretty high off the ground, Kyle. The kids would've had to be tall. I think we should call the cops."

Her words made him feel even worse.

"If it makes you feel better, call the cops. I doubt they'll do anything. But at least they'll make a report, and they might patrol our neighborhood more."

"I just don't want those creeps returning."

"Are you going to be okay if I leave?" Kyle glanced at the clock. "I'm going to be late to work."

"I'll be fine. Check outside. I'll let you know what the police say when they get here."

"Ok." Dutifully, he kissed her cheek. "Don't worry about the windows. I'll wash them after work."

"I have my six-week checkup today," she said, following him as he retrieved his thermos. "My mom's going with me to help with Samantha."

"Then you'll be able to go back to work?"

Her face fell. She avoided his gaze, staring off into the distance.

"What's the matter?" he asked.

"I was thinking." Her anxious eyes lifted to his. "What if I didn't go back to work? Samantha's only going to be a baby for such a short time. I'm breastfeeding and I haven't found a sitter I like. What if I just take off for a while? Do you think we could afford it?"

Her words didn't surprise him. In fact, he was starting to wonder when she'd bring it up.

"I suppose we could swing it. I've been getting a lot of overtime. We can talk about how to manage. It'd be nice if you could be home with Samantha. I'd like that."

Her face brightened. "At least I'll find out about birth control, and when I can start taking it."

"Sounds good." He grabbed his work jacket from the hall closet and reentered the kitchen, giving Beth a more passionate kiss, shocked when she didn't pull away. Her no sex rule was going to be lifted. He flushed as anticipation took root. The celibate life sucked. Lord knew, lately, he was an expert.

Shaking off his questionable morning, he exited the house, searched the yard, and found it secure. Hopefully, it was a once and done affair.

Chapter Seven

On Monday evening, Kyle entered Beacon's
Tavern, spying Randy sitting on a bar stool. The joint
was one of their favorite haunts and far enough away
from home for Beth not to drive by and see his truck.
The place was dimly lit without a big fanfare. Just the
way he liked it.

He took off his jacket and hung it on a wooden peg
in the foyer. The bar was busy for a weekday night, but
not overly so. Behind the bartender, a college basketball
game played out on the oversized television. The
lighting was low, giving no clue as to what time of day
it was outdoors. Soft country music drifted through the
room.

Kyle plopped down on a stool alongside Randy,
who nodded. A frothy beer was already waiting for
him. He picked it up and took a gulp.

"Hey, buddy," Randy said. "Glad you could make
it. For a minute, I was worried you'd be a no-show."

"The traffic was lousy," Kyle raised his beer in
salute, and drained half of it. "Thanks. I needed this."

"I hear you. So what's up?"

"Well, besides the fact that my house got nailed by
some vandals, not much. Can you believe somebody
soaped my windows?"

"Already?" Randy replied. "I bet Beth was pissed."

"We both were. They even used paint on our front

window. Beth called the cops but there wasn't much they could do about it. I might have to put up some cameras."

"It's not how it was when we were kids," Randy said. "Today they charge you with vandalism."

"We rang doorbells and ran," Kyle said. "I never did any real damage."

"We also threw corn at cars." Randy laughed. "Lucky we didn't get our butts beat."

"I almost did." Kyle shrugged. He had been chased by two men, but he had managed to lie down in a cornfield and they never found him.

Silence followed; both were lost in thought.

"Beth know you're here?" Randy asked, breaking the silence.

"Nope." Wearily, Kyle rubbed his jaw. "Let's keep it that way."

"That's not good."

"Things haven't been too good lately."

"Try counseling…"

"That crap doesn't work," Kyle said.

"Have you ever had counseling?"

"As a matter of fact, I have," Kyle jerked his gaze to Randy's. One brow lifted. "After my mother died. I was nine years old. I think it lasted all of five minutes. How about you? Did you get any counseling?"

"Fair enough." Randy snickered. "You got a damn good memory; I'll give you that. If you call getting smacked around 'counseling,' then I had plenty of it. It worked. I learned to shut my mouth and do as I was told. So how are you making out looking for Roy?"

"Not good," he said. "I'm not even sure of his last name. My mother's maiden name comes up as zilch.

I'm not even sure I have his right birthdate."

"Roy lived in my cottage," Randy said. "He got into a lot of fights." He paused, repositioning himself on the stool. "One day, he had been taken away, but that's the way it was. The aides never told us kids anything."

"Pop said Rose Hill was having legal issues with allegations of abuse. Any children left had to be reassigned to other institutions or returned to their parents."

"It's true." Randy said, pausing in thought. "My grandmother finally took me in. She wasn't happy about it. But Roy was a troubled kid, and he might be a troubled man. You don't need to invite a problem into your life."

"He's still my brother."

"Only by blood," Randy said. "You don't have a relationship. Why bother now? I'd drop it."

Kyle flinched, his words grave. He had dropped it but now visiting Rose Hill had brought him full circle. He wasn't getting talked out of it now. It was killing him wondering.

The friends had another round of beers, settling into their own reflections. Time ticked away. Reluctantly, Kyle glanced at his watch. He could waste another twenty minutes or so.

"I'm going back to the asylum next weekend," Randy said. "Want to come?"

"No way. I'm done with that place."

"I want to check out the morgue."

"I'm sure it's pretty depressing," Kyle said. "That place holds something unnatural. I felt it when we were walking around. Maybe that paranormal crap has some merit. There's a long history to consider. It pisses me off when I think about it."

"You're getting to be quite the advocate."

Kyle's stomach churned with the morbid talk. His thoughts turned to his dream and bile filled his throat. "I had a dream about Karen Walton. Remember her?"

"Karen Walton?" Randy repeated the name slowly, shrugging. "Vaguely." He smiled. "I remember how pretty she was. She liked to share her love. Or at least that's what she called it."

"That's a good way to put it," Kyle replied. "She share her love with you?"

"Nope, I didn't tap into that," Randy said. "You?"

"No." Kyle broke out in laughter. "She looked the same in my dream, young."

"Well, rumor had it that she was pregnant," Randy said. "She ran off with her baby's daddy." He slid his beer away from him, staring at the television. "I'm sure she's fine. I forgot about her."

"Same," Kyle said. "I think she was fifteen the last time I saw her."

Kyle considered Karen. The young woman had been happy, sweet and kind. Everyone noticed her, including adults. She never said no to sex. He'd been a boy, but Rose Hill residents weren't exactly shy about getting it on. There wasn't enough staff to stop them. It wouldn't surprise him if she'd been pregnant. It would've been hard to pinpoint a father. But who was he kidding? She'd have likely been forced to have an abortion.

"Hope she doesn't show up in my dreams," Randy said. "That would be too weird. I see you're wearing my should-be boots." He twisted his body, ogling

Kyle's feet. "Want to sell them yet?"

"No."

"Hey, sexy. Remember me?" A dark-haired woman with ruby red lips slipped her arms around Randy's neck, nuzzling his cheek. Various tattoos covered one of her bare arms. Large silver hoops bounced against her neck. She moved around Randy's shoulder and climbed onto his lap. She smiled at Kyle, holding out her hand. "I'm Kat. I'm sure Randy's mentioned me."

"Nice to meet you, Kat." Kyle's eyebrow rose at Randy's sheepish grin. His buddy had never mentioned the raven-haired beauty. If he had, he would have remembered. She was the kind of woman that stood out in any crowd. It was a struggle not to stare or notice the creamy thighs revealed beneath the mini skirt. He had to admit he was envious.

"I'm Randy's girlfriend." She slid her hand over Randy's cheek, patting him gently. "Aren't I, sweetie?"

"Sure, honey." Randy wrapped his arms around her waist. She nestled against him, leaning her head against his shoulder. Her raven hair cascaded over his chest.

Uncomfortable at the display of affection, Kyle turned his attention back to his beer. Being single had its perks. His friend was great with women. Dark and rugged, Randy drew them like magnets. He could pick them up at a snap of his fingers. Randy had vowed never to marry. The man was almost thirty-six years old. No wife. No kids. No responsibility to anyone but himself.

Kyle frowned as they flirted. What was he thinking, getting married? The notion slipped out before he could stop it. Guilt ate at him.

"I've got to go," he said. Standing abruptly, he gave the couple a dismissive glance.

"Let me know if you change your mind about this weekend," Randy said. "Tell the wife to let you come out to play. I think you need it."

"That's the last thing I need."

Chapter Eight

After Kyle refused a trip to Rose Hill, Randy decided to go it alone. But when Kat showed up at his house, he broke from tradition and took her along. It wasn't long before he knew it had been a bad idea to bring her to the asylum. What had seemed like a fun thing to do, had quickly turned into a babysitting effort. It was all he could do to keep moving forward.

"It's so cold down here," Kat said. "Why can't we go into one of the buildings? At least there would be some daylight. It's so dark, creepy. I'm scared."

"I can't get into some of the buildings without going through the tunnels. I have a map, and I want to check out parts of the tunnels. There's another tunnel beneath this one. It was used for pipes."

"Can we just go?" She stopped in her tracks, pulling on his hand. "I shouldn't have come with you. It was a mistake."

"We just got here," he said. "Can't you give me some slack?" He pulled her into his arms, sliding his hands over her back. "Come on, honey. I've been down here a few times. You're fine. There's nothing to be afraid of."

"I keep hearing footsteps behind me," she said. "I think someone is following us."

"No one is down here. They'd have to use a flashlight, just like us. We'd see it. They'd be blind in the dark."

"Then it's something else following us. I think it's haunted. I heard the rumors, and I don't like this."

"I saw a raccoon in one of the buildings. It could be an animal." It was almost enough for him to throw in the towel. "If there were any animals, they are more afraid of you then you are of them. They will stay away from us."

"Not if they're rabid," she said. "They'd have no fear of us."

His headlamp shone down on her pale face. Her bottom lip trembled. "Sunny McGarvey wanted to come here with me. I could have asked her. She'd have come running to take your place."

Her worried face turned jealous. She pouted, brows furrowing.

"I thought you weren't seeing her anymore."

"I'm not," he said. "We're just friends. But I'm looking for someone with a bit of spine, someone who can keep up with me. This is what I like to do for fun. You're not even trying."

"I'm trying," she said softly. "But I can't help it if I'm afraid."

"Try harder." He took her hand, kissing the back of it. "For me? For us?"

She closed her eyes as an inward struggle appeared to take over.

"Fine," she said. "But you'd better stay close to me."

"Of course." He slid his arm around her shoulders.

Randy led her along the tunnel as cold air whistled through the corridor. Damp, musty scents filled his nostrils.

"It won't be long before it will be too cold to do this," he said, squeezing her hand. "You think this place is cold now? Wait until winter. Winter is why they created these tunnels in the first place. A lot of the residents who lived here were in wheelchairs or handicapped. In the winter, the catwalk became an icy mess. Using the tunnels was how they got people from building to building. There was a school, a hospital and a movie theater. Also a church. They could deliver food and medicine to the other buildings. They even used the tunnel to take dead people to the morgue."

"People died here. Don't tell me that."

"Well, of course," he said, squeezing her hand tighter. Her fingers were icy in his. "This place has been around for almost a hundred years. No matter what your age, you were considered a kid. Real kids became adults. They eventually died. There's nothing scary about that. Death is part of living."

"No, it's not," she said. "Death is—well, dead. There's probably ghosts down here."

"If there are, they won't hurt you. They know you've got a good heart."

Finally, they came upon the doorway he sought. He ducked into the opening, pulling her along. Inside was a large basement, broken into sections. Refrigerators and other odds and ends were shoved against the wall. He led her past this area and into another room. His headlamp lit upon a large dental chair.

"What are you looking for in here?" she asked when he paused.

"This." He walked toward the chair.

"That…that gross thing?"

"Uh huh." He slid the backpack off his back,

dropping it to the floor. He unzipped it, while she moved her flashlight around the room. He pulled out a white cloth from his bag and began wiping off the chair.

"What are you doing?"

"Cleaning it off," he said absently.

"What for?"

"Pictures."

She didn't say anything as he finished wiping the dust from the leather. He turned toward her, nuzzled her cheek and smiled. "Ready?"

"For what?"

"This." He took the flashlight from her hands and sat it inside his backpack. He picked her up and sat her on the chair.

"Yuck. I don't want to sit on this thing."

"It's fine," he said. "I cleaned it off. It's just like new."

"No," she protested, squirming. "It could be possessed or something." She tried to slide off the side, but he was quick to push her back.

He sat down on the edge, sliding his hip next to her leg. He pressed her shoulders back against the leather. "You look incredibly sexy. I want to take some pictures of you. How cool would that be?"

"Not that cool," she said. Doubt filled her eyes.

"You're so beautiful. You could be a model."

The hesitation in her eyes lifted.

"Please…for me, honey." He touched her cheek, running his fingers along her jawbone.

"Well, then, take a few and let's get out of here," she said. "This place gives me the creeps. This chair does too. I mean, it's a dental chair. Who knows what some crazy dentist did to the people that lived here. He probably pulled out all of their teeth."

"Only if they bit someone," he said. "They claim there was a three-strike rule to get the teeth yanked out. Bite thrice, roll the dice. But that's not how it was."

"For real?"

"We're not talking about a nip or someone nibbling flesh." He picked up her hand and gripped her fingers. "We're talking about having a hunk of skin ripped out by someone's canines. How would you like having an ear bit off, or perhaps the tip of your nose?" He opened his mouth, baring his teeth. Teasingly, he bit her hand, and she yanked it away.

"You're always lying to me," she said. "You're not funny."

He reached up, took off his headlamp, shut the light off and laid it inside his backpack. The room went black. Before Kat could protest, his hand covered her mouth. He removed his hand, replacing it with his mouth. At first, she tried to sit up, resist, but then she gave in.

"I want you," he said against her mouth. "I always wanted to do this."

"You're crazy," she said. But she was already convinced. "Can't we have a flashlight on?"

"What would be the fun in that?" he said. He pressed her back into the chair. It squeaked in objection. He slid his hand up her back, pulling her shirt up with his fingers.

"What was that?" She jerked her mouth from his.

"What?"

"That noise?"

"I didn't hear anything."

A rush of air swirled over him, stirring his hair. He sat up. Something thudded against the wall.

"Randy!" She grabbed his arm, fingernails pressing into his biceps.

"Be quiet," he hissed. He stood up, straining his eyes as he felt around the floor for his backpack to get his light. His hand touched icy concrete. He felt along the floor with his foot. Where was his bag?

"Randy."

In the stillness of the room, a soft rumble of laughter began. It seemed far away and yet was right there with them. His blood ran cold. Ignoring Kat's pleas, he knelt on the floor, spreading his hand in a wide circle. He needed light, a weapon. He was as good as blind. There was no way his bag could have just moved. He grabbed at his pockets. Usually he had his switchblade inside, but it was in the bag.

In the darkness, Kat moved off the chair. Her body thudded to the floor.

"Randy," she cried.

"Stay there," he commanded.

Kat began crying. Noisily, she began to plead, "Randy. Please...please put on the light."

"I'm trying," he said. He continued his efforts, crawling across the floor. His hand touched the wall. Slowly, he stood, using the wall for leverage, trying to get his bearings.

In the dense dark, eyes watched him.

The room filled with heavy breathing. It grew louder, stilling Kat's cries.

"Who's there?" Randy demanded. "You're not funny."

Again, a rumble of laughter. Then it grew in pitch.

It went up several octaves. It filled the room, mingling with Kat's screams. Footsteps ran across the room. Then a hard thud.

"Kat! I said stay put." Using his hands, he moved along the wall. He walked out what he guessed to be around ten feet, then backtracked. Each time, he searched for his bag with his feet.

Abruptly, the laughter stopped. Kat's quiet sobbing was the only noise in the room.

"Real funny, my friend. If I get my hands on you…"

On his fifth time leaving the wall to search, his boot hit against something. He reached down and found his backpack. Quickly, he opened it. Shoving his headlamp over his head, he hit the on switch. The room filled with light. He grabbed another flashlight and flicked it on. He moved in a quick circle, searching for the source of laughter. Nothing. He turned toward Kat, who was sitting with her back against the far wall. Her eyes were huge, wet and fearful. A large knot stood out on her forehead. He threw his bag over his shoulder and went to her. She yanked the flashlight from his hand as if it were a lifeline.

Kat stood on shaky legs, warily staring around the room. "Where did he go?"

"I don't know."

"I'm getting out of here." She turned and rushed out the doorway. In the tunnel, she took a left and ran. He chased after her.

"Kat. Wait!"

"I want out of here, now!" Her voice echoed through the tunnel.

"Okay. Okay." He caught up to her and grabbed

her hand. "I'll get us out of here."

Within a few minutes, they entered the Kellogg building and exited through the cellar window. Out in the courtyard, Kat collapsed on the ground, crying hysterically.

"Thank God, thank God," she repeated. "I was never so scared."

He didn't reply, dealing with his own wild thoughts. His plans with Kat had been ruined. He liked her, more than he'd realized. She was someone he might be able to settle down with. Despite Kyle's marital problems, he envied his friend and wanted his own family. Kat made him laugh. They were compatible. She had some good traits. A few bad. Remorse set in. He should've never brought her here. What was he thinking? In the future, he'd be better armed, perhaps bring a gun.

"I'm sorry you were frightened," he said. He helped her up and hugged her shaky form. Her body quivered against his. "Let's get out of here."

As they were walking through the woods toward the railroad tracks, he came to an abrupt stop. Two men were walking around the perimeter of the complex, clipboards in hand. If he would have to guess, he would think maybe a potential buyer was touring the property with a realtor.

Abruptly, his phone rang. Spying the number, he frowned.

Chapter Nine

On Saturday evening, Stitches smiled, strutting his antics around the Worcester convention center. He was dressed to the hilt in shiny black shoes and an oversized white and black suit. He wore his favorite crested cap with bells, which boasted a flaming crown of four red and purple cockscombs. He'd spent hours on his makeup, creating his best artwork. His brows were purposely blackened, lips ruby red. Glitter adorned his eyelashes. Normally wearing a clean-shaven face, he opted to add a five o'clock shadow to his wan jawline. A yellow handkerchief protruded from his front pocket.

Oh, it felt good to be back again in public and on display. Having a Halloween convention was just the ticket to mingle with the good folks of Norristown. He paraded around the room, admiring the vendors and their wares. He giggled and bowed low to the ladies, performing sleight-of-hand tricks, mostly with cards or coins. Now and then he'd whistle and clap to the sound of his own tapping feet.

He approached a table where two bored women dressed in gothic attire sported facial piercings and sold gold and silver jewelry in a wide array of Halloween themes.

"Good afternoon, beautiful ladies." He swept the air with his arms, bowing low. "I am Stitches the clown. It's a fine day to meet such talented women."

The younger of the women brightened, smiling at him. "Hello, Stitches. Nice to meet you."

The older woman just nodded to his existence, staring down at her cell phone, fingers taping out a text.

"Why is your name Stitches?" the younger woman asked.

"Because if you twitch, you'll get stitched, silly."

He ignored her perplexed look.

"Did you make this jewelry yourselves?" Stitches bent over, staring carefully at the display. He touched a skull necklace, sending it spinning. "Nice."

"No," his greeter replied.

Stitches avoided grinning, knowing cheap crap when he saw it. He spun around in a circle, stomping one of his feet. He pulled out a black balloon from his pocket, stretched it out and began to blow. His fingers moved rapidly over the rubber, tying and twisting off the end. He grabbed another black balloon and did the same. Then he wove the balloons together, creating a black spider. He handed it to the young woman, who appeared very pleased by his gesture.

"Thank you," she said, taking it from him. "It's great."

"I aim to please," he said, bowing again. "I work for tips if you have a care."

The smile left the woman's face. She handed the balloon back to him. "Sorry, Stitches. But I'm here to make money myself. We can barely afford to pay for our table."

"Ah," Stitches said. "That's truly a sad tale. I rub your back. You rub mine. But alas, you don't help a fellow conventioneer. Tsk." He bowed again and turned to leave. His pointy shoe caught the corner of their table, jerking it off balance. Jewelry tossed around, some spilling onto the concrete floor.

"Watch it, you jerk." The older woman came to life. She jumped off the chair, urgently grabbing the tossed jewelry. "Look what you did, you klutz. You probably did it on purpose."

"You look better that way," Stitches said, bending close to her ear. "Groveling on the floor like a warthog, you ugly fat fish. That cheap junk isn't worth five cents. I wouldn't give you a penny for it. Have a tootlelishus good day."

Gasping, the woman twisted around, holding a handful of earrings. "You jerk. Get the hell out of here!"

"Gladly."

Stitches skipped off, giggling. Oh, so much fun. The old snot's facial expression was so gratifying. He moved around the convention, plying potential customers with magic tricks and then stopping at various vendor sights to beg for tips. He went back into action, creating balloon art and propositioning folks for cash. Luck began to fill his pockets.

As the evening wound down, he finally made his way out of the convention center. The bulge in his pocket told him he'd done well with tips, though he still needed to count it. The night was crisp and clear, just like he liked. Fall was his favorite time of year. His energy level was at its peak. He spied a couple of children walking toward their car with their parents. He skipped around them, patting their heads.

"Check your beds tonight, children," he said, grinning at the pretty little girl. His gaze slid to her brother; brow raised. "You never know who you might see. I might just be hiding under it. Listen carefully. I might whisper your name…"

"No!" the little girl cried out, while the brother's jaw dropped open.

"That's not true," their mother protested, drawing her arms around their shoulders. "There's nothing under your bed. Go away, Mr. Meanie. You're not very nice."

"Toodle…oo," he exclaimed, winking broadly at the boy. Swiftly, he moved on before the father came toward him.

Humming, Stitches climbed into his green minivan. He yanked the cap and bells off his head, tossing it onto the seat. With a jingle of bells, it bounced onto the floor.

"Ah, I can breathe again." He pulled down the visor, staring into his green eyes. "You handsome devil." But then he stared past his reflection, into the rear of the windowless van. "Oh. How could I have forgotten my favorite prize of the day? Oops."

He turned around in his seat, deliberately pursing his lips. The van lay in shadows. It took a moment for his eyes to adjust to the dark. It wouldn't do to turn on the light. He held his breath, listening.

"Oh, my goodness," Stitches said. "Somebody is awake. You must be hungry. We'll have to rectify that at once. Must keep up with our energy, my pretty little Donna. We have a long night to play together. I can hardly wait. And you've been such a good, good girl. I'm glad you took a nap. Tiredness would only wreck our game. I'm sure you're just as excited as I am."

Large mascara-smeared eyes gazed at him blankly. Donna tried to sit up, failed, and fell back against the sleeping bag. His gaze lingered on the track marks on her bare arm. Her addiction disgusted him, but it was an easy way to control her.

"Oh, we are going to have such fun, fun, fun." He clapped his hands. "First we will paint your face. Make you beautiful. Style your hair. Maybe then we'll eat a snack. Do you like marshmallows? And then we can have another round of hiding and go seek. I think you can do better this time."

"I…I need to get home. Please…" The woman's eyes only widened in dismay.

"What's the issue, Donna?" His gaze narrowed, tone darkening. "We've had this conversation how many times? You sell your time, and I'm a paying customer. I want to play our game. You agreed. I was thinking I'd give you a glow stick, it wouldn't be fair if I had the only light."

Donna lowered her head and limply fell into a heap. A muffled sob followed.

He started the van, pulling out of the parking lot.

Chapter Ten

On Saturday evening, Beth rocked Samantha to sleep, humming a song. The nursery was lit in soft, warm hues. The purr of the cool mist vaporizer almost lulled her to sleep. Snapping out of her stupor, she tucked the baby into her crib, staring down at her daughter. So precious. So worth the sleepless nights and mood swings.

Exiting the nursery, Beth returned to her own bedroom, expecting to see her husband asleep in bed. But Kyle wasn't in their room. Strange. She had seen him sitting on the bed an hour ago. Longingly she stared at the comforter, yearning for its soft warmth. But she was worried, she'd been worried all week. Kyle had been so distant. He'd barely looked at her, let alone talked. And when she did try to converse with him, he'd given her a wooden response. She supposed he was disappointed with her failure at finding Roy. It was a painstaking task and she had begun reaching out to social media. Still nothing.

She chewed her bottom lip. Her own mother had pointed out Kyle's reclusiveness, but she had been so tired, still tired and depressed, to bother finding out what was up with him. She missed Kyle and snuggling in bed. It was hard seeing his expression whenever she pushed him away – and she had been pushing him away. There was no denying that. Now it was he that was shutting her out.

She walked downstairs, looking for Kyle. He was asleep on the recliner. His features were relaxed, peaceful. Her heart warmed.

"Honey." She nudged his shoulder.

He didn't move.

"Honey. Wake up."

Still nothing. She got more forceful, shaking his shoulder.

"What?" Kyle jumped in the chair; eyes wild. "What do you want?"

"It's cold down here. I want you to come to bed with me." She crossed her arms.

"No," he said. "I sleep better down here."

"How can you possibly get a good night's sleep on a chair? You can't even stretch out your legs."

"Yes, I can." He was already closing his eyes. "I'm fine."

"Are you mad at me?" Gently, she rubbed his shoulders, leaning against his arm. She nuzzled her lips against his ear, whispering, "We could talk, snuggle."

He stiffened at her request, pushing away her hands. Stunned, her heart sank. It was worse than she'd thought.

"Please talk to me, Kyle." She stood, leaving her hand on his shoulder. "Don't shut me out."

"It's late," Kyle said, finally looking at her. "You should take advantage while the baby's asleep and sleep yourself. I'm fine. This has nothing to do with you so quit worrying. Go back to bed. I'll talk to you tomorrow."

"Are you sure?" Sleep did sound appealing, but she was still troubled.

"Yes."

He turned his head away, avoiding her stare. After a moment, she went into the kitchen. Abruptly, she stopped short, flicking on the light switch. Kyle's boots were on the kitchen chair. Not again. And after they'd argued over it just a week ago? What was it about those stupid boots? Angrily, she grabbed the boots, carried them into the foyer and sat them inside the closet. She resisted the urge to scream at Kyle. She balled up the newspaper, shoving it into the trashcan.

All romantic feelings vanished in a heartbeat. She returned upstairs, checked the baby monitor, and climbed into bed. Her eyes closed as soon as her head hit the pillow. Hours later, a noise woke her. At first, she just lay with her eyes closed, barely registering the sound. But then the prominent clatter against the windowpane jolted her. Her eyes cracked open. Was someone throwing stones at her window? The idea sunk in. She lay, listening.

Beth shoved the blanket away from her face and sat up. She climbed out of the bed, walking to the window. She moved the curtain to one side. Dawn was breaking over the horizon. A tall shadow hovered by the shed. She squinted, trying to make it out. She blinked. It was gone.

Chilled, she walked down the hallway to the baby's room. She then checked the middle hall bathroom and rear bedroom. Nothing. Slowly, she descended the staircase. The house was shadowy with muted light as the sun was getting ready to rise. She flicked on the foyer light and entered the living room. Kyle was still asleep on the chair.

A shudder shook her frame. She hugged herself as

unease spread over her. She touched Kyle's hand. He jumped, bolting upright.

"What is the matter with you?" he said. "Why do you keep doing that?"

"Did you hear a noise outside?"

"No. I was asleep."

"I heard something."

"You were dreaming," he said. "Go back to bed."

"I wasn't dreaming. I thought I saw someone outside."

Kyle didn't move, eyes closing as his body relaxed.

"I'm glad you're so concerned!"

Upstairs, the baby cried. Beth's heart dropped to her stomach. She hurried through the kitchen doorway. A cold knot formed in her throat.

Sprinting up the staircase, she rushed to the nursery, gathering up Samantha. Her fingers shook as she changed the baby, whether from cold or fear, she wasn't sure. Something was off.

She sat down in the rocker; eyes glued to the doorway, and nursed her daughter. She tried to make sense of what she'd seen. There had to be an explanation. She'd check out the shed in the morning light. Maybe their vandals had returned.

She swallowed hard, holding the baby closer.

Her imagination grew wild, and yet no sensible answers filled in the blanks.

Chapter Eleven

"I'm telling you, Beth, I didn't hear anything." Kyle flipped the pancake in the frying pan, patting it with a spatula. Sunday morning pancakes had become a tradition. "I didn't find anything by the shed. You were tired. Your imagination was on overdrive."

"I know what I saw." Beth sat on a kitchen chair, elbows on the table. The baby was sitting in her carrier, sleepy and content from her milky breakfast. "I'm not stupid."

"I didn't say that." Kyle plopped the food on a plate. He slid it across to his wife, who lifted her tired gaze to his.

"Let's face it, you don't get any extra rest," he said.

"Well, say whatever you want. I think someone was snooping around outside."

"Nothing's missing," he pointed out. "I didn't see anything out of place."

"It could be the weirdo who painted the front window," she said. "Maybe he came back to draw some more artwork."

"I checked the windows. I saw nothing wrong."

"Whatever," she said. "And by the way, what's up with your boots?"

"Sorry," he replied.

"That's it?"

"I didn't clean them; they were just sitting there."

"Excuses," she said, brow lifting. "Please, for the love of God, would you stop washing them."

"It was just something to do."

"Whatever," she replied, shaking her head. "There's something about those damn things. I get bad vibes." Her gaze drifted to the back door, landing on the objects of her dismay. "You said you got them at that asylum?"

"So?"

"Maybe they're cursed or something. You don't know who they belonged to. The original owner could be dead. Doesn't that creep you out?"

"No." His brow rose as he laughed. "If the person is dead, then they have no use for them." He paused, rubbing his jaw as if in thought. "Maybe a ghost wants them back."

"Don't make fun of me." She glared at him. "Didn't you ever hear of objects being haunted? I mean, they have whole television shows about these things." Irritated, she poured a hearty dose of syrup on her pancakes.

"It's all nonsense," he said.

Finished with the cooking, Kyle turned off the stove. He took his plate of pancakes to the table and plopped down to eat. He stared across at his wife, who looked every bit unhappy.

"Come on, honey. You're being paranoid. I was just kidding about the ghost thing. Randy fills my head with his garbage."

"So I'm not the only crazy one?"

"Well, he believes in ghosts. Swears he'd seen them over the years. He's been in and out of a lot of abandoned places and he's got the pictures to prove it.

But I wouldn't trust him. There are phone apps to enhance your photos. You can add a spirit to any picture. I've seen it. Randy's slick like that."

"I'm sure you would've been right by Randy's side at every place he's ever explored, if you weren't stuck here with me."

"Probably." Instantly, he bemoaned the admission. He cut a bite of pancake. There she went again with her assumptions. Her comment belied her jealousy over his friendship with Randy. "I didn't mean it like it sounded."

"There's nothing wrong with honesty. I'm sorry your life is so boring with me."

"For real?" He sighed, shaking his head. "Are you really going to jump to that conclusion?"

"Well, isn't it?"

"My life is what I expected it to be. You. Me. Our daughter."

"That's not what I'm talking about, and you know it." Her gaze tore into him. "Randy can come and go as he pleases. Don't think I don't know what he thinks about me."

"Okay." Kyle dropped his fork onto the table. "I can see you're not going to be happy until we have an argument."

"I'm just saying…"

"Just saying what?" He shifted in his chair. "I asked you to marry me because I wanted to settle down with you. I wanted to build a life together. I love you. I don't want to be with a different woman every night of the week. Randy's life isn't so great. He's already had two pregnancy scares, and recently he picked up an STD. He's always broke because he spends all his money wining and dining these women. He's got no real grounding."

Her troubled eyes lifted in thought.

"So what if I think urban exploring has its merits?" Kyle continued. "I love history. Some of the architectural aspects of the buildings are incredible. Take Hudson State hospital, for example. There's a marble church inside the complex with a beautiful staircase. There's so much beauty among the ruins. Randy has some great pictures of it, but he also said it can be dangerous. There are areas where you could fall to your death."

"That's not too smart on Randy's end," she said. "It's pretty stupid to risk your life just so you can say, 'I did this. I did that. I've been here. I've been there.' And getting the almighty selfie to prove it. I don't want you going on any more of his missions. They're dangerous. You have a daughter to think of, and me. It's not worth the risk of getting killed."

His gaze fell on his daughter, who was now asleep in the swing, before landing on his wife. Her eyes held a mixture of pain and fear.

"Rose Hill has some dangerous areas, but most of the buildings are intact," he said. "Randy has gone a few times without me, so he's familiar with any pitfalls. I'd consider going back to look around some more."

"No," she said. "Don't go back there. You have no idea how it's affected you. Just you bringing the boots here has me on edge. I think you should get rid of them. Burn them or something."

"Seriously?"

"Seriously."

"No."

"Why not?" She crossed her arms, mouth firmly set.

"Because I like them." He shoved a forkful of pancake into his mouth, chewing it slowly.

"I was scared last night," she said. "Afraid in my own house. And you were downstairs without a care in the world. You could hardly wake up."

"Well, you still managed to wake me, didn't you?"

"Barely. If there had been a real emergency, I would've been on my own, or I would've had to call the cops."

"I'm not getting rid of my boots," he said. Enough was enough. So much for keeping the peace. "You're being paranoid."

Her sour expression changed to disbelief. Score one point for Kyle.

"Then keep them outside," she said. "Or on your feet. But quit putting them on my table."

"Whatever," he said. "Do you hear yourself?" He picked up his empty plate, sat it in the sink and rinsed it off. So much for a peaceful Sunday. Beth was ruining it. Monday was looking better and better.

Rolling her eyes, Beth stood and put her dish in the sink. "We'll see who's acting irrational when that creep comes back."

"I'll be ready if he does." He walked to her, pulling her stiff form into his arms. "Look, don't be upset. I'm just teasing you. Next time just punch me in the jaw. That will wake me."

She paused, relaxing against him.

I'm going to go visit my dad next Saturday," he said. "I'm just giving you a heads-up. It's been awhile since I've seen him."

"He doesn't even know you're there," she murmured. "You come back depressed. It's hard to watch."

"It's depressing but I'm going to be there for him." He dropped his hands from her waist. "Look. If your father was in a nursing home, you'd be glued to his side. But he's dead. So I guess you don't have that issue."

"That was cold,"

"Just because you don't like my father doesn't mean I shouldn't care."

"I've never said that." She lifted her chin, face flushed. "I just said he was acting weird before his stroke. He kept hanging around here as if he didn't want to go home."

"He was just a lonely old man."

"That's not the reason." She leaned against the counter. "There was something wrong. And lower your voice."

"Because I'm pointing the obvious. Admit it, you don't like him. You never have."

"Just stop it, Kyle. What's the matter with you?"

"Nothing. Just forget it."

Her mouth opened and snapped shut.

Immediately, he regretted his words.

"Pop needs me to be there for him," he said, lowering his voice. The baby stirred but remained sleeping. "He'd do it and has done it for me. I'm making sure the nursing home is treating him right. They get paid well enough to be taking good care of him. I won't have him neglected."

"Whatever, Kyle. Have it your way." Stiffly, she did an about-face, heading toward the doorway. "Just so you know next Saturday is Halloween."

"And that means what?"

She snared him with her eyes. "It's only your daughter's first Halloween. There's nothing special about it, at least to you. I guess I'll be the one enjoying it."

"I'll go see Dad on Sunday then." But it was too late to appease her.

Chapter Twelve

The aroma of soup and baking bread filled the day room at Chester Trail nursing home. Sunlight filtered in through cracked blinds. Various individuals sat around oval tables. Many of the elderly patients had retired to the center to live out the remainder of their days.

The buffet was situated in the middle of the room, being attended by staff.

Attendants wheeled in a few aged residents and situated them either near a table or by the large windows. The overhead music changed to silly, Halloween-themed lyrics.

An aide wheeled in Scott Hampton, his head drooped slightly to one side, his eyes expressionless. The woman parked the wheelchair by one of the windows and gave him a once-over. Gently, she pulled up his white sock, which had slipped down his bony leg.

"There now. I put you here, so you can see everyone in the room. Today is Halloween and we have a special treat for everyone. I'll come back to check on you in just a little while."

Scott stared straight ahead, unmoving.

Betty moved away, leaving him alone.

The speaker's volume increased, blaring the music. From the hallway, a horn blasted. A woman came in, dressed as Dorothy from the *Wizard of Oz*. Then the

Tin Man. They were followed by a witch with a wand, and a funny-looking jester. The foursome created a lot of noise, coming into the room with broad smiles. Dorothy, her stuffed dog in a basket, moved around the room, talking with residents.

"Who would like to pet Toto?" Dorothy stopped by an elderly woman's side. "I promise he won't bite."

The Tin Man held a can of pretend oil. He stretched out his arms, walking stiffly, as if cursed by rust. "Please someone, would you please oil me?" He stopped at a table of men, who obliged the pretense, putting oil on his proffered elbow. "Oh, thank you, my good man. Thank you."

The witch waved her wand in the air, chanting pretend spells. With her wand, she touched the top of an elderly woman's head and she clapped her hands in delight. She continued along, taking the time to talk to each resident.

The jester made his way around the room. He held a small kazoo in his hands, blowing it on occasion. Then he pulled out a pack of balloons. He stopped by an obese resident and proceeded to create a dog out of a balloon. He used a marker and dotted eyes and a mouth.

"My, my, my," the jester said, patting the woman's stomach with a white gloved hand. "You have been eating your curds and whey." The woman didn't seem to mind, laughing at his jest.

The jester continued dancing about the room. He bowed and spun in circles, his purple and red cap with bells bobbing. He stopped at another table, making more balloon art.

Motionless, Scott Hampton watched the jester in his antics. The witch came closer, offered a sad smile, and continued. Dorothy also presented him her little dog, but his hands remained clenched together on his lap. The Tin Man didn't even bother to acknowledge him.

But the jester spied Scott. When he reached the wheelchair, he danced around it, singing "*Ring around the Rosie.*" Grabbing the chair handles, he released the brakes and spun the chair around in a circle, his laughter cresting.

The jester stopped the chair, leaning down. Closely, he stared into Scott's eyes. "Guess who's here?" He tapped his knuckle against Scott's head. "Knock. Knock. Anyone home?" More laughter followed. "I guess not. But my, my. What an ugly scar you have there. Looks like someone bumped his head in a nasty fall."

The jester spun the chair around again, glancing around the room. No one was paying them much heed. Not anyone that mattered. He leaned over the back of the chair, pressing his mouth close to Scott's ear.

"Remember me, Pop? Or is that brain too fried to remember anything? How pathetic you've become. Karma's a bitch."

The jester danced around the chair again, whistling and humming. He squatted down in front of Scott again, staring into his eyes. He put his gloved hand over Scott's clenched fingers.

"Want me to make you a balloon animal? How about a sword?"

No reply. No reaction.

"You're no fun," the jester said. "Tsk, tsk. Scotty is such a dull boy."

The jester squeezed the two slender hands together,

deliberately crushing the frail bones.

"Can't feel much, can you?"

The tormentor pulled a bazooka from his pocket and blew a shrill sound.

"You are really out of it, aren't you? I bet you make your precious son proud."

Noting an aide staring at them, the jester returned the bazooka to his pocket and pulled out a long silver balloon. He whistled while he worked, creating a sword. He slipped it into Scott's stiff hands.

"Mind now, don't you go hitting anyone with that," the jester warned. "You look smashing. Just like a real hero. Ready to come to the rescue." He flicked the sword back and forth, forcing the stiff fingers to move. "But we can't rescue everyone, can we Scott? No matter how big our hearts are. You know what I'm talking about, ol' boy? Some people don't matter. But time has a way of catching up, doesn't it?" He paused in his antics. "The shoe's on the other foot. You've been forgotten. I know that feeling and can relate. But seriously now, how does it feel?" He leaned against the frail knees. "It sucks, doesn't it?"

The jester pressed his nose against Scott's.

"You're probably wondering why I came here today." He paused, searching the old man's eyes. "We don't have much time, so I'll tell you. It was me at your house." He nodded, smiling. "I was watching you for weeks before I broke in. The hammer was in my hand one moment and..." He paused. "I don't remember much after that. It wasn't the reunion I'd hoped for. In some ways, it was disappointing. A real let-down. But then you survived." Stitches laughed. "It's been six months! Amazing."

"This is better though." The jester said the words slowly. "I will bide my time for a better reunion. I've been sort of good. Oh, you'd be proud. I thought of you. Did you think about me?" The jester frowned. "No, you didn't, did you? Don't sit there and lie. You know what? I don't care anymore. Now you can sit in here and wonder where I am, and what I'm doing. And there's nothing you can do about it. I told you, I'd come if you double-crossed me. I warned you. You can't say I don't keep my word."

The jester dropped his hands away from Scott's hands, but the sword managed to stay in place. He stood, noticing an old woman waving him to come over. Ah, how'd he like to flip her off. Instead, he grinned, nodding. He leaned down again, grabbed the balloon, and sharply pinched the latex with his fingers.

Pop.

Once again, the jester leaned close, staring into Scott's frozen eyes, searching. And then he saw what he was looking for.

Fear.

Positively giddy, he gave a soft chuckle.

"I found you, Scott. I see what's left of your miserable soul. You're not so brain-dead after all. I believe I've been a cure for you. But even if you do come back to life, it will be too late to protect your precious Kyle."

The old man blinked, slowly but surely.

"But just for pity's sake," the jester began. He pulled out another balloon, recreating the sword. He placed it back into Scott's feeble hands "Wave your sword proudly, Scotty. Today you can play the hero. But tomorrow, tsk, tsk. Who knows what's to come?"

The jester bowed low, spun on his heels, and waved his hands in the air.

"I'll be back again to visit soon," the jester said. He patted Scott's head as if he were a teacher bestowing an award upon a student. "Yes, real soon."

Chapter Thirteen

Twilight settled over a crisp Halloween. Trick-or-treaters had started their journey around Kyle's neighborhood. Driving home, he watched for children in the streets. After parking his truck, Kyle grabbed the letters from the mailbox and headed toward the front door. The porch was colorfully lit with several pumpkins nestled against a fall display. Nothing scary. But that was Beth. No ghouls or goblins to scare the kids.

It wouldn't be long before they began receiving children looking for treats. He'd never asked Beth if she bought candy. She was barely speaking to him. In a way, he preferred the silence.

He shrugged off his thoughts. Halloween only came once a year. Might as well enjoy it. Feeling mischievous, he rang the doorbell.

"Trick or…" The words died on his lips as the door opened.

Beth, wearing a witch's costume, peeked out through the glass storm door. Bright red lipstick and false eyelashes gave her a younger, sexier appearance. Her black dress hung just past her silk-covered thighs, but it was her cleavage that drew his interest.

"Looks like I just got a treat," he said. His wife had morphed into a stranger. Was he at the right house? He snapped his mouth shut, surely it was gaping open.

Beth's expression changed from guarded to pleased. Flicking her hair over one shoulder, she spun around in the doorway, shaking her hips. Her hat slid to one side. She caught it, jammed it on her head, grinning impishly.

In a space of a moment, his body betrayed him. So much for discord. Beth was putting on a show just for him, and he liked it. His resistance faded; she was advertising, and he was taking the bait.

"You like?" Eagerly she searched his face. "I lost a few pounds, and my dress still fits."

"I like." Aroused, his gaze slid over her form. Was this the same woman who'd ignored him all week? The scent of wine on her breath gave away the reason for her flirtatious mood. He caught himself before he could ask if the alcohol would get into her breastmilk. She'd never endanger Sammy. "You look hot. If you keep shaking those hips, I'll show you just how sexy you are."

She beamed. "Come see Samantha."

He followed her into the living room, eyes on her thighs. Samantha was awake, sucking on her fist. She had a hint of orange lines drawn on her cheeks. She wore a puffy, orange playsuit with a leaf shaped hairclip in her hair.

"Hello, pumpkin," he said, kissing his daughter's cheek. He lifted his head, eyes roaming over Beth's form. Damn. It'd been a while since he and Beth played around. It brought back memories of when they first met. Flushed, he rubbed at his forehead, brushing away the sheen. "I thought you were dressing the baby up as a kitten?"

"I changed my mind. I liked this costume better."

Beth smiled down at their daughter. "I wish we could take her out and show her off to the neighbors but it's cold and she's so little."

"Next year we can."

The doorbell rang, and they ushered in their first group of kids. Beth showed off their daughter as Kyle disappeared upstairs to take a quick shower. The water barely dampened his hunger for his wife.

Nosing around the kitchen, Kyle munched on pretzels, killing time. At eight-thirty, he lifted Samantha to his shoulder as Beth locked the front door and shut off the light. The baby was asleep. Hopefully, she'd stay that way. Upstairs, he tucked the baby into her crib as Beth stood in the doorway, watching him. When he turned around, she had vanished. For a moment, he panicked. Had he misread the signs?

Quietly, he entered the bedroom, hoping she hadn't already donned a nightgown. His heart leaped at the sight. His sexy witch was standing near the window, gazing out at the moon. Two glasses of wine stood on the nightstand.

"Such a nice night." She tilted her head, smiling.

Kyle made his move. Beth cried out in surprise as he grabbed her, spinning her around. He nuzzled her face, moving down her neck toward her cleavage, encouraged by her lack of resistance.

Hungrily, he kissed her, hands roaming over her hips as she moaned beneath his lips.

"I thought you were mad at me," he said, lifting his head.

"I want to make up. I miss you."

Her words tugged at his heart. How he had missed their intimacy. "What about Sammy? Can you drink wine?"

"I pumped a couple of bottles," she said. "I also have formula. She'll be fine."

With that out of the way, she picked up a wine glass and handed it to him. She grabbed the other glass, saluting. "I love you, Kyle." She clinked her glass to his, lifting it up. "I don't want to lose you. Lose us."

In seconds, he gulped down the wine, returning his glass to the nightstand. Gently, he retrieved her glass and placed it next to his.

His eyes never left her face as he moved closer, drawing her to him. Moonlight spilled in through the window, enhancing her eyes.

"Come here, my little witch." He lowered his head, tasting her lips. Eagerly, she drew him toward her.

"Gladly," she whispered.

Chapter Fourteen

On Sunday morning, Kyle checked in at the front desk of Chester Trail. He tried to make it a habit to come out to the nursing home once or twice a month. When his father first arrived, Kyle visited more frequently, hoping that seeing a familiar face would somehow trigger his father's memory. But week after week, no change. Just that blank stare. It was enough to discourage anyone. But Pop's heart was healthy. His mind used to be razor-sharp. He knew Pop was still there, it was only a matter of reaching through the veil.

"Hey, Pop," Kyle said, kissing the top of his father's balding head. The scar on the old man's face had healed, now vividly pink beneath wispy hair. "How've you been?"

Kyle sat in a chair, studying the thin form of his father, who was tucked into a hospital bed. He hated seeing him in this useless state. It was hard, depressing.

Six months ago, his father had had a massive stroke. Falling, he'd struck his head on the brick corner of his fireplace. No one was sure just how long he'd lain there, bleeding, waiting for help. By chance, the postman delivering mail noticed Pop through the front window. It was a miracle that Pop was alive, but this wasn't life. His father was partially paralyzed. Sure, they could prop him up, move him around from room to room. But Pop just stared off into the distance or slept.

The doctors held out hope for some possible recovery but so far therapy proved futile. Now Pop was wasting away to skin and bones, despite being fed through a feeding tube.

Kyle began rattling away about Halloween, Beth and the baby. Anything to bring a bit of life into the room. He talked about the wedding, the weather, and the coming holidays.

"It would be nice, Pop, if you could be on the mend." He sat his elbows on his knees, leaning forward. "We'd love to have you for Christmas. Hell, we'd love to have you any day." He paused, looking hard at his father. "I started looking for Roy. I'd like your input and to be able to ask you some questions. No one has any idea where he is at. It's been years since I last saw him…"

Kyle finally ran out of words. The silence stretched.

"I heard there was a Halloween party yesterday. Sounds like it was fun." Kyle stood up and moved around the room. "Remember how we used to turn the garage into a haunted house and dress up? All the kids from the neighborhood would come. Their parents liked it too. You would give out hot cider and tell your ghost stories." He looked out the blinds, and then picked up his father's cards. His eyes dampened as he read the messages of love and hope from family members and friends.

Kyle walked around the bed, looking at the quilt hanging over the rocking chair. He touched it and smiled. His adoptive mother had made it. The woman had used bits and pieces of old clothing to make her memory quilts. He wished she were alive to see

Samantha. He had no doubt she'd have enjoyed making his daughter a blanket or two.

He stopped by the nightstand. Several framed pictures of his father in various stages of life sat on the stand. He picked up the photo album his aunt had created. She had wanted the nursing staff to see that Scott Hampton was a person, he'd once had a productive life. He'd been in the armed forces, a scout leader. Spent hours at Rose Hill giving up his time in community service, even inviting a few Rose Hill kids over on the weekends for campouts. The man had the right to dignity. Now he was just an empty shell.

Kyle shifted in the chair, leafing through the album. He'd seen it a hundred times, but still the memories soothed him. There was one with Pop and his friends on a fishing trip. A few Boy Scout photos. Pictures of other relatives. Camping had always been a favorite. Another in the yard with their dog, Molly, fetching a stick. There were several of birthday parties and other events. He came to the last page.

Something new.

A nursing home picture.

He slipped the picture out of the insert and held it up to the light. Current day. It was a Polaroid picture of the day room during the Halloween party. Various people were seated around tables. Some were smiling, others talking, some eating. A witch was waving her wand near the front of the room. A Tin Man was seated at a table, legs crossed.

He froze, spying his father's image in the rear of the photo. In his fingers, Pop held something. He peered closer. A balloon in the shape of a sword? His gaze slid to the side of his father's wheelchair.

Kyle dropped the picture.

Jumping up from the chair, he stared at the picture, which had flipped onto its back. His heart did an erratic beat in his chest. He stared at his father, then at the picture. Finally, Kyle reached down and picked it up.

He walked over to the bed, holding the picture in front of his father's face.

"Who was this in the picture with you?"

No response.

"Pop." He shoved the picture closer to his father's vacant eyes. "This man in the photo, the one wearing the jester hat. Do you know him? What did he want? What did he say to you?"

No answer.

Kyle flipped the picture around, studying it. The man's lips were shockingly red, face tinted ash white. But it was the old purple and red crested cap and silver bells that held him rapt. It was spiky, ugly and unique. Exaggerated brows hung over the comic's large wild eyes. Smudged overgrowth shadowed both cheeks.

Liquid ice slid down his spine. It was uncanny.

But that was just crazy. He needed to get a grip; it was after all, Halloween. People dressed up for parties, charities or just for fun. It'd been years since he'd seen a jester's cap. Perhaps he was being paranoid. Yet, this man was giving him the creeps. He looked familiar.

He held the picture up to his father's face again.

"Pop. Please. Did you know this guy?" He leaned closer to his dad's face, pointing at the jester. "If you know him, just blink once for me. Did you know this man?"

A few seconds ticked away.

Scott Hampton blinked, slowly, deliberately.

Shocked, Kyle laid his hand over his father's. Gently, he rubbed the back of his neck.

Gurgling noises came from his father's throat. His right hand trembled.

"Nurse! Nurse!" Kyle ran out to the hallway. "Come quick. My father's choking."

The nurse came running with two other aides. She motioned for Kyle to leave the room. Slowly, he walked out into the hallway to gather himself. Inside the bedroom, suction noises filled the air. Several minutes later, the noise stopped. A nurse came out into the hallway.

"We're just cleaning him up. He'll be okay."

"He responded to me," he said absently. "He blinked when I asked him a question. His right hand moved."

"I'm sure he knows you're here," she assured him. She touched his shoulder. "Don't ever give up hope. I've seen miracles in this place."

"Thank you for saying so," Kyle said. "I was showing him pictures, trying to jog his memories. There was a picture of the Halloween party from yesterday in his photo album. Where did you find the people to dress up for the party?"

"Oh, they're just volunteers. They receive no pay. We run an ad in the community bulletin. We are always grateful when we can cheer up our guests."

Kyle didn't respond.

"Everyone had a wonderful time," she continued. "Perhaps that's why your father responded to you today. The stimulation did him some good."

She had no idea, he thought.

"Do you have any more pictures from the party?"

"Maybe a few," she said. "You could ask at the front desk."

He returned to his father's room, staring down at the man who had adopted him, changing his life. His lifeline. Pop's ashen face revealed his recent choking spell and the physical turmoil from the episode.

"Don't worry about a thing, Pop. I will check into this. You just rest now. You're in good hands. I'll come back next week to check on you." He leaned down and kissed his dad's cheek. "I love you, Pop. Now, you have a good rest. I'll be back in a few days."

On his way out of the building, he stopped by the front desk and asked about the pictures. They pointed him to the bulletin board. Walking over to it, he saw another picture of the jester's cap. His mood darkened; thoughts crazed.

Returning to the front desk, Kyle said, "No one is to visit my father unless they're approved by me and on his list. No one. And if anyone does come by to see him that's not on his list, I'd like a phone call with a name. Understand?"

The receptionist's eyes narrowed, frowning at his tone.

"Understand?" Kyle repeated. He leaned his palms against the counter, making eye contact with the woman.

"Perfectly."

Chapter Fifteen

Early Monday evening, Kyle walked around Randy's new pint-sized brick house, spying his friend sleeping on a hammock, stretched between two trees. Earphones were stuck into Randy's ears and an empty beer can lay crumpled up beneath one of the trees.

"What a life," Kyle said, shoving the hammock. "Look at you, man. In your Bermuda shorts and tie-dye shirt, and it's fifty degrees out here. Aren't you cold?"

"Nope. The sun's still shining. That's all I need." Randy opened his eyes, stared up at his visitor and smiled. "What's up?"

"I tried calling you all day," Kyle said. "I finally just stopped by. I need my drill gun."

"It's in my garage." Randy climbed off the hammock, grabbed the empty beer can and threw it into his garbage can. "You want a beer?"

"No." He followed Randy toward the garage. "I can't stay long. I got a dentist appointment at six."

Randy opened the garage door. Inside, the garage was crammed full of junk and two broken motorcycles. Two large bags of dog food leaned against the wall.

"How the heck can you find anything in here?" Kyle asked. "You just moved in, and you already got it filled up with crap. It's a mess."

"Kat is addicted to garage sales; she's been hunting for bargains."

"You'll never use half this junk." Kyle picked up an orange safety cone. Next to it sat a bucket of steel rods. "Unless you're going into the cement or asphalt business."

"Kat doesn't know what she's buying. She just guesses. I'll probably have my own garage sale in the spring. But believe it or not, I know my way around in here." Randy laughed, moving toward the rear of the garage. In the back, he picked up a case. He maneuvered his way back to the front. "Here's the drill. Thanks for letting me use it. Mine's broken."

"Anytime." Kyle took the case. "So what's up with you? Anything?"

"No. I took a vacation day today. I spent the day with Kat. She's out at the store, getting dinner."

"I think you're getting domesticated."

"She's fun," Randy said. "She buys me stuff. Loves me. She can cook. Cleans my house. The sex is good. That's enough of a reason to keep her around."

"You're shallow," Kyle said. "A true male chauvinist. Why don't you marry her? Settle down."

"I've thought about it," Randy said, grinning.

"For real?"

"Yes, for like a minute or two. Then back to reality." He laughed. "But if I change my mind, Kat's high up on my list of potential candidates."

Kyle shook his head. "Have you been back to the asylum?"

"Yeah." Randy grew serious, leaning against Kyle's truck. "I took Kat with me. I was going to take some pics and get kinky. She was freaked out the whole time. We ended up in the Quarter house building, in the basement. We had just started fooling around." He paused, thoughtfully. "There was someone in the building. He began making noises. It freaked her out."

Speechless, Kyle hung to his every word.

"I was so pissed," Randy continued. "It brought me right back to my childhood years. Remember all the crazy games we played in the dark?"

"Don't remind me."

"It might've been some guy looking for a peep show," Randy said, winking. "I'm sure he left disappointed. Kat will never forgive me for that one. We saw people outside looking at the property. They looked official, like they were there for a purpose. I read in the paper today that the state found a buyer and it's now under contract."

"Who's buying it?"

"A land developer. I don't know what he wants with the place. Probably going to build houses or a complex. But that's a lot of buildings to tear down. That alone will cost a small fortune."

"So you're done with Rose Hill?"

"No, not yet," Randy said. "It's under contract. It didn't settle. I might not get another chance to explore before it sells."

"I'd like to nose around one last time," Kyle said. "I'll go with you. How about Saturday? I want to visit before bad weather hits."

"I thought you said you were never going back there."

"I changed my mind."

"I don't think it's a good idea." Randy said. "It's really affected you. I wouldn't go."

"It has affected me," Kyle said. "And going back isn't going to change that. I'm still going with or without you. So are you in?"

"Beth know about it?"

"Hell no," Kyle replied. "And let's keep it that way."

Chapter Sixteen

Getting out of the house without arousing suspicion on Saturday was the hardest part. Kyle used the excuse that he was needed at work for a few hours. It was partially true but what he was required to do at the quarry would only take a half hour. He planned on meeting Randy right after that. He hated that he had to lie, but Beth forced him to, all in the name of peace. He loved his wife, but he didn't need another lecture or want to ruin their newfound intimacy. Now that they'd been intimate again, he couldn't seem to get enough of her. If she called his work, she'd find out the truth anyway. He didn't care if she eventually did. He just wanted to get out of the house without an earful or have her blowing up his phone all day.

Kyle drove to the quarry and met Ethan, one of the company's newest operators. After reviewing the instructions with the employee, Kyle took some time watching Ethan work the machine. Satisfied that he could handle the job, Kyle left.

He picked up Randy and they drove to Spring Forge, where they parked behind the local minimart. They crossed Main Street and walked along the railroad tracks by the river, cutting through the woods until they reached Rose Hill's broken roadway. They traveled through another patch of woods and passed several buildings, one of them demolished. They had a better viewpoint of the grounds, since some of the autumn leaves had fallen, spreading a thick carpet. It was quiet, serene.

In the distance, the huge brick buildings stood out in gloomy detail. Vines clung to the walls and broken windows abounded. They moved onto the catwalk and stopped in front of the Dalphine building. After they entered through the basement window, they moved through the cellar and used the rear entrance to move into the tunnels. Chilly air surrounded them, and dampness teased their lungs.

Like a deadbolt, the darkness hit home. Kyle had forgotten how black it was in the tunnels. It was unnerving, you couldn't tell if it was night or day outside. He almost second-guessed his decision to come. Memories began cascading over him and childhood fears surfaced. Still, he followed Randy through the corridor until they came upon the entrance into the Quarter House's basement.

"This is where I brought Kat," Randy said over his shoulder. He moved through the basement and stopped in the middle of the last room, staring at the dental chair which loomed like something out of a horror movie. "There's the chair."

"You got Kat to sit on that?" Kyle had to give Kat credit; Beth wouldn't have done it. Hell, he didn't think he would have.

"I have my ways," Randy said, flashing a grin. "I wish the creep that was in here with us would show up. He ruined my plans with Kat and I'm still pissed off over it, but I'm prepared if he tries anything today." He patted the bulge under his coat. "So let him make a show, and I'll give him something to laugh about."

"I doubt anyone was just hiding in here and waiting," Kyle said. "Whoever it was probably saw you and Kat on the grounds and followed you."

"The guy was a pervert."

"Like you?" Kyle laughed. "Kat was probably glad for the intervention. Only someone with a crazy mind would bring a woman here for sex."

"Don't knock it till you try it. It's not crazy."

Crazy. The word resounded in Kyle's mind. He hated that word. Rose Hill was a place the public called "the crazy zone." He hated the label almost as much as he hated the word "retarded."

"You're the pervert."

"Maybe I'm a crazy pervert. What's wrong with that?"

"Nothing," Kyle said. "Just forget it." Apparently, Randy saw nothing wrong with labels. They didn't seem to bother him. But labels could be cruel, degrading, and inhumane.

"I tried to spice up the old love life," Randy said. "Maybe you should try it sometime."

Ignoring this, Kyle moved around the room, checking closets and rear rooms. They moved throughout the rest of the basement, checking out the bathroom, boiler room, and office.

"Doesn't look like anyone's been in most of these rooms," Kyle said. "There's dust all over the floors. There would be footprints."

"Not anyone you can see," Randy said. He pulled out his cell phone, taking a couple of pictures. "Can't you feel something heavy in here? I'm telling you, it's haunted. Ghosts don't leave footprints but sometimes show up in pictures."

"And why do you think that is?" Kyle's brow rose. "Anyone can dissect a picture and find something weird about it. Ever hear of people that find faces in objects? I can find a face in a tree trunk or in the asphalt, but it doesn't mean anything."

"Always the skeptic, aren't you?" Randy stuck his phone beneath Kyle's nose. "Then explain this."

What looked like a shadow person stood by the back wall. Kyle lifted his gaze to the concrete, searching for what could've caused it. He flashed his light over the surface, trying to recreate the image.

"So what?" he said. "That doesn't mean anything. It's just the way the image was captured."

"If you say so," Randy said, shaking his head.

Kyle shook off his ominous words. He felt a heaviness in his chest, an uncomfortable darkness pressing against his eyes. But he was pretty good at shutting it out, not letting his imagination roam free. He'd had plenty of practice when he was a kid learning how to deal with the darkness and things that went bump in the night. "I thought you wanted to check out the hospital?"

"I do." Randy pulled the map of the campus out of his pocket, shining his light down upon the tunnel images. "I know how to get there from here. I'm getting pretty good at remembering my way around. Let's go."

They entered the tunnel system again. It broke off into two different directions. Kyle stopped in the middle of it. His headlamp shone down a menacing-looking hallway.

"I'd like to check out some of the other buildings," Kyle said. "You go and see what's up at the hospital. I'll catch up with you in a little bit."

"I'll come with you."

"No," Kyle said. "I just want some time by myself. Call it a trip down memory lane. I…I've tried so hard to forget this place. I just need some closure."

Randy considered him. "You okay, Kyle? Anything bothering you?"

"Maybe. I just need to reconnect a bit. This place is in my mind. In my dreams. I just need to put it to rest. It's nothing personal. Understand?"

"Any luck finding Roy?"

"No, but Beth thinks she has a lead."

"I don't think we should split up," Randy said. "I mean, what if there is someone else down here with us? That guy could be somewhere in one of the buildings. It'd be safer if we stuck together."

"Safer?" Kyle grinned. "Do you remember who you're talking to? Besides, you brought your gun and a knife. You'll be fine. I can handle myself in here. I know my way around. Just don't shoot me when I catch up to you."

"I wish I got phone service down here. It would be simpler to just call you. You'd better yell out your name."

"I will. Give me a half hour or so. If I don't come back in an hour, then come looking for me. I won't be longer than that."

"Okay," Randy said. "Don't say I didn't warn you if that perv shows up."

Kyle ignored him, starting down the opposite direction. Humid, moist air filled his mouth with a foul taste. Objects became clear as his light closed in on them, mostly broken furniture, trash, cans of food, and bottles. He passed several entrances to buildings, most of them with broken doors. Finally, he stopped at the building he sought and entered it.

Indistinct noises sounded in the basement as Kyle entered the rear staircase and walked up into the first floor of the building. Sunlight streamed in some of the windows, revealing wet spots on the floor as well as thick heavy dust. He moved down the hallway. Two double doors opened outward. He grabbed the handles, pulling them open.

Inside, numerous benches were bolted to the floor. In the front of the room, a wooden stage. Coughing from the dust, he felt unease spread through his limbs. He collected his scattered thoughts, which flew in every direction. Finally, he stepped into the room, walking toward the stage. He paused, remembering the sights and sounds from the past. Now the quiet was unnerving.

He headed for a doorway on the right. Inside, a small hallway led to a changing room, office, and several walk-in closets. He moved into a rear chamber. The room was in complete disarray, carpet filthy. Old clothing was lying all over the place, some of it scattered across a desk.

Ignoring the mess, Kyle walked through the room and opened another door. He flicked on his headlamp and walked into a closet. Wooden shelves lined both sides. It stank like something had died. He jumped when he spied his own reflection in a full-length mirror. He stood before his image as his heart thudded heavily in his chest. Closing his eyes for a moment, he ran his hand along the mirror's edge, found a latch and pulled. The mirror cracked open. Slipping his fingers beneath the frame, he opened the hidden portal.

Untouched for the most part, he stepped back into the past. The concealed room had been used for security. Some of Rose Hill's residents had no trouble walking off with stage equipment or costumes. Only a select few knew about the space, and certainly not the current-day trespassers.

Shelving lined both sides of the room. The compartments held clothing, gloves, scarfs and hats. Hooks held belts, suspenders, ties, and more hats. Built into the wall, long drawers lined the rear barrier. Bile found its way into Kyle's throat. He dropped his backpack to the ground, unzipped it and forced himself to open the first drawer.

Rummaging around the contents, he shoved handkerchiefs and gloves to one side. His heart was racing so fast he thought he'd pass out. Sweat poured down his face, dripping into his eyes. The stench kept him moving.

At the bottom of the drawer, a small circle latch held his attention. Slipping his finger in the loop, he pulled it up. Another drawer appeared; inside was a messy array of items.

He found packs of balloons, feathers, and handkerchiefs. His fingers lingered over some of the other contents. He sorted through makeup and wigs. Most of it was aged and brittle. Fake mustaches, eyebrows, eyelashes. Beneath, hats appeared, an array of colors stood out. Red, orange, black, and blue. No jester cap.

Slamming the door shut, Kyle searched the other drawers, finding more clothing and props. No luck.

Finally, he stopped to mop the sweat off his brow. He leaned against the wall, breathing heavily. The purple and red cap was missing. How he'd hated that thing! It was unique in the fact that it was created at Rose Hill in his sewing class. It was part of his project. It stood out not only in color, but its razor-like crested horns. Whenever someone played a villain in a skit, the cap was used. Eventually the cap was retired, and then it went missing. It showed up in the tunnels and was used during hide and seek, terrorizing the younger kids. Someone wearing a similar cap with bells had visited his father. A coincidence? Probably. Most likely, he was being paranoid. But he'd wondered about it as soon as he saw the photo at the nursing home.

Still. He had hoped the cap had still been in the drawer. An unsettled feeling resounded in his gut. Once freed from Rose Hill's grasp, he was now back in the middle of its core. He considered his life to have begun at the age of nine—he'd shoved his past into a locked box, never to resurface. Now memories were coming in bits and pieces. He wanted clarity, but fear kept him pressing the thoughts away. And now, like a fool, here he was at Rose Hill again.

Gathering himself, Kyle tried to shake his growing sense of doom. With a quick glance around the room, he exited and headed for the tunnels.

Chapter Seventeen

Cold air stirred through Beth's shoulder-length hair as she rounded the corner in the store, cart in hand. Reaching into the attached car seat, she tucked Samantha's blanket around her tiny, sleeping form. The grocery store was freezing. Didn't they know to shut off the air conditioner? It was November, not August. Thankfully, she had brought a blanket for the baby. Samantha was so little. She'd hate for her to get ill, especially with the upcoming holidays.

In the baby aisle, she paused to stare at the hundreds of infant things, toys, diapers, wipes and bottles. She touched a couple of toys, thinking of Samantha's first Christmas. Excitement lifted her spirits.

She finished her shopping, checked out at the front register, and loaded her bagged items into the cart. She pushed the cart outside, through the parking lot. Opening the rear passenger side door, she unlatched the baby's car seat from the cart and placed Samantha's seat into the backseat. She stood up, closing the door. She moved to the rear of the vehicle, opening the trunk.

That was when she saw him.

A man wearing a crazy purple and red hat was waving to her from across the parking lot. Bells were attached to the pointed-crested tips, glittering in the sunlight. His dark brows rose mischievously beneath his exaggerated ruby grin. Ghastly features stood out against the windswept day. White gloves engulfed his hands. He wore red and yellow mismatched clothes with a gaudy bowtie.

She looked over her shoulder, searching for the recipient of his wave. But no one was there. She touched her chest, gawking. He nodded yes, pointing toward her. He spun around in a circle, kicked his heels together in an odd display. His cap shifted from his actions, revealing his huge, painted forehead.

She paused, confused. He must be promoting one of the stores in the shopping center. But which one? There were several small stores attached to the main grocery store. Nothing that needed the advertising aid. And the man held no sign or logos. Perhaps he was there for entertainment; the grocery store might be having something for the kids. Still, she hadn't seen anything in their circular.

The comic's gaze remained on her. She broke his spell, placing her groceries into the trunk. Her heart galloped at an alarming pace. She shoved the bags into the car, intending on making a hasty retreat. But it wasn't to be.

"Hello there, young miss," the man said, nudging her shoulder with his.

She pivoted, unsure if she'd been assaulted. An odd scent perforated the air. She couldn't place the odor. Not exactly unpleasant and yet, not cologne.

He gave a salute. "How are you this fine, sunny day?"

"I'm…I'm fine," she managed to say. Up close, he was spookier than ever. Surely, he'd frighten a child. She glanced around, looking for other patrons. Only an elderly woman came into view, and she was walking with an obvious limp.

Dazed, she wondered what he was about. They were in the middle of a parking lot, hardly a back alley. Still, there was something off about him. Feeling stupid, she guessed she could be overreacting. It wouldn't be the first time. She shrugged off her misgivings.

The jokester dipped his head, to peer into the car window at the baby.

"I see you have a young one. Boy? Girl?"

"Girl."

"Mind if I take a closer peek?"

"Well…"

Before she could finish, he opened the door and ducked his head into the car to take a closer view of Samantha. He tickled the baby's sock-clad foot.

"Hello, Miss Sunshine," the man whispered. "Aren't you a sweet little angel?"

"No offense, but why are you out here in the parking lot?" Beth didn't like him touching Samantha. He was too pushy. She'd had enough. Using her body, she blocked his view of the baby. She was undeterred by his towering frame or the fleeting glint in his gaze. But then he produced what she was sure was a phony grin, trying to disarm her.

"The store hired me to hand out balloons to the kids today. I was just on my way in when I saw you with your little one. I thought I'd stop by to say hello."

"Oh." Now she felt rash. Of course, they hired him. There was no other explanation as to why he would be wandering around. "Well, thank you for saying hello. But now we've got to be going."

"But wait," the man said. "A gift for the little one." Fingers dipping into his front pocket, he pulled out a green and pink balloon. "A special flower for your little princess." He began blowing up the balloons, twisting and turning them into a flower and stem. He handed it to Beth. "For your beautiful daughter."

"It wasn't necessary. But thank you." Awkwardly, she grabbed her purse. "I'd like to tip you."

"Not necessary," said the man. He leaned over and kissed her cheek. "A kiss is payment enough. You two ladies have a wonderful day."

With that, he skipped away through the parking lot.

Stunned, Beth touched her wet cheek. She dug into her purse, grabbed a tissue, and rubbed it off. What a weird person. Feeling peculiar, she jumped into the front seat, gathering herself. As she was pulling out of the parking lot, she looked in her rearview mirror. Strange. The comic wasn't headed toward the store. Instead, he went to a van.

A horn blew, breaking her eye contact with the lot. She drove away, feeling a little sick.

Chapter Eighteen

Kyle and Randy stood in the dimly lit hospital morgue, listening for sounds. It appeared they were alone. Randy flicked on his headlamp, lighting up the room. Shadows splayed across the walls, and Kyle flicked on his own light. The illumination revealed a mess. Broken medical equipment was strewn about, tubes, wires, and machinery. Thick dust covered the trash.

"I wish I could take one of these with me," Randy said. He shoved a heavy metal gurney across the room. It objected with a squeal, moving only a few feet. He grabbed another gurney, looking it over with a speculative eye.

"It'd be pretty hard to get out of here," Kyle flashed his light inside a large closet. More vials and papers were strewn around inside. Nothing of interest.

"I could find a way to get it out of here," Randy replied. "I'd just have to get one of the front doors open."

"That thing is gross. Who knows how many corpses used it?" Seeing the gurneys created a deep, gut-wrenching reaction. His heart rate adjusted accordingly.

"It would be cool for next Halloween," Randy argued. "Just think of what I could do with it. I'd like to make my own haunted house, kind of like your Pop used to make in your garage. Of course, my haunted house would be a lot better than your lame-ass skeleton paper decorations and scout projects. I'd scare the heck out of my neighbors. Kat would kill me if I brought this home, but I could sell it online. There's freaks out there that love this kind of stuff. I'd make a few bucks. Why not? It's just wasting away down here."

"These tables aren't props from some store. They were used for real people. Have some respect for the people who died here. Doesn't that bother you?"

"Nope," Randy said. "Why would it? You've got to check out sometime. Doesn't matter where or when. Everyone ends up on a slab, cold and dead." He hopped up on the metal gurney and the metal wheels creaked under his weight. He threw Kyle his cell phone. "Here. Take my pic."

Kyle stared at his friend; the phone clammy in his palms. Randy was funny, but today his humor pissed him off. He shrugged away the feeling as Randy lay down on the table, pretending to be dead. His friend got goofier, hanging his head off the side, tongue lolling out.

"Come on, Kyle." Randy lifted his head. "Stop being melodramatic."

"Knock it off. You're making fun of the dead. You're right, everyone checks out eventually. I might have a kid's recollection, but I was smart enough at the time to know that this place was just plain wrong on so many levels. I saw a lot of things no kid should ever see. I know you had some similar experiences. You lived here longer than me. Don't tell me it didn't affect you in some way."

"Geez." Randy sat up, giving Kyle a once-over.

"Are you really lecturing me? Really? I'm just messing around. You're taking it too seriously. You're right, this place sucked. I hated it. I got beat up by older kids, hit for things I didn't even do. Was called names. But I have good memories. Friends. Sports. Trips. And I had you on the outside. Your dad let me stay over at your house on the weekends. It was awesome. He made me feel like family. Secretly, I wanted him to adopt me as well. So maybe I joke around to deal with it. So what? Who cares? We both survived and Rose Hill got exposed and shut down. You can't change the past, so just deal with it."

Kyle shut his mouth. Randy was Randy.

He didn't want to argue the point. Randy had been his best friend since they were kids. They had a distinctive bond. He didn't have any friends to spare, having lost touch with most of them over the years. But Randy was still around.

"I was in this morgue years ago," Kyle admitted. "It was one of the last times I'd visited Rose Hill. I think I was about fourteen. My uncle Bill was still working here, and Pop brought me to help with a holiday play. There was a picnic afterward. Me and a couple of other boys explored the tunnels, messing around. We played tag but then one of the older boys snuck us into the hospital's basement. We didn't realize the morgue was down here. We just thought it was like the other basements. It had a weird smell. There were vials of something gross, maybe blood, in the sink. And when we walked in this area, we saw a corpse beneath a sheet. One of the kids lifted a corner and we saw a bare arm. The hands were curled in an odd claw, fingernails long and blackened. We screamed and ran out of this place. I thought I'd never come back in here again."

"You never told me that," Randy said, mouth ajar. "No wonder you're freaking out. I remember you telling me you saw a dead person, but I didn't think it was in here."

"It wasn't the only time," Kyle replied. "I didn't talk about being in the morgue to anyone. I just wanted to forget what I saw. It haunted me for weeks. I also saw Adam Collier die. He was walking around the yard and fell. He grabbed his chest and was gasping for air. A nurse came running and then a doctor. His eyes became fixed as he went still. I could tell he was dead by looking at him."

"Well, the man had to be a hundred years old," Randy said.

"He was almost eighty."

"Well, he looked a hundred," Randy said. "A lot of people went into the hospital, and I never saw them again. It scared me. Even when I was sick, I faked that I wasn't. I didn't want to get sent there."

Randy shifted on the gurney, face drawn, eyes void of emotion.

Kyle exhaled. It was good to talk to Randy. He needed to confide in someone, and Randy understood how it was. He wanted to press for more but stopped himself. Why bring Randy into his dismal mind? The man obviously could handle the past better than he could. In some ways, he envied him.

"Follow me," Kyle said. "If you want to see something freaky."

Kyle led Randy into an adjoining room. Just the sight of the morgue freezer panicked him. The metal container held nine chambers. Large metal handles adorned each. He grabbed a lever and pulled hard. Rusted and worn, the inside drawer came slowly into view. Dust, bugs and hair lay on the reflective surface.

"Get on it," Kyle said, "if you're so tough. Take a real peek into what it's like to be a corpse."

"Seriously?" Randy stood, hand on hips. One brow lifted over wide eyes. "You just complained that I was screwing around with a gurney, but lying on a freezer slab is different how?"

"You want to play dead. See what it's like for real." Kyle shrugged. "Go for it. I'll be right here to get your stupid butt out if necessary."

Undecided, Randy peeked in through the tube. "I'm claustrophobic."

"No, you're not," Kyle said. "That's just an excuse. Maybe you'll have more respect for the dead when you get out."

"Now you're sounding like the Kyle I used to know." Randy held his hands up. "The one who took dares. Okay, I'll do it. But you better get me out if I scream. That thing better not be sound-proof. And if it is, I'd have to wonder why. I'm taking a flashlight."

"No, you're not. That's cheating. If you really want to experience death, then go without any light."

"Would you do it?"

"Sure," Kyle said. "It's not much different than a full-body CAT scan at the hospital. You're awake. Aware. You like taking dares so I dare you to peek into the other side of life. Like you said, when you're dead, you're dead. Only this time you get to return."

"Okay, you talked me into it. One to tell the boys I guess." Randy maneuvered his lanky body inside the tube, feet toward the rear of the compartment. He laid back his head, staring up at Kyle. "Don't leave me, dude."

Not answering, Kyle pushed the shelf inside the metal compartment. The only sound was Randy's voice, faintly muffled. He paused, troubled. Surely, Rose Hill was messing with his head. Second guessing himself, Kyle stared down at his watch. He couldn't renege now. Besides, Randy loved this kind of crap. Five minutes ought to do it. He walked away to explore the morgue.

He found the incinerator, stood before it, and bowed his head. So many people had met their end in the hospital's ward. Some unnecessarily, due to poor care.

The hair on the back of his nape stood up. Eyes bore into his soul.

Kyle lifted his head, staring in the general direction of his tracker. Nothing there, just a painted, crusted wall. He stood silent; eyes wide. The feeling persisted. Chilled, he paused. As he turned, a shadow slid from the corner, hovered for a moment, and then disappeared.

Stunned, he stopped dead in his tracks. The hard lump in his throat tightened. It was getting tiring, explaining the things he had seen at the asylum, past and present. What did it mean? Was his imagination on overload? He chose the last scenario.

"I just want peace," he mumbled beneath his breath. He wasn't sure if it was to pacify himself, or to appease his invisible guest. Whatever the thing was, it didn't feel threatening. Almost curious.

With a jolt, Kyle remembered Randy in his dark chamber. He stared down at his watch—ten minutes.

That was fast. He'd been so lost in thought he'd forgotten the time.

Foregoing his fears, he rushed back to the morgue freezer and grabbed the handle. With a loud squelch, the metal slab came out with Randy's seemingly lifeless form.

"Randy. Hey, you okay?" He searched his friend's still face. Randy's eyes were closed, hands across his heart. But the steady tic in his neck gave evidence of life.

Randy's eyes popped open. He stretched his hands above his head, yawning. "You sure know how to wreck a guy's nap. I was having an awesome dream."

"Liar." Relieved, Kyle gave Randy a shove, almost spilling him off the slab. "I should have left you in there all night and come back in the morning. See how tough you are then."

"Want a turn?" Randy hopped off the unit, sheepishly grinning. "Tough guy."

"Nope. I have no problem saying I'm too chicken to do it." Not after what he'd just seen. But Kyle kept his thoughts to himself. He didn't need an I-told-you so from Randy. "I want to get going. I'm cold and starving."

"That's not what you said earlier," Randy persisted. "You said you'd do it."

Pausing, Kyle shook his head. Once upon a time, as a teen he'd have jumped to the challenge. But he wasn't a kid anymore, and Randy's taunts and dares rarely affected him.

"So I lied," he said, shrugging.

Chapter Nineteen

Shadows crept over the house late Saturday afternoon. Beth gawked at the kitchen clock. Kyle was late. It was almost five. He'd claimed he was working overtime, but he was usually done by three. She'd hoped to be soaking in a nice hot bath by now, perhaps go out for dinner. But he remained a no-show. Typical.

Was Kyle avoiding spending time with her and the baby? It seemed he used every excuse in the book to stay away from the house. They'd been intimate, but was it enough? Kyle was preoccupied, going through the motions without any thought or reason. She hated when he was detached emotionally. It was so easy for him to do. If only she was that lucky.

What was bothering him? Could there be another woman? She stopped short; heart stuck in her throat. Was she really considering that? Her thoughts scattered in every direction. A fling? Was Kyle capable of cheating on her without her knowledge? True, her imagination could be overactive at times, and was often the source of their arguments. She jumped to conclusions without any evidence. But another woman? Her mind slid back over the past few weeks. Could hanging out with Randy really be just an alibi?

Kyle was tall, blond and good-looking. He had the charisma that most women were attracted to. In fact, Randy had the same attributes, only he was darker and a true flirt. Kyle was much more reserved. Randy always had a woman on his arm, never remaining faithful to anyone. She often wondered if any of his girlfriends would try to set Kyle up with one of their friends. Randy would love to break them up. She'd be a fool to not realize that Kyle might envy Randy's harem, or his ability to jump ship whenever he chose. Kyle might deny it, but she knew it was true. Her husband was stuck home with her. Only her.

It was no secret that Randy hated her—ever since her wedding. Randy had been Kyle's best man. Strippers were planned for the bachelor party and it caused a rift between her and Kyle. She'd gotten over it, but the damage was done between her and Randy. Ever since, he gave her the cold shoulder, preferring to hang out with Kyle anywhere except their house.

When Samantha was born, Randy had come to the hospital to see the baby. It was awkward since she hated Randy. Maybe detested was a better word. She'd tried to rise above her feelings, be the better person, but she was only human. And she had to admit, she was jealous at times. Even so, breaking up Kyle and Randy's duo wasn't her place.

Maybe she just needed to reach out to some of her own friends. Over the years, she had lost touch with them. She should have taken more care to keep those ties alive. Perhaps she'd look up some of her high school friends on social media. It might do her some good to have girlfriend time.

Beth walked into the bathroom, staring critically in the mirror. Her face was fuller, hair shorter, brownish. She looked older, mature. She had lost some of her baby weight, yet Kyle always liked her fuller curves, not like Randy's stick-figure, model types. She could join a gym, get into shape. The idea held merit. Maybe Kyle would like to join. It'd be healthy for them both, maybe bring them closer.

But that didn't help her at that moment. Beth chewed her lip in thought. She didn't want to lose Kyle. He seemed so distant; he'd alienated himself emotionally from her. They needed to reconnect. To rekindle their marriage.

Perhaps she should put on the witch's costume again. Spice things up. Or possibly dye her hair. Blonde. Red? Change her appearance. That would get his attention.

The sound of the front door opening caught her unaware. She jumped, exited the bathroom and went down into the foyer.

Kyle stood by the front door, filthy. His hair was covered in dust, dirt, and grime. He took off his boots, opened the front door and sat them out on the stoop.

"So you're finally home." She crossed her arms, watching him suspiciously. Briefly, he looked in her direction. It was on the tip of her tongue to demand to know where he'd been all that time, but something in his demeanor stopped her. Swallowing her thoughts, she forced a slight smile.

"I'm glad you're here," she greeted. "I was hoping we could go out for dinner or get takeout food for a change. Even pizza might be nice. I tried to call your phone, but you never answered."

"Sorry. I had the volume down," he mumbled. "I didn't hear it. Just order takeout."

Wow, that was a fast nosedive. Her mouth tightened.

"We could go out to a movie or something," she further pressed. "I could ask my mother if we could drop Samantha off for an hour or so. I'm sick of being in the house."

"It's Saturday night," he replied. "The restaurants around here will be packed, and so will the theater. And it's getting cold out, windy. Looks like it might even rain. Why drag the baby out if we don't have to? Order something. I don't care what. Pizza. Chinese. Whatever. I'll pick it up after I get a shower, or get it delivered."

"I guess you're right." His mood soured her own. Still, she tried again. "How was your day?"

"Don't start." He walked past her toward the staircase. "I'm beat."

"I didn't even say anything," she said to his retreating back. "I only asked how your day was. Why don't you give me your dirty clothes right here? That way I can take them to the laundry room and throw them into the washer. I don't want mud on the carpet."

Kyle shrugged but complied, pivoting around. As soon as his shirt was off, Beth scrutinized his bare skin, looking for something amiss. She blinked. What would one look for? Bite marks? Scratches. Lipstick. There was nothing. He didn't exactly look like he'd been messing around. He was foul. That was something. A musty scent emanated from his skin. She breathed a sigh of relief. Rule out the other woman scenario. She pecked Kyle's scratchy cheek, sniffing for any perfume. Nothing.

"Take your time showering." She gathered his clothing and sat the items by the doorway. He suspiciously eyeballed her, fully expecting an argument. She was glad to disappoint him. "Anything I order won't be ready for a half hour or so."

This time when Kyle looked at her, he did it with more warmth in his gaze. "Where's Samantha?"

"She's in the kitchen, in her swing. She's been a good girl today. She even got a flower from a man."

"A man?"

"Yes," she replied, noting his alarm. "At the grocery store. Or should I say the parking lot. The man was wearing a costume. He must've just arrived when he saw us and came walking over."

"What kind of costume?"

"Sort of like a clown. I guess he was a jester."

"And you just let him walk up to you without any kind of identification?" Something dark flickered across Kyle's gaze. "Where did he come from?"

"I don't know. He said he was working there. He noticed Samantha in the car and pulled out a pack of balloons. It only took him a few moments to make her the flower."

"And you let him?" Kyle asked. "Are you crazy?"

"Are you?" His tone unnerved her. "Get a grip. Why are you getting loud? He was an actor. Nothing happened. He was obviously working for the store. Why else would he be there?"

"I don't know." He lowered his voice. "But neither do you. You don't take chances, not in today's world. You don't know anything about this guy. He could've been lying to you about working there."

"That doesn't make any sense." She crossed her arms. "You sound crazy. It was fine. We're fine. Just stop already."

Kyle moved past her and walked into the kitchen. Samantha stirred in the swing. The balloon art sat on top of her diaper bag.

"That it?"

"Yes," she said, standing in the doorway. Kyle was eyeing the flower like it was a bomb ready to explode. "Why are you freaking out over a balloon?"

"Did the man say anything strange?" He pivoted around, glaring at her.

"No," she replied. "I mean it was just a brief conversation. I don't really remember. It's not a big deal."

"Describe him."

"His face was painted white with a five-o'clock shadow," she said. "Red lips. Dark brows. He was wearing a funny looking hat, kind of like horns curved upward."

"And the color?"

"Red and purple."

Blanch faced, Kyle grabbed the balloon, flipping it over. Critically, he scanned the stem and then the petals. Suddenly it popped in his hands. In her sleep, Samantha jumped, face twisting.

"Are you happy now?" She walked over to the swing, giving it a gentle push. She lowered her voice to a whisper, "Honestly, Kyle. What's gotten into you? You're acting irrational."

"Because I want my daughter safe?" He shoved the broken balloon into the trash can. "Did you even think to ask the store if this guy was working for them?"

"No," she said. "I was on my way home."

"I want you to call them and find out. Get their number."

"They're closed right now," she said. "So that ends that."

"Then tomorrow."

He was acting like a jerk. She'd just about had enough. Yet something in Kyle's frantic eyes stopped her from exploding. She checked her reaction, glancing at the baby, who fell back asleep.

"Whatever." She returned to the foyer, scooped up his clothing and headed toward the laundry room. To her dismay, he followed.

"Is there anything else that stuck out as unusual?" Kyle pressed.

"No," she said. "I haven't put that much thought into it." She dropped the clothing into a basket, opened the washer lid and dumped the basket's content into the tub. "Will you go get your shower already?"

"Was this guy alone?"

"I have no idea. I only saw him."

Alarmed, she asked, "What is the matter? Do you know something about this man? Was there something in the news? Tell me."

Kyle paused, leaning his hands on the dryer. He didn't reply for a moment.

"Did the hat have bells?"

"I think so," she replied. "I mean it was windy. My hair was blowing every direction."

"What color was his hair?"

"I don't know," she replied. "I didn't look that close. This was only a couple of minutes. His head was covered by the hat. He had on goofy looking clothes. I did find him rather creepy. He had a huge, painted grin, but he really wasn't smiling beneath the makeup. His eyes were dark, shiny, and he was wearing eyeliner. I guess that's what it was. Like I said, it happened very quickly. It's not like I just stood there and stared." She paused, feeling foolish. She shouldn't have talked to the man or let him see Samantha. Kyle was freaking her out. What if the guy took down her license plate? Followed her home. Wanted to steal her baby? Her thoughts grew darker, alarmed. Now she wished she could call the store. Tomorrow seemed so far away.

"Kyle, now I'm worried," she admitted. "I never looked at it the way you are."

"Sorry," he mumbled, shrugging. "I didn't mean to upset you. Just forget it for now. Call the store in the morning to see if they hired him. They probably did. It's just that I don't like jokers or clowns. They freak me out."

"Well, I'm not that great a fan either," she said. "But is that why you're upset? Or is there something else?"

Kyle paused; eyes guarded. She waited, while he seemed to be thinking on his reply.

"It's me," he said. "Okay. I don't want strange men around my daughter. She could've been frightened by his costume."

"Don't you think you are overreacting? Samantha is too little to have developed such fears."

"She can't talk, so how would you know if she was scared?"

"Are you serious? Do you hear yourself? She's an infant. A baby. She doesn't have the kind of fears you're talking about. It's people's dumb superstitions, other kids, or television that teaches children to fear monsters, clowns."

"Not always," Kyle said, his voice barely audible. "Sometimes kids need to be afraid. It's their only defense. The boogie man comes in many shapes and sizes. Either way, you need to learn how to run. Hide. If you twitch, you'll get stitched."

"What?" Beth's mouth fell open. "Kyle..." She reached out to touch his arm, but he retreated a step.

"Just keep anyone dressed up as a freak away from my daughter." Kyle brushed by her, exiting the room. "And anyone else you don't know, for that matter."

Perplexed, Beth followed him. "Where did you hear that rhyme?"

Her question was ignored as Kyle continued up the steps.

Chapter Twenty

People were so stupid. Predictable. Especially elderly women with their elaborate routines. Specifically, Doctor Doris Goodman and the invisible halo around her curled, gray hair.

Sneering, Stitches peered through the blinds, watching the woman inside. Situated in her favorite chair, Doris carefully laid a small towel across her lap, no doubt to avoid spills on her pristine white carpet. A pair of bifocals hung from a delicate gold chain around her scrawny neck. She wore a light blue housecoat with a pair of fuzzy slippers.

Six-o-clock on the dot. Tick tock.

Teatime. Herbal. She used the same delicate china cup, saucer, and silver tray. A small basket held tea bags, honey, and sweetener. She sat in her perfect living room with her perfect furniture in her perfect ridiculously big house.

Tsk. Tsk.

But she was alone. No shock there. Not too many people liked being around old Doris. The woman was an uppity, stupid, snotty, mean, ugly, nasty, warthog. He smirked at the names in his head. Hmmm. Rotten, puss-infected, a putrid bag of vomit. More. He liked doing this. What other names could he think of? Skank, loser, hussy, loudmouth dirt bag. Okay, so she wasn't that loud. She had a nasal voice that rose in pitch, changing to a screech. He'd been the brunt of her mouth on numerous occasions. Too many to recall. But her eyes made up for what her voice lacked. Those eyes had the ability to bore through you. Scrape your soul. Doris did her dirty work behind closed doors. More specifically, behind the closed doors of Rose Hill Asylum. At least while it was running.

He supposed she wasn't really living alone. After all, she did have her stupid, little yappy dog. Fat and lazy, the mutt hovered around its master's feet, hoping for an ounce of affection. No doubt, Doris loved lording it over the thing now that her days of reigning over humans had ended.

Doris was getting sleepy. Her wide yawn caught his stare. Look at her perfect teeth in her wrinkled face. Who would've thought her skinny jaw could hold so many? He himself had several missing teeth. Couldn't afford to fix them and had them pulled instead. That wasn't fair. Perhaps he'd yank a few of her teeth. See how she'd like that.

His belly shook in chuckles. Loud. Too loud. He slammed his hand against his mouth. She might hear. That wouldn't do. He wasn't ready yet for their reunion.

Inside, the grandfather clock struck six-thirty. The dog stood up on shaky legs, whining to go out.

Bingo.

He waited for Doris to react, take the stupid mutt to the front door and let it go do its business. So predictable. He'd watched her for three nights after seeing her interview on the local news. She'd discussed working at Rose Hill. Reminded him of the past. The local psychiatrist had a lot to say. Bragged as if she were somebody. Who cared what she had to say? He knew the truth about her. The lies she told. Although his tastes were for beautiful, young women, he'd decided to make an exception for Doris. His grin widened.

What a boring life. Oh, how he'd love to throw a firecracker in the middle of the room and watch Doris dance. But with his luck, she'd faint dead away. Not that he'd shed a tear. But he wanted some fun with the good doc.

It had taken him a week to find where she lived. She'd been married three times, but no kids. Not surprising. Mrs. High and Mighty would probably never do the nasty. He shuddered at the thought. Now he felt faint. He chuckled again. This time he pinched his cheek to still the sound.

Finally, Doris stood, wrapped her shawl around her shoulders, and headed toward the foyer. Stitches jumped from his perch and headed to greet her. He didn't have to wait long. The weather worked in his favor. It was warm for a November night and Doris noticed it. Not only did she open the door, but she stepped outside to stare up at the brightly colored sky.

The dog ran off into the yard. So easy. It never even noticed him, let alone barked.

He snuck up behind her and tapped her on the shoulder.

"Hello, doc."

Chapter Twenty-One

On Saturday night, Kyle couldn't sleep. His mind wouldn't settle. He tossed and turned until Beth snapped at him. For a time, he stared at the ceiling, but it was of no use. His legs were restless. He needed to stretch. Finally, he gave up and left the bed.

Nothing in the bathroom closet offered a sleep aid. In frustration, he went to the kitchen and drank a glass of warm milk. Aimlessly he wandered around the downstairs. He considered the television, but that would only keep him awake.

Finally, he stood before his favorite recliner. The chair had helped him many restless nights. Now that Samantha was sleeping six hours or so at a time, he hadn't used it for over a week. But now it was his only hope.

He turned on the gas fireplace, enjoying the flames. He shut off the lights, grabbed a throw blanket from the couch, and settled into the chair, stretching out his long legs.

Flames danced in merriment, drawing his regard. But his thoughts were still elsewhere. He thought about the man at the store. Then the one at the nursing home. His father's odd, almost fearful reaction. If only the cap and bells didn't look familiar. Could it be the same one he'd help make at Rose Hill? Was it possible? If so, who was wearing it?

He rubbed his temple, trying to shake the ache. What was he thinking returning to Rose Hill? Before that, he'd been fine with life. Now he was a mess.

He hated that cap and bells he'd helped create. He'd never realized it until just then. It had been fun to make at the time. It'd been a special project. Rose Hill was putting on a play. They needed a court jester. Other costumes were created, but he and two teenagers worked on the cap. They were so proud of their accomplishment.

He shook his head, lost in thought.

Once upon a time, he'd loved dressing up, pretending. He'd been involved with some of the plays. *The King and The Missing Shoes* had been written by a staff member. It was story about a theft of the king's favorite shoes, the culprit—a mouse. It was a funny tale, one the kids loved. In due time, the play was forgotten as new acts were created, but the jester cap ended up in the tunnels. Hide and seek had become twisted and cruel. *Twitches,* or the longer version, *if you twitch, you'll get stitched* had become popular at Rose Hill, at least among bullies. The cruel game haunted his dreams, followed his thoughts. Over the years, he'd avoided circuses because of clowns. Thankfully, their popularity wasn't what it once was. Even Halloween was worrisome. And he was a man, not a boy. But his heart began to race and sweat beaded his brow. His thoughts nagged at him. Faces swarmed his memory.

"Stop," he said beneath his breath. "Just stop."

A cluster of teenagers walked into Kyle's cottage at Rose Hill. He froze on his bed, listening to their voices, gripping the tennis ball in his hand. He glanced over at Ricky, a twelve-year old boy who sat in a wheelchair by the window. The boy had cerebral palsy. Dread lay in Ricky's eyes.

Ten metal beds were spread out in their section of the building, all with white bedding. Since it was lunchtime, most residents had gone into the dining area for their meals.

Kyle nervously shifted on the bed. The teenagers were now in the hallway. He could make a run for the opposite doorway before anyone noticed him, but then Ricky would be alone. He liked Ricky. They played cards and just chatted. He chewed his lip, shoving the tennis ball beneath his pillow. It was his fault he and Ricky were still in the room. It had been his responsibility to wheel Ricky into the dining area.

Acting, Kyle stood and rushed over to the wheelchair, grabbing the handles.

"I'm going to take you around the back way," Kyle whispered. He released the brake and turned the chair. It was a difficult task because it was outdated and hard to push.

"Look who we got here," a voice boomed.

Kyle froze as four teenagers entered the room. They were all bullies, but Benny was their leader.

"We're late for lunch,' Kyle said. "We got to go."

"Think I care, you piece of crap."

Kyle didn't move. Beneath him, Ricky's hands became knuckle white as he grasped the chair. Benny strolled toward them, the trio following. The teenagers surrounded them, laughing.

Benny sniffed the air. "Something stinks."

Kyle stood still, waiting. If only an aide would

come looking for them. Benny moved behind him, grabbed his pants and yanked them down.

"Looks like someone got shanked." Benny laughed hysterically. He shoved Kyle, who almost fell and was saved by his death grip on the wheelchair handle.

Flustered, Kyle let go of the handle and yanked up his pants. One of the other boys grabbed the wheelchair and spun it around. Ricky's mouth dropped open, but not a peep emerged.

"Stop it," Kyle cried, grabbing at the chair. When his efforts failed, he made a dash for help, but then he was caught.

"Where you going, punk?" Benny spun him around by the upper arm.

"Let us alone." Kyle tugged at the teen's steely fingers, digging into his flesh.

"This is a warning." Benny grabbed the front of Kyle's shirt, bunched it in his fist and yanked him closer. "Quit being a kiss ass to the adults. Do you think I don't know what you're about? You're a snitch."

"I'm not." Hot tears spiked Kyle's lashes.

"You snitched on me out on the playground. I was punished and put into the Quarter house for a whole week with a bunch of weirdos."

Kyle blinked, thinking. He hadn't said anything to anyone, but the aide, Billy Hampton, had seen what happened. At the time, he didn't think anything had come of it. Apparently, he'd been wrong.

"I...I didn't tell on you. I swear," he said.

Benny's lip curled, brows lowering. He twisted the material of Kyle's shirt, lifting him up to his tiptoes. "You tell on me again, I'm going to put you in the *hospital, and it won't be for a just a few stitches. Then I'll get that brother of yours and put him in next to you."*

Horrified at the vision, Kyle cried out.

"Benny! Let him go," a man's voice said. "Now."

When Benny released him, Kyle fell to the floor and lifted his head. In the doorway, Scott Hampton stood, his visage one of shock.

Kyle moaned in his sleep.

Clowns floated in his dreams. They were dancing, singing and prancing around with balloons. One clown juggled balls as another danced and sang. Hallways appeared. Mirrors. Music filled his ears, cresting in tempo. Kids were everywhere. Some sat on benches, others in wheelchairs. Then there were those unseen, the ones playing their favorite game, hide and go seek. Everyone was happy because the circus had come to town. Not that it was a real circus, but an imitation for the unfortunate who didn't have the physical capability to visit a real circus. Instead, entertainment was brought to them. It was low-budget, some in-house acts. But the kids didn't care.

The dream changed. He was now in the tunnels, but only he could see where he was headed. Above him the fluorescent light threw out a muted glow. Footsteps followed him. Nervously, he looked over his shoulder. Shadows played with the light, but the footsteps continued. Then he saw him, someone wearing the jester cap. Puzzled, he watched the teenager press against the wall, the cap's bells jingling as he ducked down to hide. Benny. His stomach clenched. The prankster was waiting for something. Or someone.

A child darted across the tunnel, hiding behind a door. Benny stepped out and grabbed the stunned boy. Laughter ensued between the pair.

"What are you doing?" Kyle said, moving toward them. Terrified, he tried to sound brave. "Get away from my brother!"

"I want to come with you," Roy said, stepping into the light. Behind Roy, the jester paused, then faded away. "Take me with you."

"No," Kyle said. "Go back to your cottage."

"I'll tell if you don't let me," the boy said. "I know what you've been doing, Kyle. I saw you smoking."

"Go ahead, no one will care on what you have to say. Stop with your lies."

"Please." Roy's fingers grabbed Kyle's arm in desperation. "I'm afraid to go back."

"No. You're too little." This time, Kyle gave the boy a shove. "Go back to your cottage, and if you tell on me, I'm going to be mad at you. I won't play with you ever again."

Roy's hands balled into a fist. His face turned red. Opening his mouth, he began to scream. Not a real scream. But the kind to make you react.

It worked only too well. Kyle woke with a start. His head was pounding, heart still racing. The front of his shirt was damp. He sat up, staring around the living room. Everything appeared shadowy, dark. Unnerved, feeling like he wasn't alone, he flicked on the side lamp.

After he regained his composure, he rose from the chair. Moving to the kitchen, he stopped in the doorway to flick on the switch. Shadows disappeared into the light.

Roy.

The name stuck in his head. He sat at the table, put his hands on his head and lowered his chin. A boy's face appeared in his thoughts. He tried to shake it off, but the image remained.

Roy.

Chapter Twenty-Two

In the bright Sunday morning light, Pop's house appeared lost and desolate. A realtor's sign hung haphazardly on the rancher's post. Crusted leaves had gathered along the porch, which held several old newspapers. The whole house needed new paint, perhaps a roof.

Kyle pulled into the stone driveway and shut off his truck. Usually coming home brought about a sense of warmth, family. But now, he felt nothing for the residence; only a sense of urgency to sell it and walk away from the property's upkeep. Perhaps it was time to think about lowering the price.

His thoughts turned to his father. It was such a shock the day he got a call from the hospital. His dad had had a massive stroke and fell, injuring his head. Pop had almost died. Who knew for how long he'd lain on the floor before being found. He tried to remember their last real conversation, but it wouldn't come. Pop was a quiet man, loyal to those he loved.

His father might never be the same. Kyle was losing hope. Coming to the house was a bitter pill to swallow. Without Pop it was just another building, empty, cold.

But finding Roy's whereabouts had taken precedent. Flashbacks plagued him, demanded that he remember. He'd let Roy go, along with his past. After

Rose Hill closed, Roy had been taken to another facility or group home. But which one? Where was Roy now? Damn it.

Kyle unlocked the front door, walked through the foyer and into the living room. Musty scents mingled with cedar wood hit his senses. Recollections of his life in the house were fresh. But there were memories before this life—remembered only in the mind of a Rose Hill child.

Minimal furniture still occupied the house, mostly aged chairs, and a floral sofa. Dust, stirred to life by his movements, lingered wherever sunlight manage to slip its way through the windowpanes. In the main hallway, he moved the thermostat up a couple of degrees to ease the chill. Slowly, he walked through the kitchen, dining room, and then the bedrooms. He saved Pop's bedroom for last. It appeared tidy. Most of Pop's personal belongings were now stored in boxes, kept in the attached garage.

Kyle returned to the living room, walked to the fireplace, and took off the mirror hanging over the mantle. Securely in the wall pocket sat a metal safe. He'd gained the keys from the nursing home. They had been in Pop's pocket.

It was unnerving to access the safe, an infringement of privacy, but it was necessary if he hoped to find any information on Roy. Pop didn't like anyone touching his things without his permission. But his father was out of service, so there was no way to gain consent.

After his adoption, Pop had barely mentioned Roy. Kyle supposed that if he'd have pushed it, Pop would've answered more of his questions. But over the years, it was easier to let Roy go. But now…

Kyle shook off his guilt. He needed to make things right with Roy.

Inside the safe was a small box, which held his mother's jewelry. It wasn't worth much, but Pop had been worried about thieves. Several files held Pop's bank records and cancelled checks. A couple of bonds, not worth much, sat snugly inside their envelopes. Finally, he came across what he was searching for—a thick satchel, filled with files. He sat down on the couch, opened the first file, and looked through Pop's personal records. There was a copy of the deed of the house, life insurance, marriage certificate, and a death certificate for his mother. There were copies of licenses, social security cards, and insurance claims.

He opened another file. A copy of his original birth certificate was inside, place of birth, Rose Hill Asylum. The paper felt leaden in his hands. His medical records were next. His vaccinations and school records. Then the copy of his adoption paperwork—the day of his release—a day of freedom. Kyle Hampton's life began that day, the life he'd always dreamed of. A real family, a mom and dad. He became the envy of the other Rose Hill children. When Pop came and took him home for good, he never looked back.

That was the problem. He should have.

He returned the papers into the folder. Nothing about Roy. What had he expected to find? His throat convulsed as guilt ate at him. Why didn't Pop adopt Roy? There was room in the house for one more child. He'd been told Florence, his adoptive mother, could handle only one child—him. They could've made it work.

Regretfully, Kyle lowered his head. He should've begged and pleaded on Roy's behalf. But the truth was he didn't want to make waves, have Pop change his mind. He was just a nine-year-old, scared of altercation, afraid his new life would disappear. Instead, he didn't push any buttons. Roy, along with Rose Hill, became his past.

He grabbed the last of the items, a small cardboard box. Idly, he opened it. Pictures lay inside – some black and white. Most of them were from Rose Hill. Not surprising since Pop spent many years donating his time to help the wards of the state. There were a few images of Pop's house. He studied the one with Florence sitting on a porch rocker, holding a boy, perhaps around the age of two. The baby had reddish hair and vivid green eyes. He didn't recognize him.

He began shifting through the pile, separating the Rose Hill pictures. The campus appeared tidy and orderly—groomed by the people that lived there. Group pictures began, mostly of daily activities. Images of classroom events, baseball games and art. Holiday pictures were mingled, mostly with Christmas or Halloween themes. At the end of the pile, a square envelope stood out. The name Kyle was written across it. He opened it and pulled out several photos.

Stunned, he studied a picture of an infant, a swaddled newborn. He flipped it over, read his name and birthdate on the back. There were two more pictures, each similar. The fourth picture stopped him short. His throat convulsed, absorbing the image. His mother. He hadn't seen her face since the age of nine. He didn't even know there were pictures. Why hadn't Pop given them to him? This was his mother. They would've meant something to him. His finger traced her jaw. Seated in a chair, a smile on her face. Blonde hair hung about her shoulders, her blue eyes wide and bright. She looked so childish, so angelic.

His eyes burned with unshed tears. At the age of sixteen, she had given birth to him. Her mind was that of a five-year-old, and yet someone had taken advantage of her. The result: Kyle. No one knew who sired him and if they did, no one 'fessed up. It could've been anyone. An opportunist. Screenings and laws weren't in place back then. Rose Hill was overcrowded, lacked adequate staff. There were plenty of opportunities. It was a shame the bastard got away with it. The man should be rotting in jail.

Two more pictures of his mother followed. Then the last. He lifted it closer to his face, eyes glued to the occupants. His mother was sitting in her bed, wearing a white nightgown. Sitting on the bed next to her, Roy snuggled up to her, arm draped possessively around her leg. He was holding a teddy bear, his face beaming.

Kyle gripped the photo, absorbing the image. In his mind, dots connected, then disappeared only to reemerge. His hand shook, as implications cleared. His mother was so innocent, so unprotected.

Kyle stood, dropping the picture on the coffee table. He paced back in forth in front of the fireplace. His doubts morphed into rage. His mother had been at the mercy of Rose Hill. Mentally, she couldn't agree to sex. He and Roy were both products of rape. How often she'd been raped, he hadn't a clue. So many people had visited over the years. Were they full brothers or half?

His stomach clenched. At twenty-five, his mother had died from heart complications. He was officially put up for adoption. Scott and Florence had come into his life just before his mother's death. He was grateful to have new parents. After he had been adopted, he overheard people say what a lucky boy he was. But now he had to ask why hadn't Scott taken the time to find out who had raped his mother? There were so many more innocents just like her. It wasn't right.

His mind moved to when Scott had started coming to Rose Hill. He was almost eight. Scott had spent time with the higher-functioning kids but more in a group setting. In a matter of weeks, it all began to change. His brow furrowed, thoughts slipping into his earlier life.

Baseball had been his favorite sport. He was good at it. Kyle liked to play first base. He could hit and run. He had a knack for sliding into the bases. Rose Hill had five baseball teams, a mixed bag of ages. They had one thing in common; they loved the sport.

The wind tore off Kyle's baseball cap, tumbling it along the ground. He left first base and chased after it. A few adults were along the sideline, watching the game. A man picked it up, holding it as he approached. Scott Hampton wasn't alone. An obese woman was sitting in a wheelchair next to him, smiling. A funny feeling hit Kyle's stomach.

"Hey, Kyle," Scott greeted. "Great game."

"Thank you." He took the offered cap.

"This is my wife, Florence."

Kyle stared at the woman, whose smile deepened into dimples. Without a greeting, he turned and ran back into position at first base. The couple continued to praise his efforts. It felt good.

After the game, Scott approached him. "Hey, sport.

Florence would like to talk to you."

"What for?"

"Don't be shy," Scott said. "She is very nice and has something for you."

His interest was piqued. Dragging his feet, he followed Scott back to his wife.

"You are a strong hitter," Florence said. "I see potential in you."

He had no idea what she meant. Her stare was unnerving, so he stared down at his dirty sneakers.

"I have something for you." Florence reached out her chubby hand. "Here, take it."

Kyle lifted his head, holding out his hand. She dropped two sticks of bubblegum onto his palm. Nervously, he looked at Scott. "We're not supposed to have gum. Kids stick it under the tables and chairs."

"I got special permission for you," Scott said. "I was told you could have it as long as you are careful and throw it away properly. Don't give it to any other kids, especially those who shouldn't have it. I think you know what I mean."

He nodded.

"I thought you could hang here with us and chew a piece now."

Kyle wasn't sure if he liked that idea, but he agreed.

"I want to show Florence your cottage and what area you've been living in. Are you okay with that?"

"Sure."

"You can lead the way."

After they arrived at the cottage, Kyle showed Florence his bed. He didn't know what else to do, so he sat down. The gum was losing its flavor.

"Does Benny still come in here and bother you?"

"Florence..." Scott said. "Don't."

Kyle chewed the gum, twisting it around his tongue. He popped a bubble, then said, "Not anymore."

Florence reached out and patted his knee. "You are a delight, Kyle, such a sweet boy. We'd like you to come over to our house for a weekend stay. Would you like that?"

"Just me?" His belly quivered as nervousness slid over him.

"We will pick a couple of other kids your age to keep you company."

"I guess okay."

Florence beamed. Reaching up, she touched her husband's arm. Her dimples appeared. "He's perfect."

Kyle sat down on the couch, rubbing his head. Scott had taken a renewed interest in him, only him. A variety of kids were randomly chosen to go to Scott's house for weekend camping trips, but Kyle got to pick them. He frowned in thought. He never asked for Roy to go. At the time, he was worried the Hamptons would like his little brother more and his visits would stop. Like a starved cat, he lapped up the affection they showered over him. He gave it up to luck at the time. But the truth was, Florence Hampton wanted to adopt one child: Kyle.

The pictures, like his past, were tucked away, hidden. They told the story of how he came to be. But why? Were Scott and Florence worried he'd leave them, return to his roots? Were they hiding the fact that he had come from Rose Hill from friends? He'd been told to keep it secret from outsiders. It was a small request, one he honored.

After composing himself, he slipped the pictures into his pocket, relocked Pop's papers in the safe, and headed toward the kitchen. He stood by the kitchen sink, looking out at the open yard. The yard was now overgrown, but it once held a swing, a sandbox, and a clubhouse. All the things he'd loved. Now his memories were tainted with bitterness. As bad as the asylum could be at times, nothing compared to wondering about Roy and what had happened to him.

After drinking a glass of water, Kyle headed through the kitchen doorway that led into the garage. Flicking on the light, he stared at the boxes and boxes of items blocking the garage doors. If the house sold, he'd have little time to get rid of most of the stuff. It was a future job he dreaded, but Pop's care was expensive. Even if Pop managed to recover, he'd never be able to keep the house. Pop was up in years. He had heart issues and diabetes. Selling the house had been a hard decision, but he couldn't afford to pay Pop's mortgage along with his own debts.

He stepped into the garage, struck by the amount of Pop's possessions. Cool air swirled around him. He rummaged around in the boxes, finding the tagged bin holding Pop's antique railway and trains. He'd set them up for Christmas this year. It had been a family tradition that he wanted to continue in his own home.

After pulling out the marked box, he started reading the labels on others. He was in the rear of the garage, moving a box when he heard a shuffle of feet. Just as he was turning around, something slammed into the back of his head.

He fell like a sack of flour. Someone heavy sat on

his back, hands pressing his face down and into the cold concrete. Heavy breathing came close to his ear.

"Surprise, surprise," a gruff voice whispered closed to his ear. "Looks like someone found me in the cookie jar."

"What do you want?" Blood filled Kyle's mouth. "Who are you?"

"Never mind," the voice whispered. "But listen up. You took something from me, and I want it back."

Confused, Kyle tried to turn his head. But the hand pressed it into the floor.

"What did I take?"

"My boots," the voice said. "You took them from Rose Hill. I want them returned."

"Your boots?" Kyle managed to ask. "But how do you know that?"

A long pause. More heavy breathing.

"It doesn't matter," the voice said. "On Saturday, take them back to where you found them and walk away. If you don't, I'll be visiting you and that little wife of yours. I know where you live and where you work. I know everything about your pathetic life. Don't call the police. This is not a big deal, so don't make it one. I'll be checking to see if the boots are there. If you go to the cops, they won't find me, and then I'll come back when you least expect it. Be sure of that. It's a simple request. Take back my boots. They don't belong to you. You won't like what I do if you don't." And with that, a strong hand grabbed Kyle by the hair, lifted his head and slammed it into the floor.

Chapter Twenty-Three

Belly down, Kyle woke up in the middle of the garage floor. His skull ached. Blood dribbled into his right eye. He sat up, groaning. How long was he out? It felt like hours. Spread out on the garage floor, the pictures in his pocket had fallen out. Blood splattered the photo of Florence Hampton holding the little boy. Slowly, he stood in hesitation, stomach lurching. The room dimmed. Confused, he took a moment, gathering his bearings. It all came back in a rush. He had been assaulted. The man could still be there.

Intently, he listened. All was quiet. He had the distinct impression he was alone. Still…

Tentatively, Kyle began flicking on light switches as he moved inside the house. In the kitchen, he grabbed a large steak knife and moved from room to room. Nothing. Dizzily, he managed to make it inside the bathroom, closed and locked the door. The sight in the bathroom mirror told the tale of the attack. Grimacing, he found a towel and blotted the blood from his brow and hairline. His bottom lip had a nasty cut, and it stung like hell.

He went outside, searching for his attacker's vehicle. Nothing was in sight. He returned to the house for a better search. Again, nothing. After locking up the house, he drove away into the dusk.

He fought the urge to call the police. His attacker's

warning buzzed in his head. What could he say? He didn't know who had attacked him, never saw a face. The boots had been at the asylum, buried beneath shoes. Who could possibly have seen him take them? Why would they want them back and why did he have to take them back to the asylum? He could've left them anywhere else. Blood dribbled down into his right eye, blurring his vision. Relief filled him when his house came into view.

When Beth saw his bruised and bloody face, she demanded he go to the hospital. Of course, she also wanted an explanation as to what happened.

"I fell," he said, not sure why he lied. He wasn't ready to tell her about the threat. "I was moving Pop's furniture around in the garage. I tripped and fell." It was a half-truth. He'd fallen in the garage, and he was moving around boxes at the time. He was glad she bought his story.

He needed time to think about what had happened. To reason it out before he reacted or made an irrational return to the asylum—if he took the boots back. Returning them could be dangerous. He'd been threatened. Clearly his assailant had been at Pop's house, waiting. Perhaps the man meant to rob the place but that didn't make sense. He had been ambushed. How did the man know he'd go to Pop's? It led to only one conclusion—Kyle knew his attacker.

Knowing the culprit had been around his house with Beth and Sammy inside chilled him. Everything in the house took on a new perspective. Doors. Windows. Basement. In his mind's eye, he was already thinking about how to protect them.

"I'm not going to the hospital," he told Beth. "It

looks worse than it is. I'm just a bit banged up."

"What if you have a concussion?" she said. "You could have a brain bleed or a neck injury."

"I'm fine." He grabbed a bag of frozen peas and placed it over his right eye and the huge knot. It stung like hell, but he doubted the hospital would do much more than that. Perhaps a fancier ice bag and an X-ray. He promised Beth if he felt ill, he'd let her know and she could call 911. He took three ibuprofen tablets for the swelling. It was enough to appease her.

After Beth went to bed, he wandered around the house, checking locks and doors. Deliberately, he left the porch light on and kept a baseball bat close. He now wished he kept a gun in the house. Several times he reached for the phone to ask Randy to bring one over, before he thought better of it.

He'd known there was something odd with the boots. He'd ignored his gut instincts. But there wasn't anything he could readily discern. They were military issue, aged, but perhaps not as old as he'd first perceived. He'd almost worn them to Pop's house, instead of his sneakers. What if he had been wearing them? His attacker could have just taken them. Maybe that was the plan. He'd gladly have given them up instead of receiving a face pounding and further threats.

His throat convulsed.

It didn't make any sense. Whoever it was had been at the asylum the day he'd stolen the boots. In fact, someone had been watching him and Randy all along. Perhaps it was the same guy who had screwed with Randy and Kat. There could be a squatter living there, it wouldn't be the first time. But for this man to be so attached to a pair of boots was insane. Who'd take it that far? Surely not someone in their right mind.

What other recourse did he have?

He could call the cops but that seemed like a bad idea. Having the police involved would bring up the fact that he'd been breaking into the asylum. It might stir up the past, something he'd rather not do.

The walls closed around his thoughts.

Chapter Twenty-Four

Monday morning, Kyle called in sick. He felt lousy and he didn't want to answer any questions about his face. He had barely slept. His forehead had swollen into a black and blue mass and ice had little effect on the bulge. Besides, his head was pounding mercilessly.

"Not to give you anything else to worry about," Beth said, examining his head. "But you were right about that man at the store. They didn't hire him." Worriedly, she stared at Kyle as he sat on the kitchen chair. "There are other stores there. Dry cleaning. Nail Salon. A pizza parlor. Maybe one of them had hired him. Now I'm freaking out. Should I call the other stores? Drive there and see if I'm missing something?"

"Don't worry about it, Beth," Kyle said. "I'll check it out when I feel better. I'm sorry I made you worry so much. I didn't mean to yell, either. There's probably a reasonable explanation. Just give me a day or two to look into it." He wanted to add it was the least of his worries. He now had bigger fish to fry.

Somewhat appeased, Beth brightened. Kyle allowed his wife to fuss over him, finally agreeing to have a doctor look at his head. Beth made the appointment, and yet as soon as he left the house, he called the doctor's office and cancelled it. He'd take his chances. He'd been hit before, worse than this. True, he had been younger then and healed a lot quicker, was resilient. But he'd survived then, and he'd survive now. At least that's what he told himself.

Kyle mentally replayed the attack, trying to figure out who the mysterious man had been. Once again, he considered calling the cops, but the man's threats held him back. He wasn't going to rush things.

So instead he called Randy, who agreed to meet him at Albert's, a local pizza joint.

"Geez," Randy said, the moment Kyle appeared by the table, sitting down across from him. "What the hell happened to your face?"

"I was jumped."

"By whom?"

"I don't know. I didn't see the guy."

"That looks bad. Maybe you should go to the hospital."

"No. It looks worse than it is," Kyle said. He averted his face as the waitress approached to take their order. "Coke. A slice of plain pizza."

"Same," Randy said, smiling up at the woman. As soon as she left, he said, "Tell me what happened."

"I was at Pop's house. This guy had to have already been inside. I went into the garage to get some Christmas items, and he ambushed me. I fell face-first, hard. He held me down, pressed something against my neck, and then told me I stole his boots."

"Boots? The ones from the asylum?"

"Yes. Apparently, they're his and he wants them back. He threatened my family if I didn't do as he says."

Randy's mouth drooped, brows lifting. "That's one crazy story."

"Right," Kyle said. "But as God as my witness,

that's what he said. So I'm thinking this jerk must've been in the asylum the day I took them. Somehow, he found out my address. Maybe he got it from my license plate. And he either followed me to Pop's house, or somehow got his address from the phone book." He ran his hand through his hair, shaking his head. "The crazy thing is, I think I know this guy. There was something familiar about his voice. Do you think it could've been Roy?"

"Roy?" Randy's mouth dropped.

"Yes," Kyle said. "My brother."

"I don't know. You haven't seen Roy since you were kids. You've been looking for him. Why would he attack you over a pair of old boots?"

"I don't know," Kyle said. "Maybe he's still pissed with me, or he found out I'm searching for him. Beth made some calls. We didn't exactly part on the best of terms. He hated me and told me so. He said he never wanted to see me again. That was the last time I saw him. What if he's been nosing around the asylum, same as us? Maybe he saw me and decided he wanted to have a reunion in his own way."

"For what?" Randy leaned forward; his eyes boring into Kyle's. "Being adopted? You didn't do anything wrong, Kyle. You're always beating yourself up for leaving him behind. You might not talk about Roy, but it haunts you. Don't go back to Rose Hill. It opened a rat's nest. You're a mess."

The waitress arrived with their drinks and pizza. Both men waited until she left before continuing to talk.

"I am a mess," Kyle admitted. "I know I'm grasping at straws, but I need to figure this out."

"Not if it risks your safety. You're jumping to

conclusions. It's probably not Roy. Did you call the cops?"

"No. He threatened my family if I did and said he'd already been at my house. Beth thought she saw someone in the yard just before Halloween. I think it was him. I'm not taking his threats lightly."

"So now what?"

"He told me to take the boots back to the asylum on Saturday. I am."

"Seriously?" Randy scowled. "Why didn't he just take them off your feet?"

"I wasn't wearing them," Kyle said. "I don't think it's about the boots. This guy is just messing with me, for what, I haven't a clue."

"Pretty sick." Randy took a bite of his pizza. "This guy sounds like a nutcase."

"I can't think of anyone who'd have it out for me."

"Call the authorities," Randy said, "Stop this now."

"No way. We've been breaking into the asylum. I never saw this guy. I can't describe him. It could be anyone. I think it's someone from the asylum."

"Like whom?"

"I don't know. This guy must know the place. He was there when I took the boots. He could be…" He shrugged. "Mental."

"I don't think you should go back to the asylum," Randy said. "It's not worth the risk. I'll take the boots back and drop them off for you."

"No."

"Kyle, I have a gun. I've got protection and know how to use it. Your problem will be solved."

"No way are you doing that," Kyle said. "But you can go with me."

Randy sighed; face drawn in apprehension. "I think you should give it more thought. There is no reason to risk yourself. Think."

"What's to think about?" Kyle reached into his pocket, pulled out a photo and slid it across the table.

"What's that?"

"It's a photo of my mother. Just one of several. Pop hid them from me. I realized that my mother had been raped. She had the mind of a little girl. Someone took advantage of her and who knows if Roy and I have the same dad."

Randy picked up the picture, staring at it. "That's not that shocking, Kyle. The residents of Rose Hill had sex. It happened."

"I know that. But not all were willing. The worst part is nothing can be done about it now. No proof. But that fact that I am here proves that my mother was raped. I just need to find out whose DNA I carry."

"Good luck with that."

"It doesn't really matter now. I'm taking his boots back to him. Are you in?"

"Sure."

Kyle left the pizza joint, jumped into his truck, and headed to the pharmacy. His thoughts were jumbled but talking to Randy had helped put things into perspective. He should've told Randy about the jester. Could there be a connection to the boots? Both had ties to Rose Hill.

Damn it! He should never have set foot back there. Now he was being stalked. Tying the jester cap to the incident was wreaking havoc with his imagination. It wasn't store bought, it was handmade—his awful craft project. And then there was the color—purple, red. How could it not be the same one? The cap was used during hide and seek. Whoever was the tagger put on the cap and chased down their quarry. Once found, the tagged person had to put on the cap and become "it". It had freaked him out at times. Sometimes they played outside, but other times, a basement would do. He hated the game. "Twitches," often got out of hand. The older kids could be rough. They'd hurt you if they felt like it. *If you twitch, you'll get stitched.* Unfortunately, it came true for some. Once he was shoved into a wall and broke his nose.

His temples pounded. It all seemed absurd. Surreal.

Finally, he pulled over into a gas station's parking lot. Aimlessly, he stared out the truck's front windshield. A light rain drizzled a pattern across the pane. He reached into his pocket and pulled out his cell phone, searching his contact list.

His Uncle Bill picked up on the fourth ring.

"Hey, Bill," he said. "This is Kyle. I'm sorry to bother you, but I needed someone to talk to and since Pop can't answer my questions, I was hoping you could speak to me."

"Sure, Kyle. Everything okay? You sound a bit shaken up."

"I'm all right," he lied, silencing the urge to confess what had happened at his father's house. He just needed information. "But before I say anything else, Beth and Sammy are fine. And so is Pop. I just wanted to ask you a few questions."

"Sure," Bill replied.

"This has to do with Roy."

There was a long pause.

"I've been searching for him," Kyle said. "It's been really bothering me what happened to him after Rose

Hill closed. I need to know how things turned out. I guess I'm looking for closure. Anything you can remember would be appreciated."

"I'll help if I can," Bill said.

"The last time I visited Rose Hill, I was about fourteen." Kyle paused, then added, "I saw Roy briefly a couple of times but for the most part, he pretty much avoided me. He would've been around twelve or so."

"From what I remember, Roy had anger issues," Bill replied. "I believe he was bipolar but I'm not sure what the official diagnosis was. I'm sorry, there were just so many people at Rose Hill. They were weeding out the kids, leaving mostly adults. Roy was considered violent and was abusive toward other people, even the staff."

"Anger issues? Maybe he had a right to be mad." Kyle paused, catching his breath. "Roy wasn't always angry. He had a great sense of humor. He liked being in the skits, liked school. He was thoughtful at times, considerate. Sure, he got into trouble. Had issues. So did I. I was no angel, you know, but whatever Roy's troubles were, they were exacerbated by something much darker going on at the time. He was bullied, so was I. Surviving at Rose Hill was hard at times. I should've done more to protect him. I left him alone in that place."

"Don't blame yourself. The circumstances were not of your doing."

"I feel like there should've been something…" Kyle's voice trailed off.

Guilt hit him hard. His memories took a nosedive, returning in bountiful clarity. Roy, like himself, was afraid of some of the older teens, especially Benny.

And Benny had a fondness for bullying Roy, who despite his age, stood up for himself. As Roy grew, he began to change.

"Roy was put into a group home," Bill said, breaking into his thoughts. "I'm not sure where. Look, stop second-guessing yourself. Your hands were tied and so were mine. At the time, the motto for staff was 'hands off.' Children didn't belong at Rose Hill," Bill continued. "You're living with a guilty conscience. I'm sure Roy is fine. Best to let it go."

Kyle absorbed this new information.

"Look, I've kept in touch with a few former employees. I'll reach out to them and dig around. Someone might know Roy's whereabouts. It's been many years, but I'll give it a try."

"Pop might know. I feel he might have more information. I found a hidden stack of pictures of my mother. He'd kept them from me."

After an awkward pause, Bill said, "I can't speak for my brother's decisions or my agreement on anything he's done. You'll have to ask him if he ever recovers, but personally, I think it's better to let the past go."

Kyle withheld a bitter retort. There were those famous words, let the past go. That was easy to say for someone like Bill. Someone who had a wife and kids, brothers and sisters. But he'd once had another family and he couldn't let the past go. Not anymore. He needed to know where Roy was, and he needed to visit Pop. Visiting his father was the easier task.

"Thanks for your time," Kyle said. "I'm sorry to have bothered you."

"No bother," Bill replied. "I'm sorry I couldn't be

more help."

After the phone call ended, Kyle sat in the truck, mulling over what he'd learned. Nothing really, but Bill did say he would be talking to prior staff. It might help.

With troubled thoughts, Kyle drove to Chester Trail Nursing home. It wasn't often he visited his father during the week but ever since the jester's cap had made an appearance at the nursing home, worn by someone he didn't know, he'd been worried about his dad. When he arrived, he was surprised to find the lot mostly empty. Apparently like him, most visitors came on weekends.

His father was in his room, sitting in a wheelchair, face tilted. The television was on, not that it mattered. Vacant eyes stared at a blank wall.

Kyle bent down to break his father's gaze. It didn't work.

"Hello, Pop." From habit, he kissed the top of his head, noting the scar in Pop's thinning hair. "I came for a visit a bit earlier than expected. I hope you don't mind."

Kyle moved the wheelchair into a corner and then dropped onto a chair. His father gave no sign that he recognized him. Kyle collected his thoughts, doubt setting in.

"I know I look like a disaster," Kyle said, touching his sore jaw. He leaned in, giving his father a closer view. "My face is a mess. Kind of how you looked when you hit your head." He paused, puzzled. His father had also been hurt. But what if it had been something more? Suspicion nagged at him, but he shook off his errant thoughts. "I wanted to talk to you about it. I know you can't answer but I'm going to talk to you anyway. I need to bring something out in the open."

Kyle took his father's hand. He stroked his fingers over the smooth, wrinkled skin. "I was at your house the other day." He paused, composing himself. Words struggled to come. "I opened your safe," he finally said. "I know you probably don't want to hear that right now, but it was necessary. I was hoping to find paperwork on Roy. I need closure, Pop. I need to know what happened to him. I thought maybe you had something in there with an address, or at least a clue. So even though I know you hate anyone getting into your things, I felt I had no choice." He continued rubbing Pop's hand. "I didn't find anything on Roy, but I did find my mother's pictures." He hesitated, searching his dad's face. Vacant. "I wish you'd have given them to me. She was my mom. Maybe we didn't have a normal parent-son relationship, but she had given birth to me. By all rights, they should be mine."

He cleared his throat as Pop continued to stare at the wall.

Kyle pulled a picture out of his pocket. He held it close to his father's eyes. "These are the pictures I found. I want to know, why me? What was so special that you adopted me? You had other choices—Roy. He was younger and needed a family. Why did you separate us? I'm angry, Pop, really angry that you didn't take him in." The words fell flat. He pulled out another picture, holding it up. "Does this look familiar? It's Florence, your wife, holding a child. I thought it might be a cousin. Here is the one with my mom and Roy."

Kyle returned the pictures to his pocket and cleared

his throat.

"I think that I was attacked by someone that once lived or worked at the asylum. Randy and I broke in a while ago, and I took something that my attacker claims is his. I know it sounds strange, but it was a pair of boots. This guy had to be there that day. Somehow, this man found out where I lived; where you live. He attacked me in your garage. He's made threats..."

A mist formed in his pop's stare. A single tear gathered in his right eye. It broke free, leaving a wet trail down his cheek.

Stunned by the reaction, Kyle swallowed the bile in his throat. "I see that I'm troubling you. I hate to tell you these things, but I have these crazy thoughts. I can't sleep. Yesterday, I was attacked in your house, and I'm not even sure why. Roy's been on my mind. My mother. You."

The old man stared; eyes wet.

"You promised that Roy would be fine," Kyle said. "I need to know if he is. Beth doesn't know about the attack. This whole thing has me spooked, then there's that weird guy that was here at the Chester Brook dressed up as a jester. Do you remember that cap and bells from Rose Hill? It looked just like the one I made in sewing class. Something feels wrong. My life's been turned upside down." He paused, sighing. "I wanted to make sure you're okay."

Kyle grabbed a tissue and blotted his father's face. "I think you understand what I've been saying, Pop. Mentally, you're still here. Please fight to come back to us. To me. I want you to meet my daughter. She needs her Pop-Pop."

"I'm sorry if I made you worry. Maybe I shouldn't

have said anything. I'll work it out. I needed to talk to someone. Please stay safe." Kyle stood and touched his father's hand. "I love you, Pop. Thank you for taking me in and making me your son. You've been a great father. I'll be seeing you real soon."

Another tear formed in Scott's eye, brimmed, and broke free.

Chapter Twenty-Five

Blindfolded, Doris Goodman struggled against her bound wrists. She tried to yell through the tape stuck to her lips. Her feet slid around the concrete as she tried to pry her legs free of the wooden chair. Her belly protested loudly in hunger. Ceasing to cry, she was having difficulty breathing through her nose.

Like a spider playing with its prey, Stitches watched the woman, staring at her for over an hour. She was interesting to watch. So different from the other women he'd brought to the asylum. He sat against the wall, drinking a soda. Once, Doctor Goodman had all the power, all the prestige. People listened when she spoke. She seemed so big and powerful. Had she been taller? No. It was all in his head. Now she was nothing by an aging corpse still holding a pulse. He had built her up to be so much more in his mind. How she'd haunted his dreams.

Dumb. Dumb. Dumb.

He kicked his foot out, sending a stone scattering.

Doris heard it and ceased moving.

He picked up another pebble and threw it past her head. She jerked. He threw another and another. This was fun. Like a jackrabbit, she twitched. Finally, he aimed for her forehead. Missed. Damn, he'd lost his touch. But practice made perfect. Three shots later, he hit his mark. Not a sound. It had to have hurt, but the old lady failed to utter a sound. A fleck of blood oozed from the superficial wound. Her neck stiffened, and she twisted her head.

Pausing, he stared at the crimson stain on her skin. It bubbled, then ran in a stream, disappearing into a gray brow.

"I used to be such a good shot," Stitches said. "I've lost my touch." He took another swig of soda. Memories cascaded over him. "I used to be good at softball; I could hit a homer. I was a good runner. Man, I could slide into the bases. But you wouldn't know that, would you, Doc?" He stood as rage became his friend. "You took softball away from me. The only thing I loved. No sports allowed. You said there was something wrong with me. I needed to be kept separate. I was told I was rotten, a hopeless case. What kind of doctor doesn't help someone if she believed that? You treated me like an animal. Told me I was. You put me in that padded room and left me there for days. You wrote my name down in your dirty little book. You told everyone I was a good-for-nothing. That I needed to be locked away, medicated."

He sniffed, spitting on the ground.

"But all your finger-pointing didn't work." He laughed. "People didn't care what you had to say. I was needed. Given jobs, respected. And you know what, Doctor Goodman? It's because of you I figured out who I am. You! I figured if I was going to be bad, I'd make you proud. That way, you can tell all of your friends that you were right about me." Once again, he cackled. "But you didn't expect me to come a-calling, did you? You didn't get rid of me, Doctor Goodman, 'cause here we are, together. Just like old times."

Doris mumbled something.

Stitches flicked on a spotlight, aiming it at Doris's pale face. He drew closer to her, noting the black hair along her upper lip, just above the tape's edge. He reached out and ran his finger over the brittleness. Just like tiny, black fly legs. Interesting.

"Doris, I think you forgot to shave."

That did it. She twisted her head away from his fingers. Another noise escaped her gagged mouth.

"I can't hear you." He placed his forefinger against his ear, tilting his head. "You'll have to try harder than that."

More muttering.

He ripped the tape from her mouth.

Sputtering and crying, she tried to find her voice.

"You sound so silly," he said. "Like a tiny, baby birdy."

"Whatever I've done," she blurted out, "Whatever wrong you think I did, I'm sorry."

Stitches' brows lifted. Incredible. Did she think her apology would work?

"Go on." How weak and pathetic. "I'm listening."

"I'm a good person. A human. I have my flaws, but I tried to live a good life and help others. Tell me how I can help you. We can talk about this thing that you think I've done. I can make amends. I have some money in savings. I can give it to you." Her rant went on for a full minute.

Stitches yawned, tapping his hand against his mouth.

"You're not impressing me, Doris. Your confessions are weak. I'd think you'd have more to say. You have many sins to atone for. I think I'll have to put the tape back over your whiny mouth."

"I don't even know who you are," she said. "How can I confess to any sin? Just let me go. I can't identify you. You've had me blindfolded for the most part, so I have no knowledge of who you are."

"Don't you?" He laughed, slapping his leg. "I think you do."

"No. No," she insisted. Her tongue darted out, licking her cracked lips. "Really, I don't. And I don't want to. I haven't seen your face. You have me confused with someone else. Just let me go. I can't identify you. Please. I won't say a word."

"Are you telling me that you didn't once work at the Rose Hill Asylum? That you aren't the notable Doctor Goodman?"

"R… Rose Hill?"

"Yes," he snapped. "Damn it. Don't stammer, woman. What do you think I'm talking about?"

Doris jumped at his tone, her mouth trembling.

"That was a long time ago," she said. "It's been many, many years. I have known many students and staff. I worked in other facilities."

"And did you have a favorite student in Rose Hill? A special boy?" He touched the top of the old woman's quivering lip. "Were you good to your staff? Or how about the residents that were forced to work without pay?"

"I didn't have any favorites," she said. "I loved all my charges. I did my job to the best of my capabilities. I'd like to think I helped a few and made a difference in their lives."

"Liar." His finger stopped her lip. "You don't love. You don't know love. Especially for the tainted people who ruined normal society. You only loved the power of using your stinking mouth to judge me. But that wasn't the worst, was it? No. You delighted in terror. In doling out punishments. Playing God. Some would say I'm evil. But I say you are far worse."

"No, you're wrong. I…I don't think I'm a God. You must remember—times being as they were back then—corporal punishment was acceptable. It's how I was trained. My own parents spanked me. They believed that to spare the rod was to spoil the child. But I do know how to love. I had a husband that I loved with all my heart. He died ten years ago. I have my Princess."

"Your dog?"

"Yes," she cried. "My sweet Princess. She's all that I have now. If I don't get home, she will starve to death. She needs food, water, and my love. She must be so frightened that I'm not home. Please let me go home to her."

Stitches stood, stifling his laughter. He grabbed her chair, turning it around in the other direction. His hands slid down onto her bony shoulders. He gave a light squeeze, then slid his hands up her throat, then her face. He fingered her blindfold.

"Well now, I don't think that's going to be a problem," he whispered in her ear.

With his two thumbs, he pushed the scarf away from her eyes. He picked up the spotlight from off the floor, trailing it onto the chair opposite Doris.

"Princess," Doris cried. "Oh Princess, my sweetie."

The muzzled dog sat up on the chair, wagging its tail. The canine would've jumped from her perch except for the chain attached to her collar preventing it.

"Thank you for not hurting her," she whispered. "She's such a good doggie. She doesn't need a muzzle. She'd never bite anyone. Please, take it off her. She looks so uncomfortable." Doris tried to turn her head toward her captor, but he was still behind her chair. Instead, she craned her head, staring around the room. "Where are we?"

"Don't you know?" the man said, closer to her ear. "Don't you recognize it?"

"I…I do know this place." Doris gasped. "It looks so different."

"This is what hell looks like," Stitches said. "My hell. Welcome home."

And with that, Stitches moved in front of Doris's chair and squatted down, letting her gaze into his eyes. She took one look at his face and screamed.

Chapter Twenty-Six

On Monday evening, an eerie calm embraced Kyle as he headed into his house. In some ways, it was uplifting to finally confide in Beth and lay out some of his cards. Like a soul going to confession, it was a bittersweet moment, a long time in coming. Whether he'd find any release from his stricken mind was left to be seen.

After hanging up his coat, he found Beth in the kitchen. She appeared engrossed by their bills spread out on the table, checkbook by her right hand. Without a care in the world, the baby slept in her infant swing.

Everything appeared so normal. Like nothing in his life had changed. And yet, he'd changed in just a short amount of time, ever since he'd reconnected with Rose Hill. It seemed that visiting his childhood home had set off a chain of events in his life and he was at a loss how to stop the rollercoaster ride. If only he'd never set foot there, never taken those damn boots. His life would still be simple, or at least more predictable. He'd even welcome Beth's orderly world.

"Where have you been?" Beth's chin lifted, her eyes assessing him. "You haven't answered my calls all day. I was worried sick. I thought the doctor might've sent you to the emergency room but then his office told me you never showed up for your appointment. What's going on? Did you get seen by anyone at all?"

"No," Kyle said. "I decided not to go."

"What?" Her face fell, stunned. "Why not?"

"Because I feel fine. It's just a superficial wound. I needed time to myself, so I went for a drive. I decided to visit Pop. Last time I was there, I saw signs of recovery. I wanted to reach out to him." He grabbed a glass from the cupboard, filled it with water and sat down at the table. "I'm okay. Really, I am. I might look a mess, but I'll heal."

"For real?" She shoved the checkbook away from her. It slid across the table, scattering invoices. "That's your excuse? You needed time for yourself? You basically lied to me about going for help and took off on top of that. What's gotten into you lately? I don't understand you. You've been so weird, hiding things from me." She paused; her eyes boring into him. "Are you having an affair? Is that what you've been doing?"

"An affair?" He paused, shocked. Then he laughed at the notion, shaking his head. "No, honey. You're more than enough woman for me."

Relief filled Beth's features, but her expression guarded.

"Just stop with the accusations," he said, his voice steady. "No one can ever accuse you of not having an active imagination." He sighed, took a sip of water and set down the glass, gripping it like a lifeline. "I have some issues that I need to address. I want to be able to talk to you about it but you're not the easiest person to talk to. I just want you to listen to me and not jump in."

"What do you mean?" Her face belied her hurt. She leaned back in her chair. "You've always been able to talk to me."

"No, not lately. You're too quick to judge,

criticize. You used to be different but now it's a common occurrence. Frankly, I'm tired of it." He rubbed his hand over his stubbled jaw and took a deep breath. "I don't need you mothering me. You've got Sammy for that. I don't need a babysitter, either. I'm a grown man. I decided I didn't want to see a doctor, so I didn't go. End of story. If my health suffers from it, so be it. It was my decision. Mine. Not yours."

"You could have a concussion," she said. "And not even know it. I guess I'm a bad wife for caring about you. You talk about me, but what about you? You walk around like a zombie. You don't speak to me. You're always off somewhere in your mind. And then when I do try to connect to you, you act like I'm a nuisance." She folded her hands on the table, looking lost. "I can see something has been troubling you. But I didn't dare try to ask, knowing you'd clam up. You should've told me how you felt. Communication is key for a healthy marriage."

"Communication?" he said. "A healthy marriage? Are you serious? I've tried communicating. I'd like to be able to talk to you, really talk to you. You only see…hear…what you want to believe. Everything has to be on a schedule with you, all planned accordingly. It's hard living in your world of order. I like things a little more chaotic, adventurous. You used to be fun, Beth. And now…now I don't know…"

"Well, somebody had to grow up." Her eyes glowed feverishly in the light. "Take charge of our lives. Wouldn't it be grand if I up and left? Ran off with my girlfriends like you and Randy do with each other. Go wild and let you wonder where I'm at for a change, wonder what I'm doing. Is that what you want?"

"That's not what I'm saying. You're already jumping to conclusions."

"That's what it sounds like. We have a daughter now. We have to be responsible parents."

"We are responsible," he said. "But it doesn't mean we have to live so uptight."

"What are you trying to say?" Her chin lifted a notch. "Do you want to divorce me? Is that it?"

"No." His eyes bored into hers. "Of all the things in my life that I'm not certain about, I am about this. I love you."

"You have a funny way of showing it."

He sighed, realizing he was getting off the mark. "I'm just trying to talk to you. I need you to understand what I'm saying to you."

"Go on."

"Before you say anything, just listen to me." He stared at the wall, swallowing hard. "There's some things you don't know about me. Things in my past. I need to clarify it." He paused, collecting his thoughts. "It's about my childhood."

"You had a great childhood. Your parents were great."

"No. Not my adoptive parents." He paused, waiting for her to interrupt, but she finally quieted. "When I was a boy, I was told it was better to forget the past and forge a new future. So that's what I did. But now I know I can't escape who I am and who I was."

"Honey, you're shaking," Beth reached across the table and took his hand, squeezing it gently. "Kyle, you're scaring me. Slow down. I'm here. Just tell me."

"Things were bad at Rose Hill. I never really told you how bad."

179

Her mouth dropped but she remained still.

"I had no one. My mother was a ward of the state. She had no rights. I don't know who sired me or my brother. Do you realize that someone raped her, twice that we know about? She couldn't have consented. I'm proof of that fact. I'd like to find out who took advantage of her. He should be prosecuted."

Confusion filled Beth's features. She released Kyle's hand, sliding against her chair, now guarded and tense.

"You said both your parents lived at Rose Hill," she said softy. "I had no idea she'd been raped. You never talked about your mother."

"It was just easier that way," he said. "I didn't want anyone to know I was a rapist's son." He paused, gathering himself. "I'm talking about her now. I never got to know my mother. They barely let me see her. It makes me so mad."

"I can see that."

"Then there's Roy. I need to find my brother, need to know if he's okay."

"I'm trying."

"I want you to be prepared that it might not go as planned." He paused; eyes hesitant. "What if he has issues? Uncle Bill said Roy was troubled, possibly violent. He said I should let the past go."

"You can't," she said, folding her hands. "I want you to find your brother. You need to do that for you. This is eating you up. I'm one hundred percent behind you be it good or bad."

He closed his eyes and sighed. "That's all I needed to know."

"We'll find him. It's just a matter of putting the

pieces together. If I had a correct last name that would help. Your mother's maiden name comes up empty."

"I don't know what it could be. Legally, I'm a Hampton now but it's Winston on my birth certificate. I don't know why he'd have a different last name unless he was adopted?"

"I never thought of that," she said. "Maybe he was adopted. You were."

"I also thought Roy might want to help me find justice for our mother," he confessed. "I'd like to know if we have the same father or we're dealing with two different men."

"Two predators makes it all the worse," she said.

"It makes me sick." He swallowed hard. "No one protected her."

"Tell me about your mother," she said. "What do you remember about her?"

"I suppose if the doctors had known early enough that my mother was pregnant, they might've aborted me. It was common practice at Rose Hill. Despite the segregation in place, babies were conceived. I don't even know if my mother knew she was pregnant. Understood what was happening to her. I was taken from her just after birth." He pleaded with his eyes, hoping to make her understand. "My mother had an intellectual disability. She had extensive medical problems, hearing loss and seizures. She had the mind of a child. But even though she had a mental deficiency, she wanted me. She wanted to take care of her baby, but she didn't have the know-how or reasoning. I was told by others that she'd cry and rock herself to sleep."

"As I grew, they'd let her visit me once a week under supervision. I remember her grabbing me and kissing my cheek. Squeezing me hard, a bit too hard. She treated me like a baby doll. I knew she was special, but I lived with special people with all kinds of ailments. It was normal to me. Eventually, I was put up for adoption, but no one came forward to take me. After all, I was from Rose Hill. Everyone knew what that meant. I was supposedly defective. That's what Rose Hill was for – to hide away the damaged. I didn't know any other life. I played with the other kids and went to Rose Hill School. I learned to garden and do menial tasks. It wasn't an ideal childhood, but it was the only one I knew. We were all a family; a very large family."

"Oh, my God," Beth said. "I can't stand thinking of you living in that place. It's awful to think of you, one tiny soul among all those people. It breaks my heart."

"It didn't seem like that at the time," he said. "It was normal life to me. Pop started working at the asylum when I was around eight. Then my mother died, and Scott and Florence adopted me. It was like starting over, a new life outside of Rose Hill. I begged my new parents to let me visit my old friends. They agreed, allowing me weekend visits. But then I began public school. I made new friends…well…it was just easier to not talk about it. I was embarrassed and didn't want anyone to know where I was from. I vowed never to tell anyone. Obviously, the extended Hampton family and Randy knew I was adopted."

"Randy was stuck in that place," Beth said, shaking her head. "No wonder he has relationship issues. It makes sense."

"When Rose Hill closed, his grandmother took him in," he said. "I don't know why she waited so long. It could've been a financial problem."

"Did he ever ask her?"

"No, I don't think he likes to talk about it. I think deep down he's hurt."

"I don't blame him," she said. "Is his grandmother still in his life?"

"No," he said. "She died when he was around twenty-one."

"That's sad," she said. "But Randy's always had you. You've been a great friend to him."

"I suppose, but I should've been a better brother to Roy," Kyle said. "Roy was a great kid. He had a temper and boy, could he scream. He resembled my mother, blond, blue-eyed. He was two years younger than I am. He'd follow me around and was always getting into trouble. There were older kids, a few bullies. Kids got beaten up. Being small, Roy got picked on. There wasn't much staff and in the long hours of the night, opportunity was easy to come by. Roy was kept with the younger kids, but like I said, he still got into trouble, mischief. He'd be punished. Locked up in seclusion for a while. Uncle Bill said Roy was bipolar."

"Do you think that's why the Hamptons didn't adopt him?"

"Yes." He closed his eyes for a moment, then slowly opened them. "I didn't press the matter. I was selfish, worried that the Hamptons would choose Roy over me."

Once again, he paused, gathering his thoughts. Beth's gaze was rooted to his.

"Roy was devastated that I was leaving," he said. "He cried his heart out, begged me to stay. After all, I was his big brother. I finally asked Pop to take us both, but Pop said Florence could only handle one child. That

Roy had issues and needed to stay put. That we'd visit. And we did for a few years. I was fourteen the last time I saw Roy. He wasn't the same kid, I remembered. He'd changed. There was such bitterness in his heart. He told me he hated me, wanted me dead. I never went back until I returned with Randy. Being at Rose Hill brought it all back to me; every morbid detail." He dropped a heavy fist onto the table. "How could I forget my own brother? What kind of person does that?"

"Well, if you were encouraged to forget the past, maybe it's not your fault. And you were just a kid."

"I have no excuse."

"I'm glad you told me about this. I love you. I'm your wife, Kyle. Please don't keep secrets from me." She paused, rubbing her arms. "What about your mother? What was her medical condition? It would be good to know for Samantha's sake."

"Pop said something about an accident during her birth and lack of oxygen. She'd been revived but she was never the same."

"That's awful," she said. "I'd have liked to have met her."

Kyle turned around to dig into his pocket. He lifted out a small envelope, pulled out a pack of pictures and laid a picture in front of her.

"Look."

Beth picked up the picture. "Your mother?"

"Yes."

"She was beautiful. I can see the resemblance."

"Roy looks like her too."

He handed her another picture.

"Who are these kids?"

"The one in the middle is me. The girl next to me is

Karen Walton."

"But you're all dressed up as clowns." She lifted her face to his. "Clowns?"

"The kids at Rose Hill loved the circus but many of them would never get to attend. They didn't have the physical capability to go to a show, so the circus was brought to them."

"But you hate the circus."

"I do because it brings back memories that I'd rather forget. Rose Hill was a terrible place. I didn't even know how bad it was until I left and was free." He pointed at a small clown in the photo. "That's Roy. He loved dressing up and playing pretend. He learned how to juggle and tell jokes. He was talented and could make kids laugh. It's hard to believe that he became so violent in his teen years. The Roy I remembered was bright, funny and inquisitive." He twirled the photo around, picked it up and stared at his brother. "Living in that place broke Roy's spirit. Changed him. Rose Hill was known for misdiagnosing residents. For instance, once upon a time, parents thought kids with Down's syndrome could be cured with treatment. And when that didn't happen, you can imagine their anger. But a lot of Rose Hill kids were just orphans—either taken from neglectful parents, or they were born there, like me. Who knows what they did to Roy, or what he went through?"

"That's so terrible," she said beneath her breath. "But you have to know it wasn't your fault. There was nothing you could do."

Kyle's phone ringing interrupted them. He looked at the screen. "I need to take this call. It's my uncle Bill."

Chapter Twenty-Seven

"Hey, Kyle," Bill Hampton's voice came over the receiver. "Yesterday I met up with someone who used to work at Rose Hill. I asked them if they knew anything about your brother. I thought I'd call you and go over what I found out, to give you peace of mind."

"I appreciate that." Kyle sat down on the porch swing, ignoring the chilly night air. His stomach knotted in dread.

"I was told that Roy had been living in Philadelphia. It was a group home that's no longer there. It's been years since this person saw Roy. As far as anyone knows, he had adjusted."

Kyle absorbed the words. Philadelphia, just an hour away.

"Is he using my mother's last name, Winston?"

"That, I don't know. But at least you have an area to begin searching."

"Thank you, that will help. I really would like to find him."

"I know your life at the asylum wasn't easy." Bill said. "You should know that you made my brother very happy. Scott wanted to fill the void in Florence's heart. She couldn't have any more children, and you were a perfect fit for their family." He paused and continued. "Florence's face lit up the moment she saw you, and she knew it was meant to be. I know you felt bad leaving Roy, but you were given a chance for a better life. Florence believed you'd adjust, and it seemed that she was right."

Was she? Kyle wasn't so sure. Florence only saw him on the outside. She never really knew the real him. Never saw the pain he hid every day, the trouble he'd had adjusing to family life.

"Are you there?"

"Sorry," Kyle said. "I was lost in thought. Thanks for the information." Kyle stood, shoved the swing, and stepped off the porch. The wind stirred his hair as he moved around the backyard.

"You're welcome," Bill said. "I know this is hard for you. I hope you find what you're looking for."

After he hung up, Kyle stood by the garage, staring at the darkening sky. Dark, ominous clouds crept along the horizon. Despite Bill's assurances, a bad feeling hung over him. His thoughts turned to his newest dilemma; someone wanted his boots. It'd seem crazy to think that some homeless man had hunted him down for a pair of shoes.

But he'd made up his mind. He didn't need some stranger stalking him. He was taking the boots back to Rose Hill asylum.

As he went indoors, Bill's words suddenly came to life.

Florence couldn't have any more children.

What the hell did that mean?

Chapter Twenty-Eight

Stitches opened the padlocked closet, shining a flashlight toward the rear. The bound woman inside recoiled at the sound. The tape kept her from speaking, and blinders covered her eyes.

"Good morning, Doris," Stitches greeted her. "I hope you slept as well as I did. You'll be happy to know I haven't heard a thing on the news about your disappearance or read anything in the paper. Of course, it's only been a few days. But it appears no one is looking for you." He moved closer and knelt. "That speaks a lot about a person, doesn't it? I mean, no one misses you at all. That's the mark you've left in this world."

With his pocketknife, he cut the tape from her arms, freeing her from the chair. He then cut off the tape from her legs. She began to move, reaching for the tape on her eyes.

"No, no, no," he said. "Don't be a bad girl, or I'll have to tie you up again. You must listen to my rules. You know all about rules, don't you, Doris? And the punishments for breaking them? I wonder what people would think if they knew how once upon a time the good psychiatrist would take her paddle from her desk, bend a small child over a chair, and whale his or her ass. You weren't always too careful with your aim. I wonder if some of the boys you beat were ever able to father children." He laughed beneath his breath, mimicking her voice, "Oh no, children born from the bowels of Rose Hill? They might be defective; we must protect society at all costs."

Shaky fingers lowered to Doris's lap, curling into themselves.

"That's a good girl." He patted her cheek. He reached behind her head and untied the blinders. She blinked, trying to look at him. He then pulled the tape off her mouth. She cried out in pain.

"Tsk, tsk," he said. Her lips bled from one corner. "Sorry, but it's a necessary evil."

"Please," she whispered. "Why are you doing this to me? Where's my dog?"

"In time, honey. In time. Your dog is fine. But first, a bathroom break and then a meal." He grabbed her arms, helping her to her feet. "Such a tiny woman. So fragile."

"What did you expect?" She ripped away her arm. "I'm old, you moron."

Stunned by her unexpected strength, he halted, staring down at her. Fear filled her features as she realized the imminent danger.

"I…I didn't mean it," she cried out. "It just slipped out. Forgive me."

He said nothing, grabbing her bony arm. He led her into a hallway lit by filtered sunlight. He took her into an old office, which held a dusty desk and two rubber chairs. He walked past the desk, taking her into a small bathroom.

"That is gross," she said, eyeing the commode. "The thing is disgusting. The plumbing doesn't work. Why do you insist on me using it? It's filling up and getting nastier."

"Hmm," he said, staring into the toilet. "You're quite right. Imagine that. I remember a time when the hallways had crap on the floor and so did the beds. I remember having to clean it up. I never saw you cleaning up anything, Doc. I remember kids using the same toothbrushes as the other kids. No hygiene whatsoever. Nasty, repulsive, gross, disgusting toothbrushes with other kids' spit on them. And then they'd all get sick. Go figure."

"If that happened, it wasn't my fault," she said. "I didn't make the rules. I was just one person. We were all under stress, underpaid. There were many good people who worked here, many volunteers. We were severely underfunded. There wasn't enough staff or money for improvements, supplies. Our pleas for help landed on deaf ears. I did the best I could give under the circumstances."

"You were a doctor," he said, glaring down at her. "You were supposed to help people. Find a way. But you didn't do anything for anyone. You're a liar. I have found over the years that all doctors are liars."

Doris trembled from head to toe. She swallowed hard. The bulge of her Adam's apple moved up and down her meager throat.

"I'm only human," she said. "I make mistakes, just like everyone else. Spankings were acceptable at the time. Paddling was a normal punishment for disobedient kids."

"And you got to choose who deserved the punishment," he said. "You never considered finding out the truth. You made assumptions as to who was guilty. You just swung away without any just cause.

You chose who got special treatment. Who got to leave. Played matchmaker with lives. Get to using the toilet." He closed the door, leaning his face into the opened crack. "You've got three minutes."

Feeling empowered by his treatment of the doctor, Stitches sat down on a desk chair and sighed. Underneath the desk sat a cooler. He reached into it and grabbed two sandwiches, placed them on the desk. "Let's go," he yelled toward the bathroom. "Two minutes left."

Finally, Doris opened the door. Uncertain, she stared first at him, then at the food.

"Sit there," he ordered, pointing to an opposite chair. "Eat."

Slowly, she walked into the room with a slight hobble. She sat down, staring awkwardly at him. "Why do you wear that white makeup on your face?"

"Eat that sandwich."

"Are you trying to keep disguised so I won't know who you are?"

"Shut up," he said quietly. "This is just my base layer."

"A mime?" She settled in the chair, staring at him. "Perhaps a ghost? I might not know a lot of things, but you weren't born with that makeup on your face. You're disguised so I won't know who you are. You should be ashamed of yourself, treating an old woman like this. What would your mother say?"

"Lady, you just don't know when to shut up," he said beneath his breath. "Eat while you can."

"How do I know how I wronged you if I don't know your name?"

"It will come back to you."

"That's not fair," she said. "You know who I am. Tell me your name."

"Shut up!" he yelled, slamming his fists on the table. "I'll snap your scrawny little neck. Now eat or go back to your hole."

Visibly trembling, she picked up her sandwich. She lifted the corner of the bread, scrutinizing the contents.

"Same thing as yesterday," he said. "Peanut butter and jelly." He shoved a bottle of water toward her. "Drink this as well."

"What are you going to do with me?" Her voice shook. "Are you going to kill me? If you are then just get it over with."

"I haven't decided what to do with you," he said. "You weren't in my plans. I saw your interview, talking about this place and how you once worked here. I mean, Doris"—he leaned closer—"do you really think you should be bragging like you were an angel in disguise? You claimed there wasn't any abuse going on." He laughed, snorted. "I couldn't help myself. Ol' Doris Goodman in the flesh. The paper practically led me to your house. How lucky could I be? Here I thought you were dead. What are you, a hundred years old?"

"That's none of your business," she replied, tilting her chin.

"Who cares," he said. "You look a hundred. I've thought about you all these years. Remembered how you treated me and everyone else. What you did to people who crossed you. I could come up with all kinds of ways to rid the world of you. Slow. Fast. Painful. Quietly. No one can say I don't have a great imagination." He tapped the side of his temple. "Just eat the sandwich and be quick about it. I might come up with a plan before you're finished."

Hands shaking, Doris picked up the sandwich and took a bite. She chewed it slowly.

"I feel so dirty and grimy," she said, lifting her gaze to his. "I have arthritis. I hurt all over."

"So?"

"I'd like some pain medication. I would like to wash my hands. My face. You look like you took a shower today. You smell clean. I must look a fright."

He analyzed her face. She looked like a prune. Dark smudges from week-old mascara gave her the appearance of a raccoon. Her hair was wild about her head.

"Yeah, you're pretty scary looking."

"Humph." She took another bite of her sandwich. "You're not a very nice man."

He smiled and shoved his own sandwich down his throat.

"Thanks for the compliment," he said. "I don't think killers are supposed to be nice, do you?"

Words hitting their mark, her pallor changed to stark white.

Satisfied, he grabbed another sandwich from the cooler and thrust a chunk into his mouth, chewing. He paused, studying her. "And by the way, my name is Stitches."

Chapter Twenty-Nine

In the days that followed, an unnatural calm settled over the household. Kyle began securing the house. Dead bolts, new locks, and motion lighting were added to their décor.

Beth appeared distant, preoccupied. Kyle hated the pity in her gaze. Still, she was unbelievably sweet. In fact, he'd welcome a bit of discord.

Kyle kept his thoughts to himself, content to allow Beth to wait on him. He had no doubt that she was getting closer to finding Roy. In some way, he was glad because she was doing the research he wanted to do. But he was disconnected. He couldn't stop thinking about his attacker and the threats to his family. His anxiety was at its peak.

Second guessing his decision to return the boots replayed over and over again in his mind. His assailant wanted them Saturday. So why not mix up the cards, do it on Friday? Screw up any waylaying tactics. Maybe this guy really did just want the boots, end of the issue. He smiled to himself. He'd like to leave a little something inside the boots as a parting gift. He shuddered; the image hardly appeasing. The stress of the situation was warping his brain.

But on Friday, he decided against returning the boots early. His fear had been replaced by curiosity; besides, he wasn't making any mistakes. He'd be ready if it was a trap. He wouldn't mind getting a little payback if possible.

With his decision made, he found some peace. Come hell or damnation, he'd face what was to come.

On Saturday morning, Kyle rose, wondered if he'd regret his decision. There was still time to call the cops if necessary. That gave him a lifeline if needed. Beth thought he was going to work, and he intended to keep it that way. He didn't want any kinks in what he was doing, or her trying to stop him.

If Beth had any suspicions, she kept them to herself. He kissed the baby, then Beth, and then left for work, lunchbox in hand. He drove to Randy's house, honking the horn in the driveway. His buddy came out, giving Kat, who stood at the front door in a silky robe, a wave.

"It's chilly," Randy said, sliding into the front seat. He noticed the lunchbox. "Wow. Beth thinks you're going to work?"

"Yeah. So?"

"Not my concern." Randy shrugged. "Whatever."

"Did you bring your gun?"

"Yes," Randy replied. "It's in my holster, beneath my coat. You're acting so edgy. Worried we can't handle this?"

"As a matter of fact, I am," Kyle said. He started the truck, backing out of the drive. "We could be walking into a trap."

"Then why are we going?"

"I don't want to piss this guy off and have him come after my family. I'll call the cops if things get worse. After today, I'm buying my own gun."

"Where are the boots? I don't see them on your

feet."

"I've got them," Kyle said. "They're in the rear of the truck. I haven't worn them since the attack."

"You're way too stressed out," Randy said. "Let me drop off the boots. I'm armed. There's no reason for you to put yourself in danger."

"We've already been over this," Kyle said, glancing sideways at Randy. "I appreciate the offer but we're in this together. I just hope you don't have to shoot someone."

"Damn," Randy replied, laughing. "I was looking forward to it."

"Real funny," Kyle said. "How can you joke around when I have a serious problem?" He paused, dealing with his rising temper. "I've got a knife. We should be ready for anything."

"Does Beth know you took one of her kitchen knives?"

"Cut the crap," Kyle said. "Just lay off Beth. She doesn't know about any of this. If she did, the cops would've been called days ago. Things are better at the house, we're getting along. I give her credit for trying to work things out. I haven't been easy to live with lately."

"Man, you're uptight," Randy said, shoving back against the seat. "Just chill out."

"Well, then listen to what I'm saying. This bastard threatened my family. I don't know who this guy is or why the boots are so important to him. The whole thing is weird."

"That's why you should just let me go." Randy whistled beneath his breath. "That way only one of us has to deal with the consequences if things go south."

"No," Kyle said. "Drop it. This is my mess."

"Some dude ripped into you and you're just going to hand them over?" Randy shook his head. "That doesn't sound like the Kyle I used to know."

"I won't risk Beth or Samantha for paybacks, but if it's an ambush, I'll be ready," Kyle replied. "Call me a coward if you want. I don't care."

"This could be the same dude that was spying on me and Kat. I think we should jump him and give him a taste of his own medicine."

"No." Kyle shoved his foot on the brake. The truck jolted to a halt. He looked over at Randy, noting the eagerness in his gaze. Randy liked trouble. He had to stop it before it began. "We don't know who we're dealing with. This guy's been watching me, watching my wife and my daughter." He paused, heart racing. "I got to get this settled."

"Kyle. Maybe you should stop and rethink this whole thing."

"No, I've come this far." It was hard being away from the house. Worry took over his fear. "I need to stay focused. Let's just dump the boots and go. The sooner I get home, the better."

"Whatever," Randy said. "Do you remember anything else about this guy? Anything?"

"His voice, it was deep, raspy. Probably on purpose. He was strong. He held me down with his weight. This is one guy you don't want to mess with."

"There's two of us," Randy said. "We're not exactly small men. I can handle myself in a fight. And I've got my gun to back up my fists."

"I don't want you shooting at anyone. We're trespassing on Rose Hill property and taking in a weapon. Do you know how that would look to the cops? We'd be the ones arrested. No way. I just want to drop the boots and get out of there, no questions asked. If you're going to do something crazy, then you can just get out now. Understand?"

Randy sat against the seat, rummaging around in his backpack. After pausing a moment, he turned toward Kyle. "Fine. Whatever. We'll be ready for anything. I wanted to look around some more, but I guess that's out of the picture for now."

"It's out. At least for today. Besides, the place will have a new owner soon. This guy's going to become his problem. I hope they arrest him for trespassing."

Randy didn't say anything, glancing out the window. Finally, they came to the small shopping complex in town and parked behind Jake's Bar. They traveled onto Rose Hill property the usual way, up the old railroad tracks, cutting in through the woods.

Uneasily, Kyle stared around the property, looking for any signs of human life. Nothing but birds. He held the boots over his shoulder, gripping them like a lifeline. Part of him just wanted to throw the boots somewhere on the grounds or by a building, but his attacker had been very clear as to where to leave them. He wasn't taking any chances. Besides, Randy having a gun gave them some leverage. An avid hunter, Randy knew how to shoot. It gave Kyle a bit of reassurance since it had been years since he himself had shot a gun.

When they got near the Dalphine building, they climbed in through the basement window, affixed their headgear, and began their walk into the tunnels. All was quiet.

"Stop breathing so loud," Kyle said to Randy. "I'm

trying to listen for any noise."

Randy didn't reply, nor did his breathing relax.

They moved at a steady pace, checking behind doors and walls before continuing into the dark tunnels. It was colder than the previous visit, but the air seemed less musty because of it. The corridor was damp, floors crusted over by bits of ice, creating slippery spots.

They found the Kellogg building's basement doorway, entered, and took stock of their surroundings. Randy motioned for Kyle to begin searching the rooms on the right, while he searched on the left.

They continued, finally ending up in the largest of the rooms. Kyle nodded in the direction of the last room.

"That's where I found the boots."

"Well, go put them back," Randy said. "I'll keep watch while you do."

Kyle moved into the doorway, looked around the small room. All appeared the same. The clothes were still piled on the ping-pong table. Beneath it, the box of shoes held his gaze. He knelt and yanked out the box, spilling several shoes on the floor. He breathed a sigh of relief when nothing popped out. He sat the boots on top.

"Done," Kyle said, moving toward the doorway. He flashed his light around the adjacent room, then moved toward the connecting tunnels. "Randy?"

Silence followed.

Uneasily, he stepped into the tunnel, listening. Stillness.

Flashing his light in both directions, he cursed himself from separating from Randy, though it was only a few more feet. What could've happened to him?

Damn it. He was alone.

And Randy had the gun.

Now what to do?

Chilly air drifted over his feet as he stood there, undecided. He leaned against the tunnel wall, suddenly reconnecting with his childhood. In seconds, he returned to yesteryear, Roy's face appearing in his mind.

"Let me play with you," Roy had said, trailing Kyle. It was a common thing for Roy to follow him. "I want to play, too."

"No," Kyle replied, jerking around. His other friends paused, waiting for him. "You're too little. You'll get lost in the tunnels."

"No, I won't," the boy exclaimed. "I know my way. Please. I can keep up."

"I said no," Kyle said. He held up a fist. "I'm gonna punch you if you keep following us."

Roy paused, eyes wide.

"But I don't want to walk back alone." Roy's eyes were huge in his face. "I'm afraid. Can you walk with me?"

"That's exactly why you shouldn't have followed me," Kyle said. "Now go back to your cottage."

With slumped shoulders, Roy turned around, dragging his feet as if a ball and chain were attached.

"Come on," Kyle said to Steven and Joel. The two boys shoved one another, and then were off running. Without a backward glance, Kyle raced after them.

Up ahead, a big boy stood in the hallway, silhouetted in muted light.

Kyle and his friends paused.

"Let's go back," Steven said, tugging on Kyle's arm. "It's Benny the creepo."

Fearfully, Kyle stood his ground, eyes glued to what was behind Benny. Steven and Joel raced off behind him. He could barely breathe.

"Go back to your cottage," Kyle yelled to Roy.

"Stay put," Benny said. He grabbed Roy's arm, dragging him next to him.

"Let my brother alone," Kyle said. "He's got nothing to do with you or me."

Benny laughed, digging his hand into Roy's arm, who yelped. He released his grip on Roy, who stumbled, caught his balance, and stood, hesitating.

"Run, Roy!" Kyle cried. "Don't worry about me."

Roy bolted, racing down the hallway, disappearing around a turn.

Relieved, Kyle took a step back.

"I warned you, Mr. Goody-Two-Shoes," Benny said. He dug into a duffle bag on the floor, producing a purple and red cap. He slid it over his head. "Look what I got."

Kyle's heart leaped to his throat. He hadn't seen Benny in weeks. He thought he'd left Rose Hill. He never would've played in the tunnels. Now it was too late.

"If you twitch," Benny said the words slowly, "you'll get stitched."

Kyle turned and ran. He was fast and thrust out his legs. He passed other kids, who stared at him as he flew by. Footsteps followed, and the dreaded bell's tinkling.

He rounded a corner, running into the janitor. Catching his breath, he looked over his shoulder. Benny was gone. In the distance, the jingle of bells resounded.

Kyle broke from his memory, chilled to the bone. Just the thought of Benny increased his heart rate. Would it have been that big a deal to take Roy with him that day? Or any other day after that? Roy was just a little kid. Lonely. Sad, vulnerable. Looking for someone to cling to. And what did he do? He left him behind with Benny the creep.

"Hey," Randy called from down the corridor. "You done?"

"Where were you?" Relief made Kyle's knees weak, even as anger quickened his strides toward Randy. "You were supposed to keep watch."

"Chill out," Randy said. "I needed to take a leak."

"You couldn't wait for a couple of minutes? You know I'm on edge." He shoved by Randy, increasing his strides. "You're never serious."

"Any sign of your friend?" Randy asked, catching up with him. "I didn't see anyone. I think we're alone."

"Lucky for me," Kyle said beneath his breath. "Glad to see you've got my back."

"Don't be like that. I know what I'm doing. I was close. Nothing was going to happen."

Kyle didn't bother replying, increasing his strides.

They traveled back the way they had come, taking the time to make sure no one was following them. Kyle began breathing more even with each step he took toward freedom.

Finally, they came to the Dalphine building's doorway, entered the cellar, and crawled out of the building's basement window. Kyle leaned against the brick wall, breathing heavily. He hadn't known he was trembling until he noticed his hands shaking.

"You okay, man?" Randy asked. "You don't look

too well. You're as white as a ghost."

"That scared the hell out of me," Kyle said. "I didn't know what to expect, but I expected the worst. I'm just glad that's over."

"Let's go then. You look like you could use a drink. Since we're parked by Jake's tavern, I'll buy you a beer."

"I could use a drink," Kyle said. "Let me just touch base with Beth and give her a quick text." He grabbed his phone and sent her a message, asking her if she needed anything on his way home. She replied, "No."

"She's okay, so I guess I could have a beer or two. Or second thought, a shot of whiskey would be better."

Chapter Thirty

It was late afternoon. After trying to reach Kyle, Beth finally threw her cell phone on the table. She hated when Kyle would text her, and then refuse her call. Frustrated, she sat down in the rocker and nursed the baby. She had told herself she wouldn't call his work to check up on him, but now she was doubting his overtime story. Something nagged at her. She couldn't shake her premonitions. As much as she was trying to understand his moods and deal with his past, she was failing miserably. And his lying had to stop. If they couldn't be honest with one another, they weren't going to make it as a couple. The thought was depressing.

After tucking Samantha in for her afternoon nap, she put in a load of laundry and sat with her cell. Finally, she called the quarry asking if Kyle was working and his expected time for release. She'd already guessed the reply.

Angrily, she sat for a few minutes, staring at the wall. He'd lied to her and it was becoming a common occurrence. She tried his phone again. Nothing.

Trying to take her mind off Kyle, she pulled her laundry from the dryer and folded it. She carried the basket to their bedroom and put it away. She was placing boxers in the top dresser drawer when she paused. Beneath a few socks, a manila envelope caught her eye. She pulled it out, sat on the bed, and released the metal clip. The items scattered across the bed. She picked up the first picture, holding it up to better view. It was aged, black and white. Many kids played kickball in one of the Rose Hill courtyards. A couple of the pictures were ones Kyle had already showed her, but there were others he hadn't revealed. There were colored photos of groups in various activities, such as weaving, gardening, or sewing. Then there were pictures of various stage plays, Rose Hill entertainment.

Kyle's name had been written on the back of what appeared to be a party photo. She couldn't figure out who was who, since the kids wore makeup. There was one themed Indians. Another appeared to be Christmas. Then she came across a group picture. Four kids stood in the photo, being silly and obviously having a good time. Kyle wore a red wig and a mustache. She recognized his bright smile. He wore a silly yellow shirt with suspenders hanging over his slender frame. Another boy similar in size stood with an arm draped around Kyle's shoulders. Next came a smaller boy, posing with his hands in the air. Then there was a tall, pretty girl with golden yarn braids that matched the fake freckles painted on her face. Most were dressed similarly, except for one boy's cap and bells. All wore circus-like clothing. On the back of the photo, Roy's name was written next to Kyle's. Then she paused.

Puzzled, she stared at the image again. Indeed, the boy next to Kyle had dark hair and a cocky grin. She had a nagging suspicion that it was Randy. What did she really know about him? They had been Rose Hill buddies; Kyle had said as much. The asylum had its own school. Randy had to have been a pupil. She really didn't know much about Randy's former life. Kyle kept their relationship to himself. They were friends way before she came into the picture.

Beth sat on the bed, thinking about the men. Randy was a bit eccentric. Although he was Kyle's friend, he was all about himself. For one, he was a skirt-chaser, always with a different woman on his arm. He frowned on marriage and commitment. He was a wanderer, even a loner. Randy had pursued the friendship with Kyle, more so than the other way around. There were times she thought Kyle felt bad for Randy, often helping to direct him.

She picked up another, similar photo, only this one was blurred. In the background, she could make out Kyle's father along with his Uncle Bill. They were facing one another as if conversing. Despite what Kyle said, Kyle appeared to be happy in the photos and being a part of the pack.

The house phone rang on the bedside table. She hurried to answer, stopping the noise from waking the baby.

"Hello," she breathed into the receiver, hoping it was Kyle.

"This is Emily from Chester Trail Nursing home," came the response. "Is Kyle Hampton available?"

"No. He's not home."

"May we leave a message with you?"

"Certainly, I'm his wife. Just a moment while I get a pen and paper." Grabbing the items, Beth gripped the phone. "Is everything all right with his dad?"

"We would like Mr. Hampton to give us a call at his earliest convenience."

"Is there an emergency?"

A brief pause. "No. Not an emergency. Just an

update on Mr. Hampton's father. I'm not at liberty to say."

"My husband has given permission at Chester for me to be able to take messages," Beth said, fuming. "I'm on the list. You can tell me if it's anything important."

"Just a moment." After a pause, the woman returned to the line. "You're right, Mrs. Hampton. I do apologize. I can tell you that it's a bit of happy news. We don't want to speculate yet on what it means, but Mr. Hampton's father began to speak today. His nurse reported that when she went in to make up his bed, he was alert and wanted to communicate. At first it was a bit garbled, but she could make out a few words. Mr. Hampton was very frantic to reach out to his son, Kyle. We promised him we'd call. Of course, the doctor will be running some tests tomorrow. In the meantime, I was calling to share the news. Your husband wanted to be kept updated on any progress."

"That's wonderful news," Beth said. "Kyle will be so happy. Did anyone write down his pop's message? I'll make sure Kyle gets it."

"Well, it's a bit strange," the nurse replied. "I'm not sure if it will make any sense to your husband or not. But here it goes."

Beth scribbled down the words, then hung up. She stared at what she'd written. What the heck did it mean?

Stay away from the asylum. Need to talk. Important you come.

Chapter Thirty-One

After having a double shot of whiskey and now nursing a beer, Kyle and Randy tossed cash into the bartender's tip jar and rose from their stools to leave.

"Thanks, Randy," Kyle said, leaning against his truck. "I needed this. I didn't know how stressed out I was until now."

"Glad to be of help." Randy glanced at his phone. "Kat will be here any minute to pick me up. We're driving to the mall to shop for a birthday gift. You did what you needed to do. Catch your breath and just relax. The boots are out of your life. Go home and get some rest. We'll talk next week."

"Are you sure Kat's coming?" Leaving Randy was hard after what they been through, yet Randy looked none the worst over it. His own pulse had finally returned to normal. "I could wait a few more minutes."

"Nah. I'm fine. She said she'd be here at five and it's ten of. Kat's a stickler for time, so no worries."

"This whole thing was crazy. I hope I can put this behind me."

"You did what the guy wanted. Problem solved. I'd keep an eye out but the worst is behind you. Hopefully, it's just a bad memory. One for your scrapbook."

"Like I needed some more crap to add to my life's story," Kyle said. "This was definitely the last time for me going to Rose Hill. I'm done. I'm not taking any

208

more risks. Besides, there's too much baggage for me there, anyway. It's taken its toll on me, at least mentally. Made me remember things I didn't want to remember. I'm going to concentrate on finding Roy, but I wanted to get this boot thing off my plate. I've been so on edge. Thank God everything went smoothly. Now time will tell if this jerk disappears."

"Call the cops if he doesn't." Randy shrugged, brows dipping in thought. "Don't mess around playing superman. Any progress concerning Roy?"

"Sort of," Kyle said. "I got a lead from my uncle. He says Roy was living in Philadelphia. It's so close. I wish I had known sooner."

"Like anyone in your family wanted you to know that." Randy shook his head. "Seriously? I'm sure your Pop knew exactly where he was the whole time. You've got to remember that your new family didn't want you to be in Roy's life. If they did, they would've made sure you stayed connected. It's their fault, not yours. Adults were in charge over you. They told you what you were doing and how you were doing it. So quit beating yourself up over something you had no control over or could do anything about."

"Maybe back then. But this is now. I could have tried to find Roy years ago, make amends. But I didn't. I have no excuses."

"Did you ever consider that Roy doesn't want to be found?"

"Yes," Kyle said. "Or maybe he's incapable of reaching out to me. Who knows if he even remembers me or what condition he's in, mentally."

"You were good to him." Randy picked up a loose pebble and threw it across the rear lot. "You might have had your moments, but for the most part, you cared. Roy knew that."

"I didn't care enough."

Randy opened the truck door, grabbed his backpack off the seat and eased it over his shoulders. Finally, he said, "I guess you're only going to make yourself happy by suffering in your guilt. I'm telling you to just let it go. Let Roy go. It wasn't your fault, and it's still not your fault. Go home to your family and leave the past in the past. That's my suggestion. Move forward."

"Thanks for helping me put it into prospective," Kyle said. "You've sure got a lot of stuff in that bag. What's in it?"

"Food. You never know when you're going to need a meal." Randy laughed. "I'm always prepared. I hoarded food as a kid. And socks. I've always got an extra pair. It carried over into my adulthood; it makes me feel secure. You never know when you might need an extra pair." His grinned deepened. "I suppose I've got my own hang-ups to deal with."

"Closet eater. Nice." Kyle laughed, climbed into his truck and waved, driving onto the main drag leading out of town. When he braked for the third traffic light, he grabbed for his cell phone in his front pocket to call Beth. Empty. He searched his coat pockets and pants and slid his hand over the seat. Finally, he pulled the truck over and rummaged around his backpack. He checked the floorboards and beneath his seat. His phone was gone. Beth must have called him at least a dozen times by now. The last time he'd used the cell was at the asylum.

"Damn it," he said, hoping it was at Jake's bar. He

had used the bathroom, probably left it on the sink. He had to find it. At the next light, he looped the truck around the block, facing south again. He drove toward the bar, pulling into the rear lot. Only three cars were parked in the area. Slowly, he circled around. No Randy. Although it had only been about five minutes, he surmised Kat must've picked him up.

Kyle parked and then entered the bar. Inside it was even emptier. Only one patron sat on a stool and it wasn't Randy. The bartender and waitress stood conversing behind the counter, barely noticing him. He first checked the bathroom—no phone—then went up to the bar and asked the bartender if she'd seen his phone. She assured him no and jotted down his wife's number should it turn up.

"What about the guy I was with just a little bit ago?" Kyle asked. "He come back in here?"

"Not that I'm aware," the bartender replied. "I doubt it. I thought you were together."

"We were," he replied. "But he was getting picked up by a ride."

"Well, mystery solved," she said, winking. "His ride came through."

"Thanks," Kyle said, moving toward the door. "If he shows up, please let him know I was looking for him. Again, my name is Kyle Hampton."

"Will do," she said. "And if the phone is handed in, I'll let you know. I'd check around the lot."

"I intend to," Kyle said. Angry, he went back outside, stopping at his truck to grab his backpack. He pulled out a flashlight and then slid the bag over his shoulders. It was dusk; not much light left. He could call the cell company and have them send a signal to the phone, find a general location. But he needed the company's phone number, and he didn't even have a phone on which to call. Retracing his steps was his best bet. He must have dropped it on the way back from Rose Hill. It could be anywhere. That was great. Now he had to return to the asylum, just after he'd vowed to never set foot on the property again. This day was getting worse by the minute.

Dreading the inevitable, Kyle moved to the corner of the parking lot and walked onto the railroad tracks. Thick weeds sporadically dotted the line. Once upon a time a train carried supplies into the asylum. As a kid, he'd loved the sound of the whistle, the roar of the engine. Of course, that was many years ago. He took a few steps, eyes sweeping the ground.

It would be dark soon. He didn't have much time. He should've called Randy from the bar; Randy might even have his phone. If he didn't find it in the next few minutes, he'd go back and try to do exactly that.

He traveled down the railway, taking the same path they had used earlier to get to the asylum. In the distance, the river stood out. Finally, he moved off the tracks, sweeping the light along the open ground. Nothing.

He strained his eyes to see into the woods, now shadowy and dim. Stunned, he came to an abrupt halt. "What the…"

In the distance, Randy shuffled toward the asylum.

It was on the tip of his tongue to call out, but something held him rapt. Suspicion took root. What the hell? What was Randy doing there? He was advancing as if he didn't have a care in the world. Randy stopped to pick up a large rock. He rolled the stone in his hand, then dropped it into his coat pocket, ambling onward at a steady pace. Clearly, Randy wasn't worried about running into the man who'd threatened Kyle if he didn't return the boots. Then again, Randy was armed.

Crazy explanations raced through his mind. Perhaps Randy thought he'd made the whole boot thing up? Or maybe Randy was seeing if the perpetrator had returned to get the boots, and wanted to confront him? Could Randy be that stupid with his own safety? He frowned, itching for answers. Randy might want to explore. He'd said as much earlier. Randy probably didn't want Kyle worrying about him.

Kyle trailed him at a safe distance. When they reached the asylum courtyard, Kyle hid behind a large oak, peering around from his vantage point. Sure enough, Randy headed straight for the Dalphine building, climbed in through the basement window, and disappeared.

Kyle swore beneath his breath. Randy was brainless. Reasons came to mind as to why he should leave. But in the end, allegiance won out. He'd have Randy's back, whether it was needed or not.

Torn on how to proceed, Kyle waited a moment. The minutes ticked away as the sun lowered. Damn, he could use his phone about now.

Irritated, Kyle moved forward and entered the basement via same route as Randy had. He stopped, pulled off his backpack and grabbed his headlamp. He put it on his head but left off the switch. No sense giving away his position to anyone else who might be wandering around. Randy was probably headed toward the boots. At least it gave Kyle a general direction. He used the smallest of his flashlights for just enough light, inching along the basement and its many sections. He hated exposing himself to the many crooks and crannies, but he didn't have time to search every area. Finally, he came to the entrance to the tunnel, peeked out and shone his light into both sides of the structure. Randy was nowhere in sight.

He took a right turn, heading toward the Kellogg building. He crept through the tunnel, oblivious to the encroaching dark. He'd once known the tunnels like the back of his hand. If this had been his first time returning, he would have had trouble navigating his way. But having recently explored the tunnels with Randy had its benefits. Getting lost was the last of his worries.

His anxiety over Randy's safety now overran his fear for his own. It dawned on him that he didn't have much in the way of protection. If anyone other than Randy was in the tunnels, he could be in trouble. He had no weapons, save for the pocketknife. God forbid if Randy might think he was the creep with the boots and start shooting at him. His friend had no idea he was being followed. Right now, Randy assumed Kyle was at home with Beth. Getting shot was a very real fear.

The cold began to seep into his sneakers, chilling his legs. Plops of water fell from the ceiling into his hair. Still, he continued, rounding another corner. Another flash of his light revealed that no one was up ahead. He turned off the flashlight, stood quietly for a moment, listening for noises, and scanned the area for any light source. Nothing but darkness.

The quiet was unnerving. His breath roared in his ears. Despite himself, the words from his youth slipped into his mind. "If you twitch, you'll get stitched." His childhood memories of hiding in the dark came rushing back. Being shoved, hit, or bullied. Hide and seek was meant to be fun – but not the version he was forced to play. Staying still during the game was your only recourse; hiding, waiting for someone else to get grabbed. Then you'd hear a thump. Crying or pleading would follow. Occasionally a scream. Later you'd hear about someone's injuries. A black eye, a nosebleed, or a busted mouth. "Accidental" was the excuse given to the aides or nurses but all the kids who played the game knew the truth. And no one ever told. It would be worse for you if you did.

Kyle leaned against the wall, trying to quiet his racing heart. His imagination was getting to him. The dark pressed against his eyes and a rush of frigid air touched his face. Time to keep moving.

Finally, he came upon the Kellogg building's doorway. Chilled to the bone, he peeked around the corner, peering into the gloom, finger ready to press on the flashlight. There was no discernable light source in the basement. Some of the rooms were obscured to his view. Slowly, he crept along the wall. Using his hand, he covered the flashlight's plastic cover and turned it on, creating an indistinct small glow. It gave just enough light for him to move ahead.

When Kyle reached the last room, it was dark. He was sure Randy was inside. Perhaps he was hiding, waiting in the dark, expecting a visitor, only it wasn't who he was expecting. Once again, thoughts of Randy's gun worried him.

"Randy," he whispered, taking a chance. "Are you in here?"

Nothing.

Kyle removed his hand from the top of the flashlight, throwing more light into the room. He flashed it under the ping-pong table, over the crate beneath. Finally, he made his way over to the table, pulled out the crate and stared down at the piles of shoes. The boots were gone.

Somewhere off in the distance, he heard a jingle. He jumped, bumping hard into the corner of the table, dropping his flashlight. He crouched down to pick it up. As soon as he reached it, he rolled it into his hand and pressed the off button. Now it was pitch black.

He stayed crouched down, waiting while his heart thudded.

Then something shoved him, pitching him face-first to the floor. The jolt revived his recent facial pain, sending a crashing wave into his skull. Whoever hit him took off running, disappearing from the room.

"Randy!" Kyle yelled, sitting up. "Is that you?" He scrambled to his knees, grabbed the flashlight, and shined it across the room. Shakily, he stood. He reached into his back pocket, producing the folding knife. He opened it, warily stepping forward. Finally, he exited the basement, peering into the tunnels. He flicked on his headlamp, lighting up a part of the expanse. Decision time; should he follow whoever just shoved him, or opt to get out? He froze, indecisive. Maybe Randy was in trouble. Or maybe Randy was screwing around.

Against his better judgment, he opted to go the opposite way, heading away from his nearest exit, and following the way he believed his attacker had gone. He needed to find Randy and get the hell out of there.

Chapter Thirty-Two

Beth tried to call Kyle again, then threw her phone onto the bed. It was no use; he wasn't answering. Frustrated, she sat down on the quilt and finally picked up the phone. Now she called Randy, despite hating to go that route. Also, no answer. She then tried Randy's house phone. To her surprise a woman answered.

"Hello?"

"Hey, this is Beth Hampton. I'm Kyle's wife. I was wondering if Kyle is with Randy at your house?"

"Hey, Beth," came a friendly voice. "I'm Kat. Randy told me all about you. I'm sorry, but no, Kyle isn't here right now. But I know he is with Randy. Your husband picked him up earlier this morning. He said something about them hanging out today. I'm pretty sure they're over at that asylum; the one Randy took me to. Talk about a scary experience."

"Are you sure they went there?"

"Pretty sure. I heard them talking on the phone. And Randy packed his gear, took some food and water, the works. That's a sign he's exploring."

"I tried to call both Kyle and Randy. Neither one answered or texted me. I'm worried. It's getting late."

"Randy hasn't called me for the past few hours," Kat said. "But that's not unusual. He gets very absorbed in what he's doing."

"Did you try to call him?"

"No. I've been busy all day. Boys will be boys. Let them have their fun."

"But that place isn't very safe," Beth said, gritting her teeth. She wondered how old Kat was. She didn't sound very mature.

"Tell me about it. I mean, some crazy guy was hiding in the dark when we were there. It was pitch black, and then this whistling sound came out of nowhere. I screamed and smashed my head into the wall. Randy couldn't find his backpack and by the time he turned on a flashlight, the guy was gone. Poof! I swear it sounded inhuman. That place is haunted by something dark. It was so scary. I will never go back there again. Ever. I'm not sure why Randy loves it so much, but I agree with you on the danger part. I'm terrified he's going to run into something terrible."

Like an icy shawl, Kat's words fell across Beth's shoulders, chilling her. Pop's message also came home to roost. What was it about Rose Hill that held Kyle spellbound? If anything, he should want to stay away. Randy and Kyle were playing with fire again. So stupid! She thought Kyle was done with that place. What was he thinking? What if the men had an emergency and couldn't call for help?

"When was the last time you spoke with Randy?"

"Around one," Kat replied. "Randy just said he wouldn't be home till later. He didn't say anything about Kyle."

"Would you mind calling Randy after we hang up?" Beth pressed. "Please ask him where Kyle is and have him phone me. I'm worried sick. It's almost seven o'clock. It's not like Kyle to be this late without calling."

"Will do," Kat said. "I'll text you if you'd like."

"Perfect."

Beth sat on the bed, giving Kat time to reach Randy. Minutes ticked away, then her phone chirped. She glanced down at the text message. "Randy's not answering me either. I called three times and left several texts. I'll let you know if anything changes."

Unsettled, Beth tried Kyle's phone again. Voice mail. Her imagination was getting the better of her. Kat's story had been a bit too graphic. Images of Kyle falling, trapped, or injured filled her thoughts. A bad premonition gripped her. She decided to drop the baby off at her mother's, drive out to Rose Hill, and see if anything was wrong. Hopefully, Kyle would return home by then, or at least call.

Beth left her bedroom and changed Samantha into pajamas. Within minutes, she readied two bottles and grabbed the baby's diaper bag. She slid her cell phone into her purse. Minutes later, she was headed out the front door with a sleepy baby in hand. She drove the ten minutes to her mother's house.

"Call me later to let me know how long you'll be," her mother said, cuddling Samantha. "That's wonderful news about Kyle's dad responding to his nurse. Most likely, he'll improve from here on out."

"Yes," Beth said. "I can't wait to tell Kyle the news." She pasted on a smile, shutting the front door. Guilt lingered as she got into the car and turned the ignition. She had fudged the truth, so her mother wouldn't ask a million questions. Better she didn't know where her daughter was off to. Her mother thought she was headed to Randy's house to give Kyle the news about Pop. If only that were true.

Chapter Thirty-Three

Kyle moved steadily through the tunnel, stopping every few inches to listen for footsteps. The tunnels accessed most of the buildings, though a few were in bad shape. He paused by the doorway into the Adams building. Although he knew the cellar's layout, it had been some time since he'd been in the building. He stepped into the doorframe and waited. Once again, he shut off his flashlight, listening intently. In his hand, he gripped the pocketknife, ready to press the spring into action.

A noise sounded behind him in the tunnel. He turned around, facing the corridor. Stepping back against the wall, he kept his eyes trained on the tunnel and whoever was approaching out of the darkness.

A light trailed along the ground. Randy's telltale gait gave him away. Kyle was just about ready to jump out in front of him, demand an explanation, when he saw something hanging over Randy's shoulder; the boots. His blood ran cold. Why did Randy have them? Where was he taking them? Was Randy the one that shoved him in the Kellogg building? It didn't make sense. But then, nothing about the boots made sense. He tried to wrap his mind around reasons, but he came up short.

He stopped, considering Randy's motive. Perhaps Randy wanted to apprehend whoever had attacked him at Pop's house and threatened Kyle.

No. If that were true, Randy would still be waiting for the creep to show up for the boots. There wasn't enough time for him to have done that. He wouldn't be holding them over his shoulder.

Kyle thought hard about the past few weeks. Randy had wanted the boots for himself in the beginning. He'd offered money to buy them; joked that they were haunted. Did Randy want the boots so badly that he'd waited for Kyle to put them into the crate, only to take them for himself? It was a strange scenario. Then again, Randy was a bit strange. Then a new thought struck home before he could shake it away. No. That couldn't be right. Randy wouldn't have attacked him at Pop's house. An inner voice told him to be cautious. Not to jump to conclusions.

Randy moved past the doorway, slogging along the tunnel. After his footsteps were farther up the hallway, Kyle stepped out of his hiding place to follow.

Trailing Randy in the dark was a tricky feat. Trying to do so quietly was also a challenge. Kyle held back, using the distant light source as a guide as he followed his childhood friend.

Randy turned a corner, headed toward the school and dining hall. He stopped, entering the basement of the auditorium. Kyle moved closer, peeking around the doorframe. Now Randy flicked on his headgear, lighting up the expanse. Clothing, crates, and broken props stood out in the gloom. Chairs, desks, toys, and trash littered the rooms.

Kyle waited by the entrance, straining to see what Randy was about. The boots dropped heavily onto the ground. Kyle stepped inside, moving into the first closet he came to. He pressed back into the wall, shelves digging into his back. He heard a shuffling noise, then a loud thump.

Kyle's breath caught as he listened. His heartbeat drummed away in his head. Frantically, he tried to control his breathing, to slow his racing heart.

A jingle of keys sounded. Movement. Then a door closed, clicked, and the sound of the keys again.

Kyle's thoughts raced. What was Randy up to?

Footsteps resounded on the rear staircase, heading up to the first floor. Kyle took the opportunity to move out of his spot, undetected. He turned on his flashlight, shining it inside the various rooms, checking knobs of closed doors. In the back corner, he came upon a locked room. He jiggled the lock. Pressing his ear against the door, he listened for any sounds.

Inside, something stirred. He jumped, alarmed.

"Who's in there?"

As he turned, something slammed into his head. He fell onto the concrete, his vision doubling. He tried to turn his head to see who'd hit him. Shocked, he could only stare at the strange-looking jester staring down at him. *If you twitch, you'll get stitched*, he thought as darkness descended, throwing him into oblivion.

Chapter Thirty-Four

Footsteps by his head, a nudge of a hand. Kyle came to, disoriented. Pain radiated through his skull. The icy floor cooled his bruised features. He realized he was on his stomach, face forward.

He stifled the groan that almost leaked from his mouth. He listened to the voices in his head, arguing. At first, he couldn't make out the words, but then they began to clarify.

"So stupid. What were you thinking?"

"I did as you asked," Randy replied.

"No, you didn't. You were supposed to bring him at three and leave him behind. Instead you came earlier than expected, and then tried to save him."

"Okay, maybe I did," Randy replied. "But that's because you're not thinking rational. We don't need this right now. This wasn't our deal. I brought him here like you asked, gave you those damn boots. You said you just wanted to screw with him. Now you're taking it too far. Just let him go."

"It's none of your concern what I do," the raspy voice said. "I should never have counted on your help. You're weak and pathetic. You want to leave, go. But he's not. I've been waiting for this day for a long time. You're not robbing me of it."

"I want no part of this," Randy said. "This isn't about the boots. This was always about payback. You never told me about this crazy scheme. I would've never agreed. None of what happened to you is Kyle's fault. I want to dump him out on the property and beat it out of here. He won't remember a thing. There's no reason to continue this any further."

"I already told you, you can leave. But I'm not through with him. Besides, he's a liability and has a big mouth. You think I'm taking any chances? I need him out of my way. We've got to get rid of him."

"No. This is nuts." Randy paused. "He's a good man; we're friends. He's got a kid, a wife. People will look for him. He's not just someone who won't be missed. His wife will send out the National Guard if she has to. Let's just leave him up the road somewhere."

"No! I can see you're not up to the task. I'll handle what must be done, but you're helping me along the way. Don't make me sorry that I trusted you. You don't want to be on my shit list. I might even put you at the top. Your girlfriend will be next. Understand me?"

A long pause followed.

"Understand, Randy?"

"Sure."

Then Kyle was being dragged by his arm across the hard floor. The motion stopped, and then he was lifted by the armpits and thrown over a shoulder. Up the staircase they went. His head bounced against the man's back, jarring his senses.

The hallway was murky and held just enough light for him to see the dusty floor as they moved. He turned his head sideways. Walls. Familiar. They were on the first floor of the Assembly building. He heard Randy's voice. Who was carrying him?

They entered the auditorium. Rows of benches

passed by his blurred vision. The man carried him down the center aisle, made a right and headed into a stage room. When they reached their destination, Kyle was dumped onto the floor. Closing his eyes, he feigned unconsciousness.

The room filled with heavy breathing as the perpetrator stared down at him. Although he couldn't see him, Kyle felt the eyes boring into his face. He didn't dare move or blink. The man left the room. He cracked open his eyes, staring at the stagehand chamber.

Just outside the doorway, he heard voices, "Where'd you put him?"

"Back there." Randy said, "He's out for now."

"Did you tie him up?"

"No," Randy replied. "I need more rope. We have time; he won't wake up for a while."

"Do you think I believe you? I'm, not taking that chance. I don't trust you. I'm checking on him."

The jester burst into the room, moving toward Kyle. He stood over him, staring down at him. With his foot, he nudged his arm. "Look at who got caught. Precious Kyle Hampton, here in the flesh. I've been waiting for your return. Thanks to Randy, we almost missed our date with destiny. You're such a disappointment. You gave in and brought my boots back; never even once tried to confront me. I expected more, maybe a game of wits. Coward. I thought being a man, you might've changed. You're, soft, always been soft. Now you've got a bigger problem than you already had."

Kyle remained silent, the man's words penetrating the silence. Sweat beaded his forehead. His heart thumped painfully against his ribs.

The jester began pacing by Kyle's head, cap and bells jingling.

Kyle opened one eye a slit, staring up at the man. The purple and red cap stood out. Terror struck him. The jester was muttering to himself, rubbing his hands together.

Then the man left the room.

Again, the jester's agitated voice sounded outside the doorway as he spoke to Randy. "Don't fail me now. Get your feelings in check. We've got two problems to get rid of tonight. Not one but two."

"That wasn't part of our deal," Randy said. "Now thanks to your personal vendettas we got three. You still got that woman downstairs."

"She's not part of this. I'm not done with her yet. She'll be going home with me."

"Unbelievable," Randy said. "You're making stupid decisions."

A stinging slap filled the air.

"Watch your mouth, boy. Who do you think you're talking to? You ain't any better than me. You got blood on your hands."

A long pause followed.

"You're the reason we got two problems," Randy said, voice quieter. "You just couldn't leave Kyle alone. After tonight, I'm done with all this. I wish to God I never brought Kyle back here. You lied to me. You always had it out for him and used me to do it. He'd have been safe."

"Would he?" The jester laughed. "He'll never be safe from me. Kyle stole what's rightfully mine. Now he's going to pay for ruining my life, and so will the old doc, who made her recommendations. If I go down, you're going down with me. You hear me?"

"Yes."

"Then we've got to fix this problem now. Move the old woman to the morgue, and then get back here. I'm tying Kyle up before we move him. While you're gone, I'll figure out how to handle this."

"What about the doctor's dog?"

"Dog?" Something snapped as if someone angrily hit or threw something. "The dog is at my house, not here. I took him home. When this is all over with, then you can have the beast."

Kyle moved his head, looking around the room. He had to get out. The jester wanted him dead; he didn't even know why. But the man was clearly pissed off. He didn't have time to figure it out. There were two doors, both closets. He felt around his back pocket. His pocketknife was missing. He'd either dropped it, or they'd taken it. He had nothing to use for a weapon.

Kyle tried sitting upright. The room spun. Gingerly, he felt the bump on the back of his head. His fingers came away with blood on them. The men were still outside the room, now distant and hard to hear. Slowly, he got to his feet. His belly heaved and he pressed his palm to his mouth. Now wasn't the time to throw up. He moved toward one of the three windows in the room. All held thick metal screens. He managed to get over to one that looked out onto a parking lot. It would be darker soon. This might be his only chance to hide. He had no idea what he was up against, or what Randy or the jester intended to do with him.

The turn of the doorknob jolted him from his thoughts. He struggled to move at a quicker pace, hoping to reposition himself on the floor, feign sleep.

But his vision blurred. He dropped down on one knee, trying to regain his composure. Finally, his eyesight cleared. When he looked up, he could only gasp.

It was the jester again, only now he had a better view of the man. Burly and tall, the man was menacing. The purple and red cap was spiked to perfection, bells reflective. His face was painted white, shadowed along his jawline with crimson-tinted lips. Black eyeliner enhanced his eyes and brows. He wore dark clothing at odds with the jester's disguise as if he'd forgotten that part of the assembly.

"Roy? Is that you?"

With that, he lost his balance, falling at the jester's feet.

Chapter Thirty-Five

Beth drove by Randy's house, noting the man's driveway was empty of vehicles. But that didn't mean anything. Randy drove a motorcycle and shared a car with his live-in girlfriend. The woman could be out in the car. But Kyle's truck wasn't there. So the men were probably still together. Her hopes that Kyle would call faded with each passing minute.

She opted to leave without knocking on Randy's door. She didn't want to get Kat involved because if it all turned out to be senseless, Randy would have a lot to say about her anxiety. No thanks. Besides, she was fairly sure Kat would've texted her by now or at least gotten Kyle to call.

Instead, she drove toward the center of Spring Ridge, reached the old railroad tracks, and passed the river. She pulled into the mini shopping center, searching for Kyle's truck. She drove past the stores and Jake's bar. She drove around the buildings. Bingo! There in the rear of the lot was Kyle's truck. She parked next to it, noted the cab was empty. She laid her palm on the hood, but the engine was cold. The truck had been sitting awhile. She went into the bar, scanning the rooms. After a few minutes, she came out, frustrated. The bartender had said that Kyle had come in earlier looking for his missing phone. That explained why Kyle wasn't answering her calls. Why didn't he borrow someone's? Her husband was nowhere to be seen, so he must still be looking. It led to one conclusion; he had returned to the asylum to search.

She had heard Kyle talking to Randy about how to get into the Rose Hill grounds without drawing too much notice. Beth assumed Kyle and Randy were now searching for the missing phone. She opened her car door, looking in the glovebox for a flashlight. True, she had her cellphone, but she didn't trust her battery. Luckily, she found a slender green light. After locking her car, she followed the railroad tracks toward the asylum. With any luck, she'd see the men searching the grounds. Or at least she hoped. The place gave her the creeps, but she was also curious about Kyle's former home. The darkness and isolation was formidable. She didn't want to get arrested for trespassing. She'd only go onto the property a short way.

As she moved, she realized that the place was much larger than she'd anticipated. She didn't need to get lost on the grounds or run into some other trespasser. The place was a target for vandals, or so Kyle had said. She continued into the woods, warily listening for the rustle of the leaves.

As she crossed into open ground, she paused. A teenager stood near the woods. The girl wore a white nightgown with long blonde tresses. Beth froze, staring at the spectacle. There was something very odd about the girl. It was her hollow eyes. She had no facial expression; just a fixed gaze, as if her vision were off. Then the teen turned around, walking behind the trees.

"Hey, wait," Beth said, following her. "Miss. Can you help me?"

Beth rounded the set of trees, intent on finding the

girl but the teen had vanished. A cold chill washed over her face. Her skin prickled, sending cold snags along her shoulders.

Regaining her composure, she shook off the notion that she'd just seen a ghost.

Get a grip. You're definitely losing your mind.

She hurried out of the tree line, back onto open ground. She found the blocked roadway into Rose Hill and followed it along its curved path toward the asylum. She passed several brick buildings, overgrown with weeds. She'd only seen pictures but now the place terrified her. It was hard to image Kyle living in such a huge place. How would a child have ever coped?

Beth rounded a bend, coming to the first building on the campus. Huge brick buildings were spread out in a cluster with courtyards and a catwalk. The building in the middle seemed to be the central location because of the tower on its roof. She'd never find Kyle in this place. She'd be lucky to find her way back out. She grabbed her cell phone and tried to call Kyle. She'd left a message, telling him where she was. Then she called Randy's phone. No answer. Even if Kyle didn't have his phone, Randy did. She had to wonder if Randy would deliberately not answer her calls. He'd done exactly that in the past, most likely to spite her.

Frustrated, she turned to leave the way she'd come. But then up ahead someone yelled. She froze, trying to see if it was Kyle. It had sounded like a male. But now it was quiet again.

Slowly, she began to walk to one of the distant buildings, listening intently.

Chapter Thirty-Six

The jester wouldn't speak to him. Kyle tried to get the man to interact, but it was useless. Instead, he grabbed Kyle by his arm, hauled him to his feet, and forced him through the doorway into the auditorium.

Kyle was shoved into a first-row chair. The man tied a rope around his chest, securing him to the back of the seat, then bound his hands and feet.

Watching the jester, Kyle tried to distinguish his identity behind the makeup. For the most part, the artwork was precise. He couldn't help but ask again, "Are you Roy?"

The man paused, gawking at him. He then looked around the room as if searching for the answer from someone else, though no one was in sight.

"You seem familiar to me," Kyle said. "Who are you?"

This time, the jester looked perturbed. His painted smile turned ugly, curling. He grabbed Kyle by the throat, shoving him against the chair.

"Don't talk to me!"

"Why not?" The fingers bit cruelly into his neck.

"Because I said," the man replied. "Shut up."

"It's a simple question." Kyle pressed his luck. "Are you Roy?"

"No."

Kyle withdrew into silence, while the jester tugged

on his ropes to make sure they were secure. The man moved down the row, dropping down on a chair. He put his hands on his head, staring at his feet as if he were pondering a problem. He began to rock.

"Where is Randy? What is he involved with? I've got a right to know."

"Shut up."

"What do you want from me?"

The man continued to ignore him.

"So they're your boots?" Kyle noticed that the jester was wearing them. "What's so special about them? I did as you asked so how about keeping your end of the bargain and let me go?"

"I told you to shut up," the man said. "I'll hit you. Make you bleed."

Kyle paused. All he needed was another rap to the head. At this point, he'd have permanent brain damage. He thought about Roy, the brother he once knew. The brother he'd forgotten. Could this menacing man be his brother? Roy had enjoyed silly pranks and was always laughing over something stupid. Today, would his brother remember any of their good times? Was blood thicker than water? If this man was Roy, then it could be good or bad, but especially bad if his brother hated him. It could be good if they reconnected on some personal level.

He realized now that he'd barely known his brother. How pathetic and sad. They were family, blood. Guilt ate at him. It wasn't Roy's fault if he'd been born at Rose Hill. It was because of the boy's love of magic and dressing up that made him wonder if this man could be Roy. His brother liked making people laugh by doing tricks, or at least attempting them.

Sometimes it was funnier when a stunt went wrong. Before Roy began to change into a darker version of himself, his brother had insisted that when he grew up, he was joining the circus. If this man was his brother, it could explain the weird jester fetish. Or was it more sinister? No matter what, the whole thing was a nightmare. He had to be smart and get free.

A voice echoed from the top of the room. "I see he's awake."

"Randy. What's going on?" Kyle frowned, straining his head to see Randy. "Is this a joke? Let me go. You owe me some answers."

"This is your fault." Randy moved in front of the chair, eyes narrowing in on Kyle. "I told you I'd return the boots, but you wouldn't listen to me. I tried to keep you from coming here, to protect you. If you would have gone home like you were supposed to, you wouldn't be in this mess. Why the hell did you come back?"

"My fault?" Kyle exploded. "I lost my phone and started looking for it. Then I saw you coming back here. I was worried something bad would happen to you. That you were being stupid, like confronting this guy." His gaze slid to the jester. "I was watching out for you, but apparently, it was unnecessary."

Randy flinched. He glanced at the jester, then looked toward Kyle indecisively.

"This wasn't how it was supposed to be," Randy said. "You've stepped into something you weren't meant to be a part of. You should've just dropped off the boots and left. It was all I needed you to do to appease him, but nothing in my life goes as planned."

"The boots again?" Kyle scoffed. "Maybe you

should've offered me more dough. This is all over those boots? What's so important about them?"

"Shut up," the jester said, coming to life. He rose to his feet, glaring at Randy. "You're making too much noise. None of it matters, especially the boots. I'd have tracked him down with or without the boots. I just wanted to see if he'd show up today."

Randy frowned, but shut up.

"And did you find your phone?" The jester leaned down to stare into Kyle's eyes.

"I found my cap and bells," Kyle said. "On your head. Did you know I picked out the colors and sewed most of it together?"

"Why do you think I'm wearing it?"

Kyle was at loss for words. Fear circled his heart, squeezing it into panic. He thought of the other boys who had helped him with the cap. Their names were lost to him.

"Again, did you find your cell phone?" The jester fingered one of the cap's bells, toying with it. A soft jingle rattled the silence.

"No." Kyle tried to sit up straighter against the unyielding chair. The man's eyes were strange. Contact lenses, that could be it. There were making his pupils larger than normal. If not, then perhaps meth. The guy could be strung out on drugs. This man wasn't Roy, but he was familiar. "People know I'm with Randy," Kyle continued. "The cops will come looking for me. You're better off letting me go now, before things get ugly. I don't care what's going on here. I won't say a word about it. Just free me."

"No one knows you're here," the jester said. "You lied to your wife and you told her you were at work. I'd say she bought the story."

Maybe at first, Kyle wanted to say, but Beth was shrewd. She had to know by now he'd lied. For once, her suspicions might benefit him.

The jester paced before Kyle, rubbing his gloved hands together. He sauntered past Randy, bowing low to Kyle. He knocked his knuckle on Kyle's head. "Hello?"

"Earlier, I told her that," Kyle said. "But it's getting late. She'll figure out that something's wrong and call the cops. Besides, I kept my end of our bargain. At any time, I could've gone to the police. For all you know, they could be on their way as we speak."

"Called them without a phone?" The jester threw his head back and cackled. "That would be a hard trick even for me. Besides, Randy told me what you told Beth."

"Randy!" Kyle called out, but Randy wouldn't even look at him. "What's the matter with you? Come on, this is absurd. What did you get me into?"

"I'm afraid Randy doesn't have anything to say," the jester said. He walked over to Randy, rubbing his head like he was a pet. "Randy can be a little defiant at times, but he knows where his loyalties lie. Unlike you."

Randy's head lowered, his throat convulsing.

"Seriously, Randy?" Watching his friend's submission was repulsive. "You're going to bow down to this creep?"

If Randy was afraid, then he was in some serious trouble, Kyle reasoned. The implications struck him full-on. Something terrible was about to happen. and he was smack in the middle of it. If only he could speak to

Randy alone.

"My name is Stitches." Eerie laughter erupted out of the jester's chest. He glanced down at his watch, then looked at Kyle. "Remember me now?"

"But Stitches is a game, not a person."

"And who made up the game?"

"Who cares who made it up," Kyle said. "Everyone was playing it. It was hide and seek, a warped version."

The jester let out a war cry, walked over to Kyle and slapped his face.

"Calm down," Randy said, pulling on Stitches' arm.

"Time's wasting," Stitches said, jerking his arm from Randy's grip. "We need to take this one over to the hospital. We have to see how to proceed with his medical care."

"What?" Kyle froze in horror. "What are you going to do to me?"

"Whatever I want," Stitches said. "Your diagnosis will be deadly accurate. I've been waiting for paybacks for a long time."

"Paybacks, for what?"

"I suppose for being too sweet and kind. The perfect little boy, an adoptable boy. La, la, la. Your goodness makes me want to throw up." He glared at Randy, who was nervously watching him. "It's getting late. We need to get done and him out of here before his wife sends out the brownie troops. Such an uptight little prissy."

Stitches spoke as if he knew Beth—unless Randy had filled him in with details of their marriage. Still, it was spoken like first-hand knowledge.

"It doesn't have to be this way." Kyle blinked,

trying to stay calm. "I still don't know what I've done to you. I lived here at Rose Hill. Obviously, so did you. We were all a family."

"Family!" Stitches sneered. "You know nothing about family. Just because Scott and Florence adopted you, doesn't make you a real Hampton. You're an imposter, a fraud. Not a lick of Hampton blood resides in your stupid veins." He paused, considering Kyle. "Do you know what it's like to have your family walk away from you? To choose another little boy to take your place?" He paused, leaning close to Kyle. "To pick out the perfect boy to replace you?"

Kyle's mouth fell open. "What are you saying? Who are you?"

"I'll let you wonder."

"The picture," Kyle said. "You were the little boy in the photo."

"Now we're being clever." Stitches tapped his chin.

"You were their son?"

"Bingo."

Shocked, Kyle grappled with the information. No wonder the guy was so pissed off.

"I don't understand," Kyle said. "They left you here at Rose Hill?"

"It started out as a punishment," Stitches said. "At least, that was one of the terms they used. I was to be placed here temporarily. Thanks to Doctor Goodman, I was made to stay. At first, like any good parents, my mom and dad visited a lot. They kept an eye over me. My uncle Bill worked here to help out. I had hoped I'd go home, but I started liking it here. I was boss over my life. No one could tell me what to do. Mom and Dad, well, they grew frustrated that I didn't change to their liking. Sadly, that's where you came in. Mom wanted a replacement and guess who replaced me?"

"That wasn't my fault," Kyle said. "I had no idea who you were or what was going on. I didn't ask to be adopted. It just happened. No one asked my permission. I understand now. I don't blame you for being pissed off." He paused. "I haven't seen your face, and I wouldn't throw Randy under the bus. Let me go. I'll just walk out of here. I can find my own way home."

"I watched you around him," Stitches said, ignoring Kyle's plea. "Scott Hampton. Oh, you couldn't do enough to please him or Florence. Your manners were impeccable. You were helpful. Sweet. Oh, so full of sunshine and goodness. They forgot all about me because they had you—a perfect little boy."

"My God," Kyle said, heart racing. "I'm not perfect, I was just a kid."

The jester pranced around in a circle and bowed low. Wickedly, he grinned. "They couldn't stand the sight of me." He clamped his hands together, raising them in salute. "In time, they actually gave me money to stay away from them. Can you imagine that?"

"So you're going to kill me in cold blood because of something I had no part of?"

"Probably, but not sure if it will be cold blood." Stitches tapped his chin. "Perhaps hot blood. It can be messy, messy, messy."

Kyle tried to wrestle out of the chair, but the ropes held fast.

"Why did they put you here?"

"Because I'm..." the jester tapped his chin. "Incorrigible." He clapped his hands together. "I guess that word sums it up. Apparently, Pop didn't like that I killed his cat." He tilted his head. "Florence was afraid of me. It was really her fault. Pop tried to make it work. Really, he did. But in the end, he was weak. She cried a lot, and he gave in, put me here. But you know what Kyle, I flourished here." He spread his arms wide. "Rose Hill is my true home. My true family. I didn't need *them*. They meant nothing to me. But *you*!" He stopped, staring at Kyle. "You just swallowed up being adopted, gaining a new family. Gag me."

"You can't blame me for wanting a real mom and dad."

"Oh, yes, I can." Stitches laughed. "Really, I can. You should've stayed at Rose Hill with the rest of us. You belonged here more than me. You were born here and had a brother. But you abandoned him, just like my parents abandoned me."

"That's not how it was," Kyle said, face flaming.

"Tell me how it was?" Stitches leaned closer, cupping his ear at attention. "Roy wasn't good enough to join the Hampton family. He wasn't sweet enough. You never looked back."

At a loss for words, Kyle's mouth dropped.

"So you knew all of this, Randy?" Kyle yelled. "And you never told me! Aren't you going to help me? Speak on my behalf. Think about it. We can all work this out."

Kyle's words fell on deaf ears. Even as he was pleading with Randy, a "no vacancy" sign crossed his friend's face. Randy avoided Kyle's gaze, turning away.

"I gave you the boots, Stitches." Kyle said the name in disgust. "You said if I did, you'd leave me and my family alone. Be a man of your word."

"I lied," Stitches said, grinning. "And you know what, Kyle? Those boots aren't even mine. They're Scott Hampton's. I took them from him many, many years ago. Call it a memento of sorts. It's funny you stole them. All this time, you've been wearing them, and never even knew they were your own sweet Pop's." He chuckled. "Let's get him out of here." He moved toward the doorway.

Randy came to life, moving behind Kyle, tugging him free of his bonds.

"Randy," Kyle said beneath his breath. "Please…"

Before Kyle could even move, Randy grabbed him, pulling him up from the chair. "I've got my gun, so don't try anything funny."

"Does it really matter if I do?" Kyle said, struggling against his grip. Something poked his back, reassuring him Randy meant business. "Sounds like ol' Stitches has it out for me."

"Don't speak to him, Randy," Stitches said. "It's his death march. He's a sneaky bastard. Keep him in your sight and get moving. If he does anything stupid, kill him. Time's wasting."

Forced to the rear of the auditorium, Kyle was shoved forward by Randy. Despair washed over him. He couldn't fathom what the pair could've been doing in the asylum, or what they were trying to hide.

"You're not going to really let him kill me, are you?" Kyle said quietly. "Who is he really?

"Don't talk," Randy said. "I don't want to have to shoot you."

"Come on, Randy. This is crazy. Think about what you're doing. Even if I die, the truth will come out. Do you really want to spend the rest of your life in jail?"

Randy ignored him.

"I swear to you I won't say a word."

If Randy wouldn't help him, then he had to find a way to help himself. Then, a ray of hope. He could escape in the tunnels. For once, the darkness would be his ally if he could only get free. He wouldn't go down without a fight; he wasn't missing his daughter's life. She wasn't growing up without a father. He'd find a way or die trying.

Randy kept a tight rein on him, prodding him along. He grabbed Kyle's arm, directing his prisoner down the flight of stairs into the basement. Randy paused to flick on his headlamp.

In the basement, Kyle wondered where Stitches had disappeared to. Sordid ideas filled his mind. He pleaded with Randy some more but to no avail.

He tried another tactic, trying to reach through Randy's barrier. "Do you remember playing hide and seek down in the tunnels when we were just boys?" Kyle said beneath his breath. "We always stuck together. We always looked out for one another. Did you forget that?"

"I'm sorry," Randy said. "It's too late. You should've just gone home. Stitches lured you here with the boots. I tried to intervene and to throw him off with the time. It would've worked until you returned. You would've been safe until I could've found a way to get you off the hook."

"Why are you helping him? What's he got on you?"

Randy's breathing grew heavier.

Not sure if he was onto something, Kyle prayed he

could reach Randy. "We can get out of this together. Whatever he's got on you, I won't say a word. We can figure it out."

"Don't ask questions," Randy said. "I need to think."

A spark of relief flickered to life in Kyle's heart. Did that mean Randy was going to help him?

"You're my best friend," Kyle said. "You know that..."

The hand holding his arm was ripped away, then quick as a rattlesnake strike, Kyle was snatched by his throat and pinned to the wall, his feet several inches from the concrete.

"You are persistent," Stitches said. "You just never shut up."

"Don't," Kyle said, grabbing at the steely fingers. He struggled to breathe as the room spun. His vision dimmed. Suddenly, he was let go, falling onto the floor. He gasped for air, curling into himself. He saw the boots again only inches from his face.

"Please," he said. "I've got a little girl. I'll do whatever you ask. Do you want money? Anything? Just ask."

The jester reached down, grabbed his arm, and lifted him up.

"Just shut up," Stitches said. "Do you think I care about your brat?"

"Well, what do you care about?" Kyle said. "There must be something you want."

"There is nothing you have that I want," Stitches replied. "Except your silence."

Astonished, the truth hit Kyle deep in his heart. His life meant nothing to this man. He would be snuffed out, and all because Scott and Florence Hampton adopted him.

"If you're going to kill me, I'd like to know by who? Who hides behind a jester's disguise? Why not show your identity?"

"What's it matter?"

From behind, Stitches shoved Kyle, forcing him deeper into the tunnels.

"Did you know my brother, Roy?" Kyle asked, deliberately walking as slowly as possible. "My mother, did you know her?"

A jab of pain hit below Kyle's ribs. He grunted. Then a hand snaked around his neck, pulling his head back against the jester's chest. Stitches slid his face alongside his ear, growling low.

"If you twitch, you'll get stitched."

The words rolled over Kyle like liquid ice. So the man was playing the game and he was wearing the jester's cap. He needed to connect, someway, somehow.

"This isn't hide and seek," Kyle said, trying again. "You obviously lived at Rose Hill when I did. If you were upset that Pop was adopting me, why didn't you say something then? I didn't ask him to take me. It just happened. I'm sure you were hurt." He tripped over the words. "That was a rotten thing they did to you."

No answer. He tried another tactic.

"Sometimes we'd play 'Word Jester' when we were caught during hiding and seek," Kyle said. "The seeker would say a word to describe something. A caught person could say a similar word. They'd continue back and forth until someone ran out of ideas. If the caught person had the final word, he'd get another chance to hide." Not often, he realized. Because whoever was bigger usually decided the outcome. "Did you ever play 'Word Jester'?"

Again, the agitated breathing. Kyle hated having the jester behind him where he couldn't see his face. His childhood fears resurfaced. Where was Randy? Was he following them?

Swallowing hard, Kyle pressed his luck.

"I'd say a word like, boy…"

No response.

"Then you'd might say a word like, male," Kyle said, answering his own prompt. He wasn't sure of Stitches' mental capacity, but "angry adolescent" came to mind.

"Man," Kyle said. Frustration made the situation hopeless. The tunnel walls closed in on him as they walked. His walk to the gallows.

"Dad. Father. Son. Men." He struggled to find words. "Husband. Male. Guy. Gentleman."

His thoughts scattered, thinking of words meaning male. Seconds ticked away. The thud of their feet on the hard ground echoed through the corridor.

"Pa, Pop, Papa…"

"Bastard," Stitches said, breaking the silence. He cuffed Kyle's ear. "That describes you."

Chapter Thirty-Seven

The morgue's atmosphere felt heavy and ominous. The air was cold, musty, and stung Kyle's nostrils. He supposed it was due to fear, but he was also angry. Angry that Randy had betrayed him, and even angrier that Stitches enjoyed toying with him.

Trying to make sense of this senseless puzzle was driving him nuts. But he was clueless as to what he could say to appease Stitches, or why Randy was his pawn. Maybe it was better he didn't know. It might be worse than he ever imagined.

Stitches shoved Kyle down into a chair, blinding him with his headlamp. He walked over to a table to turn on a battery-operated lantern. The room lit up, creating eerie shadows.

"Don't move," Stitches said. "I won't hesitate to kill you."

"Where is Randy?"

"You were told not to talk, and yet you won't shut up. You're just like the old lady."

"Are you referring to my wife?"

"No, stupid. Doctor Doris Goodman. Surely you remember her. Scott Hampton's best friend."

"I remember her," Kyle said. "I didn't know they were friends."

"They liked to sit behind closed doors and discuss me."

"Where is she? Did you do something to her?"

"Maybe."

"I remember Randy saying she was mean," Kyle said, trying to engage Stitches. "Did you kill her?"

"Not yet."

"I get that you want to hurt me because of the adoption. But why is Randy involved with you?"

Stitches eyes narrowed, then lifted into round orbs.

"You never told me if you knew Roy," Kyle said, hoping he wasn't going to get backhanded. If he kept Stitches talking, perhaps he could avoid getting tied up. Still, the man had a gun trained on him. In just one second, it could be all over. "If you lived here when I did, then you'd know him." He struggled to talk through his clogged emotions. "I haven't talked to him in such a long time. I was given no choice but to leave him behind. I'm sure he could've related to what you felt, having your parents walk away. I miss my brother."

Stitches grabbed a chair, pulling it into the middle of the room, only a couple of feet away from Kyle.

"Do you know where Roy is?" Kyle persisted.

No response, just that odd stare.

"This doesn't have to be this way," Kyle said. "In some ways, we're like brothers. Please. You don't have to kill me. The Hamptons never told me about you. I would've refused to go with them." He lied, wondering if that was even possible. "It's not too late to stop what you're doing."

"You're no brother of mine. You're exactly where I want you to be. You made it so easy."

Kyle's breath caught. This man had no regard for human life. His situation was perilous. Where the heck was Randy? Was the jester waiting for Randy to come and finish him off?

"When is the last time you saw Pop?" Kyle asked. "Did you visit him in Chesterbrook? I saw a picture."

Stitches laughed, shaking his head. "You're pathetic."

"You must still care if you visited him."

"I'm not like you," Stitches said. "I don't forgive."

Kyle's heart sank further into desperation. Pop was in danger from this maniac.

"What about Randy? What's he got to do with all of this?"

"Randy is my friend," Stitches said. "Loyal, unlike you. He owes me favors, and I called in a debt. But he wasn't counting on how big a debt he'd be paying. He's got a soft spot for your miserable hide. You make him weak."

"Why does he owe you a favor?"

"Let's just say I helped him clean up a mess."

"What kind of mess?" Kyle sat up straighter. "What did he do?"

"You don't know him," Stitches said. "Not like I do. I think you remember Karen Walton." He grinned. "Karen was pregnant. Who knows who the daddy was, but Randy claimed it was him. She wanted him to run away her, so they could get married and keep their baby. But Randy didn't want to leave. He tried to convince her to stay. They had a fight out by the railroad tracks. It got physical. She fell and hit her head on the metal rail. Randy came to me for help. That's what best friends do for one another." He paused, sighing. "When I found her, Karen was in bad shape, bleeding, convulsing. She died in my arms. Randy was devastated. We buried her out back in somebody's unmarked grave. I've kept his secret, now he keeps mine."

"It sounds like an accident," Kyle said. "Randy would never deliberately hurt a woman. You could've gotten her help. Maybe she could've been saved."

"What for? She would have ruined Randy's life. They'd have said he attacked her, and he'd be in jail. The kid probably wasn't his, anyway. She was a lost cause."

Astonished, Kyle could barely grasp what he was saying. Karen Walton had lived at Rose Hill all her life. It was hard to picture her so callously disposed of. She had epilepsy and suffered from seizures. He had witnessed several, feeling her embarrassment when she recovered. It had been scary for him to see her suffer. He supposed she just wanted someone to love her. All Rose Hill children longed for affection.

"Karen was my friend," Kyle said. "She was everyone's friend. She didn't deserve to just be thrown away like trash. Randy must've been desperate, not in his right mind." He shook his head. "Randy didn't attack her."

"Not intentionally," Stitches said, his voice sullen. "Or so he says. Randy was in love. They'd go off for sex, hide in the woods. She was nothing but a whore, and Randy was a fool. She had him wrapped around her finger. He says it was accidental, but the marks on her throat told a different tale."

Kyle absorbed the words. He had kissed Karen a few times, usually in the stage room. It was during his last few visits to Rose Hill when he was around fourteen. Karen was promiscuous and all the boys knew

249

it. Now he knew how wrong it was for them to take advantage of her. But at the time, he was just as infatuated as the others.

"It sounds like you were the last one to see her. Maybe you decided to help Randy out, and it was you who made the marks on her throat," Kyle said.

"How presumptuous," Stitches said. "I left it up to Randy if we should get help. He begged me not to tell. Didn't want his life ruined. Cried like a baby. I agreed. He was grateful. I knew someday Randy would be useful. And he has been, over the years."

Kyle's thoughts slowly clarified. The last time he had seen Karen was during one of his visits with Pop. They had come to help with a Valentine party. There had been music, food, and crafts. Karen had been wearing a pink dress with a red bow in her hair. She had looked so happy and carefree. What a crime that she was dead. That was the last time he'd been at Rose Hill. He had begun his new life. Pop was careful to hide any news from Rose Hill, and at the time, Kyle just didn't care.

"Where is her body located?" He stared at Stitches as his blood ran cold. "Please. I need to know."

"I told you. Buried in the cemetery."

"And her family never asked questions?"

"Of course," Stitches answered. "But it was determined that she ran off. The years slipped away, and she was forgotten. End of story."

"I don't believe your version of things," Kyle said. "Randy is no murderer. If you were the last person to see her alive, you strangled her. You lied so he'd owe you for this so-called favor."

The jester stomped his foot on the ground, chair

groaning in protest. His breathing grew labored as he held his hands over his ears. His head bobbed as he pressed his palms flat.

"Is that what this is about?" Kyle asked, puzzled. "Did you kill Karen and blame Randy, and now he's helping you do what?" His voice rose. "Tell me, you bastard!"

Stitches suddenly stopped moving, eyes narrowing in on Kyle's face. Then he grinned. "It would be simpler if it were only Karen," Stitches replied. "It's worse."

"Worse? What could be worse than the death of an innocent girl?"

"Another strangled girl, of course." Stitches grinned. He held up one finger. Then two. Another finger shot up. Then finally his pinkie. "Oops." He laughed, tapping his chin. Then spread his hand wide. "Or was there five? Is a thumb considered a finger? I really can't remember."

"You're a sick freak," Kyle said. "No wonder Pop left you here."

Head down, Stitches kicked Kyle's chair, knocking out the legs. Kyle fell hard. He lay on the floor, catching his breath. All his joints ached. At this rate, he wouldn't even be able to walk, let alone run for help.

"Okay. Okay," Kyle said. "I see you're upset. And strong." Slowly, he sat up, dragging the chair with him. How could he reason with someone who had an unstable mind?

He decided to try another tack. "So do you have a girlfriend now?" He scanned the room, looking for an escape route. "Or someone special in your life?"

"All my ladies are special," Stitches said. The

jester's eyes were hooded, obscured. "I loved them all."

"Okay," Kyle said, holding up his hands in a mock truce. "Okay, you answered that question. Where've you been living since you left the asylum?"

"Shut up," Stitches said.

"Do you do tricks? In our play, the court jester danced and had fancy footwork. Some of the other kids could juggle, make balloon art." He closed his eyes, remembering. "Jokes. Sometimes magic. Sounds. Whistles…"

Bingo. This time Stitches' eyes changed ever so slightly. The man's chin lifted. Clearly, he liked his jester attire and his talents.

"My brother Roy could make balloon animals." Kyle slowly stood, righting his fallen chair. He gripped the wood, gaining momentum. "He could make flowers for the girls. They really liked his parrots. I remember a fishing pole and the fish. And his laugh. he had such a great laugh. He'd pull a quarter from behind people's ears and make a hankie disappear. I never did figure out how he did those tricks. He was good with his hands. Can you do any tricks?"

In the absence of a reply, Kyle rambled on. "How about card tricks?" He inched his way to the side of the chair. If he could make it to the tunnels, he might be able to outrun Stitches, whose hulk suggested a slower gait. But he'd be blind in the dark. Stitches had adequate light. He wasn't sure what he had in his own pockets, or if he'd been searched while unconscious. And then there was Randy. He could come in at any second. Or worse, he could run into him in his bid for freedom. He was still reeling in shock over his friend's betrayal.

"Can you show me a trick?" Kyle asked. Stitches was so odd. One minute cold and calculating, then lucid. "Or do you know some new ones?"

Stitches tilted his head, as if considering the request. He looked so peculiar in his jester getup, face white, lips scarlet red. One painted eyebrow was partially missing. His scarlet eye shadow was smeared, contrasting with the purple and red cap.

"I've got tricks, but I can't show you any." A smirk crossed the man's face, revealing specks of red lipstick on his teeth.

"That's a shame," Kyle said. "I might never get a chance again. How about balloons? Do you make something special?" He hesitated, hating his next words. "Are you the jester who made my daughter a flower?"

"I did." Once again, a blank expression entered Stitches' eyes. It was bizarre. Was he medicated or off his meds? Kyle couldn't decide. Whatever the case, it was clearly irrational behavior. Thank God the man had forgotten to tie him up.

Stitches tucked the gun into his waistband. He dipped his large hand into his pocket, producing a limp balloon, Kyle waited with bated breath. The man tugged on the rubber, stretching it out. Then he put it to his lips, eyes rolling. As he blew, he tested the length with his fingers, stretching, pulling.

The jester's absorption in his actions was enough. In a split second, Kyle bolted. As he ran by the table, he flung out his hand, knocking the lantern to the floor. He raced through the basement, aided only by memory. His feet took on new life as he rushed into the dark tunnel. He took a right, hoping Stitches would think he went left, the easier route. In his mind, he tried to remember the way, needing to outthink both his opponents.

Shouting came from behind as Stitches gave chase. Using his right hand, Kyle kept it outstretched, touching the tunnel wall as he ran. Several times he tripped over things, managing not to fall. In terror, he waited for a hand to reach out and grab him. The thought propelled him forward. It was inky black, not a drop of light. The hallway split into four and he opted to take the left, hopefully heading toward the outer buildings. He needed a place to hide until he could figure the best way out.

He felt for doorways, flinching when something slimy slid beneath his palm. His feet sloshed into icy water. Still he kept on. His hand touched space, an open doorway. He had no idea which building it was, or if it was even safe. He stepped into the basement. His eyes bugged out as he strained to see. He ran into a wall, then tripped over something hard, guessing it to be rubber mattresses. He sat, catching his breath. The silence was deafening to his ears. He had to remain quiet. Composing himself, he stood, picturing the layout of the room. With outstretched hands, he began to walk.

Finally, he ducked into what seemed like a utility room. He felt around his pockets for something to use for light. Yes. He'd forgotten, his penlight was inside. He took a moment, running his hand over the metal. In some way, the light was his lifeline, but he dared not turn it on. Not yet. Despite the cold, he was sweaty. His heart thumped away in an anxious pace.

The chilly air dried his skin. He felt around his back pockets, hoping to find something else of use but there was nothing. While he searched, he listened for approaching footsteps. He needed to get further into the tunnels to find a place to hole up or go through a basement to get into a building or out a window. He would have had the advantage if his opponents weren't so familiar with the tunnel system.

He left the utility room, holding the pen light to use if necessary. He moved deeper into the tunnel, listening and watching for sounds of pursuit or signs of light. He came upon another doorway. Yes, the entrance was open. He slid into the darkness, walking toward the middle expanse. It was hard to know which building he was in because many of the basements were similar in design. Sometimes you could tell by what was stored or left behind. He flicked on the light for a second. He recoiled, almost losing his footing. On a wall was a huge portrait of a woman's face. It was the same gruesome image painted on his front window. Stitches had been the one who painted it. The thought made him sick to his stomach. His family had been in danger and he never even knew it.

He had little time to reflect on his find. Broken furniture and trash were scattered about. Most likely it was one of the women's buildings. He had been heading toward the upper campus, cursing himself for not keeping track of how far he'd run. But at least there were several ways to get out of the building.

In the rear of the building, a staircase lay undisturbed, thick with dust and spider webs. He opted to take the closest route. Slowly, he climbed the steps, flicked on his light, and barely missed falling into a missing step. At the top he moved into a small foyer. Another choice. Climb another staircase? The building held a second and third floor, but he needed to be on the ground level to get out. On the other hand, it might be wiser to wait until dawn to escape.

Once again, decision time. Scanning the foyer, he saw that indeed, it was one of the women's cottages. He trailed his flashlight along the floor, avoiding too much illumination. The graffitied walls appeared endless, with rooms on either side. Diffused moonlight touched the shadows; not much, but enough that his eyes could adjust a bit. He'd have to be careful that his light moving around in the building couldn't be seen from the courtyard. The men could be searching for him in the tunnels, or one of the many buildings. Having so many structures to choose from was in his favor.

As he moved, his thoughts turned to Randy. What if Randy found him? Would his friend shoot him dead? Was he capable of such a deed? Stitches had suggested that Randy had killed before. The prospect was grim.

Maybe Beth would call the police and figure out where he went. His breath stopped. She must be frantic. And she'd call Randy to find out where he was, surmising they were together. Would Randy harm her? His family had been threatened. It was a possibility.

He had to find a way to get the hell out of there.

With renewed resolve, he moved into the first room he came to, keeping his penlight on the floor, avoiding the windows. It had been a standard office for staff, but now was an empty room with scattered debris and dirt. Standing next to one of the huge windows, he peered out into the courtyard. Moonlight lit it up in a ghostly glow. A fine mist lay low to the ground. Towering trees encroached along the borders, along with the remnants of an old swing set. A light moved into his line of sight.

Two silhouettes approached from among the trees.

Maybe Stitches and Randy were giving up searching for him and were now leaving. Even as he thought it, it didn't seem likely. They wanted him dead. He knew about Karen and now the other victims, too.

Hope filled his heart. Maybe it was the cops. If so, he could call out for help.

As he watched, the couple moved out of the dark, and rounded a large tree. They passed by the building adjacent to his location, then they moved closer into open space.

In horror, Kyle gaped. No, it couldn't be. His wife was walking with Stitches, as if the pair were taking a casual stroll. He couldn't imagine why Beth would be there. But then again, he could. She'd obviously realized where he was and had come searching for him. But where was Samantha? Did she bring the baby with her?

His heart sank to his feet. Fleeing was no longer an option. Stitches had Beth, and if the man had no mercy for him, he certainly wouldn't have any for her. He couldn't even think what the jester was capable of.

As they came closer, he could clearly see something in Stitches' hand. It was a gun pointed directly at Beth's head.

Chapter Thirty-Eight

Still in shock, Beth couldn't help but stare at the jester's features. He was the same man that she'd met in the grocery store parking lot. She'd been singled out that day, but why? What did the man want with her? What did he want with Kyle?

When someone had come rushing out of a building, calling her name, she'd thought it was Kyle. Happy to see him, she'd hurried toward the man, only to discover it wasn't her husband. With the moonlight aiding her vision, the horrifying truth was clear. She didn't know if she was more afraid of the gun, or the horrible spectacle aiming it at her. Now he was parading her around like a trophy. But who was watching the parade?

"Who are you?" she mustered up the courage to ask. "Do I know you?"

"My name is Stitches." The man grabbed her arm in a painful clasp. "Stitches at your service. Surely you remember me?"

Fighting off panic, she tried to yank her arm from his steely grip. "What you want? Let me go right now!'"

"Shut up, Beth, and do as I say." He leered at her, aiming the gun toward her chest.

Fear curdled in the pit of her stomach. "How do you know my name? Have you been following me?

Where is my husband?"

Stitches stared into her eyes, smirking. "In time, darling, you'll have your answers, but for now you're going to listen to me, and do exactly as I say, or I will hurt you. Understand?"

Slowly, she nodded, gulping. She had to get a grip, or…

"Good girl. No questions. No answers. Unless I ask you something. Can you handle that?"

Once again, she nodded. He let her go. She rubbed her arm, breathing hard, her heart pounding.

"Please. If you want money, I have some in my car. We just need to walk back to it."

"You don't listen," he snarled. He slapped her, shoving her to the ground. "You women are all the same. You don't listen. Next time you say something, you're not going to like what I'll do to you."

She opened her mouth to speak, then snapped it shut. Tears came to her eyes.

"Now, one question. Where is your baby?"

"She's not with me." Terror struck her. What did he want with her daughter?

"And who has her?"

"A friend, a babysitter…" She grabbed at his leg in a plea. "Please. Leave her alone." He kicked her hand away.

"Think I want your brat?" The jester spat on the ground. "Think again."

She had little time for relief. The man grabbed her shoulder, yanked her to her feet, and gave her a shove. "Walk." She complied but dragged her feet.

As the minutes ticked away, Stitches grew more agitated. She feared what he was going to do next.

"Keep moving," Stitches said close to her ear. "If you want to live."

His threat slid over her like thick syrup. Unanswered questions filled her mind, especially ones about Kyle. Where was he? What had Stitches done to him, and why? What had she stepped into? More importantly, the man seemed to be waiting for something, a signal perhaps.

She frantically scanned the huge brick buildings. Was Kyle staring at her through one of the windows? She couldn't shake the feeling of being watched. But by whose eyes?

The jester suddenly grabbed her from behind, putting her in a chokehold.

"You better hope your husband comes for you," he snarled against her ear. Then she was flying face forward into the hard ground. Dirt and leaves littered her clothing and hair.

"Please, Stitches," she said, rolling over. She fought bitter tears. "There's no need to get violent. I'm somebody's mother. My daughter needs me. She needs her daddy, too. Please let me go."

"She needs me," he said in a mimic voice. "She needs us. Who cares?" He nudged her with his foot. "I'm sure your mother will step up to the plate. Ol' grandma to the rescue. Maybe your daughter would be better off without you as a mother. Did you ever think of that? We wouldn't want her to grow up to be like you."

Stitches grabbed his cell phone from his belt clip and stuck it against his ear. "Any luck finding him?" Then he was mumbling and cursing under his breath. "Come out here then. He'll come for his wife."

Stitches hauled her to her feet, forcing her to walk again. She blinked back tears of rage. Tears of regret. What if she died? What would happen to Samantha?

"You always have to keep tabs on Kyle," Stitches said, giving her shoulder a slight shove. "Don't you? You can't even let a man be a man. He's put up with your whining and your temper tantrums. I'd have kicked you to the curb a long time ago. Do you really think Kyle is happy with you?"

"I…I don't know," she said, wiping away an errant tear. The words stung. But how did this man know about her marriage? Who was he to them?

"Well, he's not. But still he remains ever faithful to you. Then again, that's Kyle. *Mr. Goody-Goody Gum Drops*. Always putting others before himself. But now you've stuck your nose into something that if you'd just minded your own business, it would've kept you home and safe. But you just had to come track him down. Drag the dog home and chain up his collar."

"You're wrong. I love Kyle," she said, jerking around. "You don't know me, or how I feel. Who are you to judge me? No one is perfect. I make mistakes, but that doesn't mean I don't love my husband. Every marriage has troubles, but we get through it." She frowned. "Who are you? Why is my marriage a concern to you?"

"It's not." He sneered. "I just wanted you to know that you suck at it."

Her blood ran cold as his voice became smug. She swallowed down her panic. Better not to ask. Better not to know. Perhaps disagreeing would doom her.

"Keep moving." The jester grabbed her arm, spinning her around.

As they moved between two buildings, another man stepped out of the darkness. At first, Beth hoped it was Kyle. But then her feet skidded to a stop.

Randy flashed his light over Stitches' ghastly face.

"Randy? Where's Kyle?" she asked.

But a guilty glimmer in Randy's eyes quickly faded into nothing.

"I… I don't understand. Where is Kyle?"

No reply.

"I'm sure you know Randy," Stitches said. "He's going to take care of you for a while."

Chapter Thirty-Nine

Kyle began a frantic search for a weapon, any weapon. He had trouble seeing the floor, let alone finding anything of use. After moving through several rooms, he managed to obtain a few long rusty nails and tucked them in his pocket. He also found a piece of metal with a jagged tip.

He raced back to the window, scanning the courtyard. Stitches was nowhere in sight. His wife was now walking with Randy. Although he couldn't see her face, the way she hugged herself betrayed her fear. The weapon in his hand felt useless. He hoped Randy wouldn't do anything crazy. It was hard to believe that his childhood friend would hurt Beth. If he took out Stitches, maybe Randy would come to his senses. It was his only hope.

He left his hiding spot and entered the basement stairwell. It was time to face Stitches. He had a better chance with a one-on-one encounter, instead of facing both men, and he wanted to take out the bigger opponent. Quietly, he snuck into the basement, only using his pocket light when necessary.

As Kyle backtracked through the tunnel, he had the feeling he wasn't alone. Once again, he wondered if the place was haunted by lost souls. There were no sounds, but something was there, watching him. If only he could call out to see who answered. Spooked, he hurried in his stride.

Creeping up on the hospital morgue, Kyle gripped the metal rod tightly. Although the weapon gave a pretense of security, it would be of no use against their weapons. He had to find a way.

"Kyle."

Kyle jumped at the sound of his name echoing farther down the tunnel.

"Kyle," Stitches called. "Come out, come out, wherever you are, or Beth will die. She's just outside with Randy. If you don't want her blood on your hands, then you'd better give yourself up."

Kyle paused, pulse pounding. If he gave himself up, he and Beth would both die that night. Samantha would be an orphan, just like he had been.

Shoving away his misgivings, he moved forward toward the sound, feeling along the wall. Down the lengthy corridor, Stitches stood with a headlamp on his forehead, making the jarring purple and red cap off-balance. He began to giggle, then spoke in a sinister voice. "If you twitch, you'll get stitched."

The words had their desired effect, freaking Kyle out. But it was the jester's laugh that was truly evil.

He heard the click of the gun and ducked. A bullet whizzed by him, ricocheting off the wall. Several more followed. His only hope was using the darkness to his advantage. Stitches couldn't see him; he was aiming where he thought Kyle was. He backed up against the wall. Slowly, Stitches approached, searching for him. As the light neared, Kyle backed up again, then again, always just out of the light.

He came upon a juncture in the tunnel and ducked into the opposite corridor. Now Stitches would have to move forward to see in which direction he'd gone. He waited with bated breath for the jester's approach, holding up the rod.

Light trailed along the opposite wall as Stitches moved closer. Then suddenly it went out. Poof. Now they were both as good as blind. Then a quiet dripping from somewhere in the distance.

Kyle tried to slow his breathing. His heart drummed in his chest.

Suddenly, a rush of movement. Stitches ran around the corner with a hair-raising scream. The attack caught Kyle's abdomen. He lost his grip on his rod. Kyle shoved hard at Stitches, grabbing the jester by the throat, punching him with his fist. They fell onto the damp floor, each struggling to get on top of the other. Although Stitches was heavier, Kyle managed to shove Stitches flat against the floor. He gave as good as he got, punching the man's face. Warm blood and makeup seeped over his fingers, making his hands slippery. But then he felt it. The tip of the gun pressed against his throat.

"Don't," Stitches warned. "I'll shoot. Get off me, slowly."

Kyle moved to a kneeling position, then stood. Stitches kept the gun only inches away. With a flick of the switch, he managed to right his headgear, blinding Kyle with light.

"Let's start walking. If you make any sudden moves, I will shoot you."

"You'd shoot a man in the back?" Kyle said. "Why am I not surprised?"

They left the tunnel. At the first floor, they stopped. Stitches held the gun to Kyle's skull. "Don't move."

"I got him," Stitches said into his cell. "I'm bringing him down toward the morgue. Meet me there."

As Kyle listened to Stitches' voice, a shock of revulsion hit him. He could barely breathe.

"Let's go," Stitches said, grabbing his shoulder. "Back down to the tunnels."

"I know who you are," Kyle said. "It makes sense now. I remember everything you ever did to me."

Stitches spoke close to his ear. "I was wondering when you were going to figure it out."

"Pop knew you were bullying me and my brother," Kyle said.

"I saw how he was with you," Stitches said. "How he adored everything about you, and you sucked it up. My parents took you in. They gave you everything they took away from me, my bedroom, my things, my future. They stopped loving me; they loved you."

"They must've thought they were helping you by leaving you here," Kyle said. "That is love."

The gun jabbed his ribs, making Kyle double over. After a moment, he caught his breath. "You enjoyed tormenting me. You were always terrorizing Roy. Loved it, in fact, but he wasn't adopted."

"He was flawed, like me," Stitches said. "You were a snitch. You turned my father against me. You knew the rules about snitching."

Kyle thought about his words. He'd told Pop that Benny had been hurting Roy and the other boys. Pop had been one of the few adults that listened. He'd appeared sad at the allegations. Now Kyle knew why. Pop's own son was a monster.

"Yes, I told Pop what you were doing to the kids."

"Tattletale."

"I wanted you to leave Roy alone," Kyle said. "He was so little and scared."

"I did as I please. I still do."

"I was told you were sent away from Rose Hill," Kyle said. "Where did you go?"

"I was committed to another state hospital, but I didn't stay there long. I escaped. I fell through the cracks, changed my name. The rest is history."

"Except here we are."

"Here we are," Benny repeated. "I've lived here off and on for the past twenty years."

Stunned, Kyle said, "That's a long time."

"From time to time, I checked in with Pop. Watched him from afar. Then one night, I decided to give him a final farewell. But the old goat managed to live." He snorted. "He couldn't even die right. Eventually, I'll catch up with him again. We will have that final curtain call."

Kyle didn't reply. Poor Pop.

"They're selling this place," Benny continued. "It's time for me to clean up my mess and get out of here."

"What kind of mess?" Kyle's heart raced, waiting for the dreaded words to come.

"Emily."

"Who is Emily?" Kyle asked.

"Someone I've loved and lost. I've moved on. She won't be missed. Dope makes people stupid, and it was easy to tempt her with a promise. She stayed with me for a time." He paused, a happy sigh. Then he swung his arms wide. "Right here, in this spectacular place. I had a bit of fun. So what? All she had to do was play by the rules. I didn't intend on killing her. I was going to set her free. Who'd believe her crazy shit? But I confess it got out of hand. We played hide and seek here in the tunnels. She wasn't good at the game, sat and cried. But what a screamer. Wow. I still hear that sound in my head. I gave her a chance to win her freedom, but she wouldn't even try." He paused, grinned, then shook his head. "I took some great pictures."

"You're sick," Kyle said. "Deranged. You're nothing but a cold-blooded murderer."

"Emily was a waste of life. She would've overdosed on her own. I did the world a favor. My itch comes back occasionally. It's hard to control at times. I keep telling myself that each game will be my last." He laughed. "I have a new girlfriend. Donna is a better opponent, at least for now. Then there's Beth. I didn't plan on her being here tonight. What a bonus. I can't imagine the challenge."

"Leave her out of this, you bastard. Just let her go."

"Not for a million dollars."

They approached the doorway to the morgue.

"I taught Randy how to survive. How to take what he wants in this cruel world. His only downfall was you. You made him weak."

"Weak?" Kyle said. "You should know that word well. I remember how you were. You had your pick of young, vulnerable kids. Knew the ropes. Preyed on the weak. You used fear to control them, pretended friendship to others. They were innocent victims." Dawning occurred as his memory flowed like a runaway train. He turned around, facing Benny. "I remembered you following the girls around. It's beginning to make sense." He swallowed hard. "I saw you sneaking into their cottages. You were always finding ways to be around them." He stopped, mouth gaping. "You were even around my mother. Did you touch her?"

"Touch her?" Stitches laughed. "With ol' Pop around? He was waiting for her to die, so he could take you home with him."

"He knew she was dying?"

"Of course. She was in heart failure. It was only a matter of time. Sorry, but I liked my women a little feistier…and younger."

Kyle mumbled an oath. He could barely grasp the implications. His mother had meant nothing to anyone but him.

"Roy hated the dark," Benny said. "He was pathetic. But in the short time I toyed with him, I made him stronger. He learned to fight, survive."

"You had no right terrorizing any of the kids."

"I had every right!" The jester snorted. "My parents put me here. I did what was natural. My father was a fool. Over the years, he mailed me money. As I grew, he promised that if I stayed away from my mother, he'd send me more dough. Do you know how hard it was to have to beg for money? Money that he freely handed to you! You weren't his flesh and blood son. I was! He tried to keep me on a budget. Claimed he'd make sure I was covered if I agreed to stay out of trouble. I did for many years. Then came the day he told me he was going to have you take over his finances. I couldn't believe it. He was going to confess his sin! That wife of yours would've enjoyed making me beg. So I went to see him to discuss a solution. We argued and it got ugly. I hit him with a hammer, and he fell, hard. Everyone assumed the stroke was to blame.

No questions asked. Afterward, I stole his bank account information, and forged his name to get access. It was a good payoff, and long overdue."

"He's your father, you bastard."

"Don't care. Tonight, I'm correcting a wrong. No Kyle, no Beth. Next in line—Pop. I'm taking over my father's house. I'm the rightful heir. He might not have much, but I'm taking whatever he's got."

"If your father dumped you at Rose Hill," Kyle said, "he made the right decision. I see it now; you were born evil. Pop saw it. You tied his hands. I can smell your stench from here."

"Maybe just a tad evil," Stitches admitted. "So what? You got everything you wanted, a cushy life with your new family. I got this." He spread his arms. "I thrived here."

The horror of Rose Hill sank into Kyle's mind. It was a suitable place for a predator. Benny was just a teenager, but he'd been big and strong. How many lives had he destroyed before being caught and sent away?

He swallowed hard. What a fool he'd been. All these years he had the power to do something for the nameless victims. He'd failed.

"I was told to forget about Roy," Kyle said. His throat convulsed. "But the truth is, I wouldn't have left Rose Hill to go live with your parents if you weren't such a screwup."

"Shut up." Stitches shoved Kyle. "Roy hated you. He would run to you for help, but you'd push him away. You were a pathetic brother. Tell me, Kyle. What is your relationship like today with your precious brother? Hmmm? I'm curious."

"Nonexistent," Kyle said. "Just like yours and your

father's. But you already know that. I'm glad I told on you. I'm not sorry that you were taken away from here. The people at Rose Hill were safer once you left. You're the monster everyone feared in the dark."

Kyle stopped in the morgue doorway, as Benny pressed the gun into his back.

"I was a terrible brother. I'll admit it. I was selfish. But you—Jester—are sick. What you're doing tonight shows just how right everyone was. Pop made the right choice in sons. Unlike you, I will never betray him."

"You're going to pay for that." The gun dug painfully into his back as Benny breathed into his ear. "Did you think you were afraid as a boy? That was just a drop in the bucket. I have plans for Beth, but first I want to watch you say farewell to her."

"You'd better not lay a finger on her," Kyle said. "She's got nothing to do with any of this."

"Right." Benny laughed behind his back. "I'm just going to let her walk right out of here. Tell her tales. Beth would love to be the one to put the cuffs on me, much like she does her husband. No. I don't think so. You have no idea who you're dealing with. I admit, I got sloppy. Comfortable. Now that this place is under contract, people will be looking very closely at the asylum, the buildings, and grounds. Who knows what the new owners will do? Move the graveyard? Check over their investment? Murder is a messy affair. My last angel was a bleeder, but oh, was she strong. What a challenge. She hurt me. Put a few dents in my skull."

"Good for her," Kyle said. "To bad she didn't kill your rotten hide."

"Randy tried to spare you all of this. But you came back to me. Walked right into my web. That day at your

Pop's house, I was going to end it. But then I had an idea. A final game, just between you and me. Randy lured you here, boots in hand. I never thought he'd try to stop me. I'll deal with him later. In some ways, this is like a family reunion, don't you think?"

"If you think you're going to keep getting away with murder, you're sadly mistaken," Kyle said. "Other people know I'm here. They'll put two and two together and come looking for us. You'll never be able to wipe away all your stains from here."

"I'm not going to be the one to kill you. Randy is. He's been looking forward to it."

Fear struck Kyle to his core. Looking forward to killing him? Did Randy hate him that much? Was their friendship just an act? His soul hurt.

"Bastard," Kyle said, swinging around. He grabbed for the gun, but Benny jumped away, pointing it at his face.

"Stop, or you're dead," Benny said. "I'm done talking. Move."

"Come on," Kyle said, digging in his heels. "Beth is innocent. She doesn't deserve this. We have a daughter."

"You're getting pitiful," Benny shoved the gun in Kyle's rib. "Man up and take your medicine. Now move, or I'll end this right here. At least you'll get the chance to say goodbye."

With the gun digging painfully into his skin, Kyle took a step forward.

Chapter Forty

Awkwardly, Beth walked in front of Randy, deliberately dragging her right leg in the pretense of an injury, stalling. She wasn't sure what she was hoping for. She only knew that he had talked to someone on the phone, probably that awful jester, and was told to take her somewhere. Whatever that meant, it sounded bad.

"Why are you doing this, Randy?" she said over her shoulder. "What are you involved in? How can you claim to be Kyle's friend?"

"This isn't my fault," Randy replied. "It's his."

"How can you say that? What's he done?"

"He's stupid," Randy said. "Keep moving."

"What does that mean?" She rubbed her knee, pausing. "What did you get him involved with?"

"Always me, isn't it, Beth?" He poked a finger in her spine. "Did you ever think that Kyle gets himself into his messes because of you?"

"Don't try to turn this around on me," she hissed. "I'm not the one holding a gun."

"Move." The finger dug in. She jumped forward.

"Is Kyle hurt? Is he okay?"

"He's fine."

"Does he know I'm here?"

"He will."

She bit her lip, thinking. Why would he know she was there? Once again, she considered the buildings, wondering who watched them.

"What are you going to do with me?"

"Just shut up, Beth. I'm tired of your mouth."

"Please…" Despite her best efforts, emotion was taking its toll. "Whatever it is, Randy. You're Kyle's best friend. He loves you. He'd do anything for you. Whatever this is, please help him. Help us. We have a daughter. A baby. Please…"

No response.

"Are you going to kill us?" The words came out in a whisper.

"I didn't want this, Beth…"

"Then help us."

"I can't," Randy said. "It's too late for that now. I would if I could."

"You can," she said. "You just don't want to."

She shuddered at the blank stare directed at her. Did this man have a soul?

"What about the jester?" she continued. "Stitches. Who is he? I saw the pictures of you and Kyle when you were boys. Kyle said you were in skits, dressed up like clowns. So what is this? Reliving some sick fantasy? My God, he's dressed up as a freak, Randy!" She shook her head. "The man's crazy. I can see it in his eyes. What does he want with Kyle? Why are you helping him?"

His silence made her panic.

Randy grabbed her shoulder and pushed her into an open doorway of a brick building. Darkness enveloped her. She stumbled and was righted by the hand on her shoulder. "I'm afraid of the dark," she said. "I have been ever since I was a child."

Suddenly, there was light as Randy pulled a

flashlight out of his pocket. But seeing the shocking conditions of the building's interior gave her no comfort. White paint chips hung along most of the graffitied walls. The floors were littered with dust, trash, odds and ends. Just as she thought it couldn't get more ominous, Randy forced her down a staircase toward the basement.

Beth froze in the middle of the steps. She could barely breathe. He grabbed her arm, forcing her to move. A sob escaped her.

At the bottom, he walked her through the basement, which was huge and hard to see. Hopelessly, she tried to memorize the way, knowing it was fruitless. She'd never find her way back out, especially without any light. Then they were in the tunnels. Kyle had told her about them, tried to describe them. But seeing them was terrifying. She couldn't imagine being a child in such a place, playing in the endless corridors.

They passed several doorways, then came upon an open one. Randy steered her through the portal, into what appeared to be another massive basement, only this one had medical supplies strewn around; gurneys, tubing, vials and metal trays. They came upon a huge room with more gurneys. They walked around a wall and she saw Kyle, standing in the middle of the room. Stitches held a gun toward her husband's temple. Some of his makeup was smeared. Stitches whistled beneath his breath, an odd ditty. Hearing their approach, the jester grinned hideously.

"Welcome to your nightmare, Beth. As much as I regret not having more time to play with Kyle, you, on the other hand, I'll find time to send straight to hell, Stitches style."

Chapter Forty-One

Kyle swore beneath his breath. His wife's tear-stained features tore at him. She was terrified and his helplessness made him angry, but he avoided making a foolish mistake. He'd wait for an opportunity to try and allow her to escape. If he could just distract Benny and Randy, maybe he could buy her time to get away.

"Kyle!" Beth cried. "Oh, my God, what's going on?"

"I'm sorry," he said. Helplessly he held out his hands, then dropped them in defeat. "Where's the baby?"

"With a trusted person."

"Thank God for that." Relief, though bitter, swept over Kyle.

Randy stood in the middle of the room with Beth, waiting for orders. He kept a firm grip on Beth's arm, while Benny stood next to him, gun in hand.

"Go on, you two," Benny said, grinning. "I'll give you a few moments to speak to one another. After all, you are husband and wife—at least until death do you part."

"Oh, Kyle." Beth flung herself into Kyle's arms, burrowing her head into his shoulder.

"I love you," Kyle said against her ear. "I always have. I am so, so sorry for all of this. I got us into this mess and should've warned you."

"None of that matters now." She lifted her face and kissed him. "I love you. No matter what happens. I have always loved you, and always will. They can't take that away from us."

"Okay, enough already," Stitches said. "I'm getting sick to my stomach with all this talk of love. Take Kyle's wife and put her in the top drawer of the freezer."

"Don't," Kyle said, grabbing Beth in a bear hug. "What kind of sadistic prick are you?"

"The very best I can be," Stitches said, his eyes lit in pleasure.

Randy grabbed Beth's arm, pulling at her. Kyle held fast to his wife, who became the object of a tug of war. She screamed as they jerked her around.

"No," Beth cried. "What are you doing? Kyle, don't let me go!"

Then Stitches' gun was in Kyle's face, cocked. "Release her."

Kyle lost the battle as Randy half-dragged, half-carried Beth through the open doorway, toward the morgue. She dug her feet in, clawing and scratching.

Kyle started after them, halting when Stitches' gun was again in his face.

"No, you don't. Don't move or it will be all over."

From the other room, Beth began screaming and pleading. There was a loud screech of protesting metal, then sobbing.

"Now you can move," Stitches said, pointing the way. "But slowly. Follow them."

Kyle rushed through the doorway. Beth was lying on the top metal slab, hands and feet bound by wire ties. With her feet facing inside the metal structure, her head was the last to be shoved into the opening. She pleaded and begged.

"Take her out of there!" Kyle screamed. "Randy, don't listen to him. Please. You're my friend. Help us."

"Push it in," Benny said. "I'll deal with her later."

"Coward!" Kyle yelled at Randy. "You've been bought and paid for. You're disgusting."

"I don't disagree," Randy said, pausing with his hand on the metal handle. "You know, I don't like doing this."

"At least he's honest," Benny said, mockingly smiling at Kyle. "More than you've been over the years. Don't you think?"

Randy pushed the drawer in. Once again, metal scraped metal in a chilling clatter. Beth's sobs became faint.

"Check the other drawer," Benny said. "Hopefully the ol' Doc died of heart failure."

In shock, Kyle watched as the middle drawer was pulled open, revealing an old woman. Unlike Beth, she was head-first and alive. She wore a flowery nightgown, stained and soiled, with a pair of bobby socks.

Benny walked over to her and stroked her face. "My, my, my. You're a stubborn one, ain't you, doctor? Don't worry if you can't find a way to die on your own, I guess I'll just have to help you along."

"Moron," the woman managed to whisper. "Go to hell, Benny…"

The jester winced when she said his name.

"You are a bad, bad, boy. A disgrace to your family."

Stitches bellowed in a loud roar. He pressed his

hands against his ears, walked over to the wall and banged his head. Dust and debris filtered onto the floor.

"It's okay," Randy said. "She's not important." Quickly he shoved the drawer into the freezer.

"I thought I knew you. Look what you've become. Inhuman. Soulless."

"Evil," Randy said beneath his breath.

"Help us," Kyle hissed, staring at the broad back of Benny, who had his head pressed against the wall as if deflated. "Please, he's nuts. Don't listen to him. He's just using you. He told me about Karen. It wasn't your fault. He as much admitted that he killed her and all to make you a part of his schemes. It's your word against his. You know this is wrong."

"Shut up," Randy said. He slammed the gun across Kyle's face. "Don't talk about her. Karen was an accident. Benny helped me dispose of her. No one would've understood. I was so young. I've had to live with the guilt all my life. All my life! You don't know what that's like. The blame. Wondering if anyone would've believed me. Karen was just a girl. I deal with that every day. Not you; you've got the perfect life."

"I don't understand," Kyle said, spitting out blood. "You never said you were unhappy. Never once. You have Kat. She's a good woman who loves you. Maybe I did get to leave here. But adults decided our lives, not us. I've always been your friend. I would do anything for you. I'd have understood about Karen. I might've been able to help." He caught his breath. "He's lying to you. He killed her so you'd owe him. That should make you angry. You're his pawn. When's it going to stop? He can't do anything alone. He abused women, kids. His own parents. You're not a child, you're a man. Act like one."

Something flickered in Randy's vision. A warning. His hand shook, slightly.

Beth's muffled cries came from her metal box. The people he loved were being destroyed by evil. Suddenly, Kyle rushed at Stitches, who had turned toward him. He propelled into Benny's chest with all the fury of hell. The movement caught his nemesis off-guard. But his victory was short-lived. Benny managed to right the gun, pointing it between his eyes.

Kyle held his breath, waiting for the shot. A weapon discharged. The sound was deafening. Stitches crumbled to the ground, holding his chest. Benny stared at Randy, shock in his eyes, before collapsing onto the floor.

"Bastard," Randy said, gun pointed toward Kyle. He spat on the ground.

Kyle's relief quickly fled, unsure of Randy's next moves. His heart galloped.

"I just killed Benny Charles," Randy said. "Or should I say, Benjamin Charles Hampton. He would've killed you, then me. And God knows what he would've done to Beth. That's what the cops will discover when they sort through this mess."

Kyle waited, eyes glued to the gun, still pointed in his direction.

"What are you doing, Randy? Put the gun down."

"You've already told the cops someone was at your house," Randy said, ignoring Kyle's plea. "You set the stage. Someone wanted to harm you. They will say Benny was sick, deranged. He killed women for pleasure, your wife, the old hag, and then you, because Benny was the nut that finally cracked. It will all be tied up in a neat little package. And while the police are trying to figure this out, I'll be on my way to Mexico."

"So that's it?" Kyle was stunned. "It ends here? Everything we've ever done or been through together was all for nothing? You were my best friend. Doesn't that mean anything to you?" He shook his head. "That hurts." He straightened his shoulders, his gaze dissecting Randy. "But your plan will fail, because no matter how careful you think you are or were, there'll always be a piece of evidence left behind. You've overplayed your hand."

"Well, you won't be here to see if your premise comes true, will you?" Randy said. "Your wife and the old woman won't be found for days. Be glad it's me taking them out. I'll have mercy. I'd already planned out this scenario way before tonight. You weren't originally part of this, but Benny would've eventually killed me. You don't know what he's capable of. What he's done in the past. What I did, and now regret. I know you think I don't care about you, but I do. But I'm not going to prison. I lived years in this hellhole; I'm not living out my future in another one. I'm sorry, but it's either you or me. And I'm choosing me. Maybe some of the pieces of the puzzle won't exactly fit, but in the end, everything will turn out all right. Your little girl will be raised by Beth's mom. She'll be safe, and at least that part of you will live on."

"You think you've covered everything," Kyle said. "But earlier, I lost my phone somewhere along the main street. Or maybe along the train tracks or in the woods. My truck is parked at the bar. I told the staff where I was going and exactly who I was looking for. You. Someone will come looking for me. There'll be an investigation. You'll lose precious time trying to find my phone before the police can. They'll be able to follow the cell's signal. So you better find it before they can because my text messages point directly at you. I was suspicious of what you were up to. I wrote it all down and sent it to several people. They'll put two and two together and come to the one and only conclusion—you. You won't have a prayer."

The partial lie took on new life. For the first time, he saw a crack in Randy's armor. The man faltered, panic reaching his eyes. It was as if he were just waking up to the situation he'd put himself into.

"Then I'd better hurry," Randy said, raising the gun toward Kyle's chest.

Kyle dove low into Randy's legs and toppled him as he fired. The main lantern was knocked to the ground, throwing the room into muted light. Kyle grabbed the hand holding the gun, wrestling with it. He dug his fingers into Randy's wrist, twisting and pointing the gun toward the ceiling. It went off and plaster rained in a cloud of dust. Despite Randy's punches, Kyle held on. They fell back against a gurney, sending it crashing into the wall. Randy stood and Kyle clasped him around his chest, and they collapsed together onto the floor. Randy lost his grip on the gun and it skittered over the floor, into a corner.

Kyle scrambled to his knees to crawl after it. Randy jumped onto his back, arm across his throat. Stars flecked Kyle's vision as he tried to break the hold. He grabbed into his back pocket, pulled out a nail and jabbed it into Randy's wrist. The man howled in pain. He kept pushing, shoving it until it hit bone. Blood splattered out, spraying him in the face. He managed to roll over, toppling Randy onto the floor. But Randy came up swinging with a piece of wood. The blow to the head took Kyle's breath away. The room spun as he fell. In a blur, Randy's hand drew back to slam the board into his head again, but the board was ripped away.

"You twitched," a voice murmured. "He's mine." Benny's arm slid around Randy's throat, lifted him. His body was flung across the room into a wall. With a sickening crack Randy's head connected with the wall. A thud followed as his body fell.

Half-unconscious, Kyle struggled to keep his eyes open. Rolling to his side, he crawled across the floor. Stitches' blood stained the floor. The cap lay stuck in the crimson flow. Benny grabbed his foot, twisting him onto his back, straddling him with his legs.

Kyle kicked with all his might, hitting the man's belly. Benny toppled to one side, gasping. Kyle pivoted around, scanning the scene. Randy lay still but the gun was in sight. Crawling on his knees, Kyle reached the weapon as Benny staggered toward him. Kyle rolled onto his backside, took aim, and fired. Benny stood still for a moment, then fell into a heap.

Chapter Forty-Two

Kyle trained the gun on both men, catching his breath. He reached into Randy's pocket, took out his cellphone and searched for a signal. Nothing. With one eye on the room's occupants, he grabbed the handle of Beth's morgue drawer, pulling it out.

Her eyes were wide, and she sobbed his name. The shock and relief on Beth's face would last him a lifetime.

"There's a woman in the other drawer," he said, cutting her zip ties. "We have to get her out."

Kyle yanked out the other drawer, stunned by the old woman's condition. So frail, thin and cold. With Beth's help, Kyle managed to sit the woman up, legs dangling over the freezer slab. The elderly lady seemed numb, as if she didn't realize she'd been rescued. She could barely hold herself up, clinging to his arm. Yet when she glanced up at him, the old woman's eyes were shrewd.

"Who are you?" she asked.

"Kyle Hampton," he replied. "Are you Doctor Goodman?"

"I am."

"You're safe now," Kyle said. He remembered the doctor worked at Rose Hill, though he'd had little interaction with her. There were stories though, tales of abuse and excessive punishments. "We need to get out of here."

"Are they dead?"

"I think maybe," Kyle said. "The cops can figure it out."

"Beth? Are you hurt anywhere?" He turned toward his wife, noting the purplish lump above Beth's eye, the dirt on her face. She hugged herself, shivering.

"I don't know," Beth replied. "I think I'm okay."

Kyle grabbed the lantern, handed it to Beth. "You need to hold this. I have to carry her. She's too weak to walk." He scooped up the doctor, conscious of not hurting her.

Beth took the light, and they exited the room.

Carrying the doctor, Kyle followed Beth up the staircase, to the first floor of the hospital. The front door was unlocked. They stepped through the opening into the cold, starlit night.

Being outside was exhilarating. Kyle never thought he'd see the moon again. His thoughts raced, competing with his heart. Randy's betrayal stung.

Kyle carried the doctor to a stone bench, gently sitting her down. He tucked his coat around her bony frame. Beth watched him, hugging herself, her eyes vacant. He wondered as to her physical and mental state.

"You need to sit," Kyle said to Beth. "Take the other bench. You're in shock. I don't know how badly you've been hurt. You both need medical help."

"So do you." Beth's voice was barely audible. "Your forehead is bleeding."

Kyle touched his damp skin. Slick blood slid over his fingers. He brushed it away and grabbed Randy's cell phone from his pocket, thrusting it into Beth's hand. Nervously, Beth glanced over his shoulder, shuddering. He grabbed her arms, staring into her eyes. "It's okay, Beth. Relax. Call 911 and get the cops here. Tell them to bring an ambulance. I want to check over the doctor."

"Don't leave me," she said, coming to life. She grabbed at his hand as a sob escaped her. "Wait till the cops get here. They can check her out. Not you. Please." More tears brimmed into her eyes, crested, and then fell. He kissed her forehead.

"Call them," he said. "You're strong. Hang in there."

Kyle moved over to the other bench, checking on the old woman. She blinked at him, unfocused.

"I know you," she said. "You're Kyle Hampton. The boy Scott adopted. I gave the referral for your adoption."

He remembered Doris Goodman being around Pop, but he had to wonder how she could give a referral when she never spoke two words to him. When she gave orders to staff, they jumped. He had witnessed the doctor in action a few times when he was visiting Rose Hill. The kids feared her.

"How did you end up here with Benny?" Kyle knelt by her. "Did you know him from before?"

"Yes."

"Were you my brother Roy's doctor?"

"Yes," she said. "But not for long. He was transferred into foster care. I lost track of him after that."

"I need to find him," he said. "If you have an idea where he is, please tell me."

"I don't." She closed her eyes, her mouth set into a

firm line.

Frustrated, he quelled the urge to demand answers. The woman was in no condition for his interrogations.

"Was there someone else here besides you?" Kyle asked. "I heard noises in a basement closet."

"Stitches stole my dog," Doctor Goodman said, her eyes snapping open. "Maybe she's in there. Please, her name is Princess. I hate to think what that horrible man did to her. Please, find her for me. Go look."

"The cops are coming. I'll let them know." Kyle hung his head. It could be her dog, but it could be the other woman that Stitches had mentioned. Tiredness washed over him. The nightmare was over. He walked back to Beth, sank down beside her, and pulled her into his arms.

"I called the police, and they're coming," she murmured against his shoulder.

Chilled to the bone, Kyle held Beth's hand, waiting for the cops. His head pounded and every part of his body hurt. The wait seemed endless.

"You're sure the cops understood what you were saying?"

"Yes," Beth replied. "I told them where we were, and about Randy and Benny. I told them what I could."

A noise sounded somewhere off in the distance. Sirens.

"They're here," Kyle said. Eagerly, he stood and signaled his light toward the road. Headlights filtered into the darkness. More emergency vehicles followed.

Kyle reached down, grabbed Beth's hand, and squeezed.

"We made it, Beth. We made it."

Chapter Forty-Three

"The Rose Hill murders have been all over the news," Beth announced when Kyle walked into the kitchen. She put down the pot she'd been washing, wiped her hands on a dish towel and faced him. "I hope they keep our names out of the media."

"They will for now," Kyle said. "At least while it's being investigated. But eventually we might have to testify against Randy. Something I'm not looking forward to."

"If they catch him," she replied. "I can't believe he got away."

"They'll get him," he assured her. "It's just a matter of time."

"It's so hard to believe that Donna Jordan was being held against her will and Randy never tried to help her," she said. "The woman is lucky to be alive."

"If Randy wasn't going to help me, then why would he help her?"

Beth's voice lowered. "It's hard to believe at times."

It didn't take long for the news to reveal the story of serial killer Benjamin Hampton, alias "Stitches," and his six female victims, ranging in age from seventeen to twenty-five. All of the young women had gone missing within a fifty-mile radius. Two victims were found at the bottom of a nearby pond, bound and weighed down by rocks or bricks. Other victims were found at Rose Hill Asylum, buried in the former graveyard. Benny had scattered wood and leaves over the graves to blend them in with the scenery.

Benny's computer gave credible evidence that there could be other victims. A timeline was established. After being expelled from Rose Hill, Benny had spent time at another state mental institution. It appeared that for a while, he had lived a normal life. Years, in fact. But then, over the past two years, the killings began. Pictures of the women in duress were displayed on his computer, many of them wearing costumes. Stitches had created his own gruesome artwork, used psychological torture, and hunted down his victims to strangle them.

"Did you go see your Pop?" Beth asked.

"I did," Kyle said. "Apparently, Benny was violent even when he was a little boy. He'd been killing neighborhood animals, just for fun. That was the tip of the iceberg. He began stalking a twelve-year-old girl at his school. After a failed rape attempt, he beat her up pretty badly." He paused, letting Beth digest the news. "Benny grew increasingly violent and attacked his mother. After that, Pop committed him to Rose Hill. Benny was fourteen. He improved with medication, or so it seemed. At fifteen Benny was sent to another facility." He exhaled. "Pop had trouble discussing it, but he admitted that Florence was terribly depressed over Benny and they thought they were doing the right thing."

He placed his hands in his pockets, leaning against the wall.

"Scott adopted me to basically take Benny's place.

Someone who wouldn't give them any trouble. It really makes me angry to think they traded children without thinking of the consequences. No wonder Benny hated me so. Pop apologized and said that he intended on telling me one day, but he kept waiting for the right time. The right time never came."

"I'm sorry, honey." Beth's face echoed his pain. "I know you're angry but maybe one day you can forgive him. It's been an emotional rollercoaster for you."

"To put it mildly," he said.

"Did you ask your pop about your biological father?"

"I'll probably never know who he was. Pop has no clue. I can search, but most likely, I'll be wasting my time."

"What about Roy? Does your Pop know his whereabouts?"

"No. He didn't keep in touch. I called the hospital to talk to Doris Goodman to see what she knows, but I was a day late. She was discharged from the hospital, so I drove to her house. A neighbor said she would be staying with a family member for a while and to check back in a couple of weeks. It's really frustrating."

"I'm sure Roy is still living in Philadelphia," she said.

"Possibly. He might've seen the news, although our names weren't mentioned as of yet. I won't give up till I find him. Benny liked rubbing salt in old wounds, reminding me how I left Roy behind. The things he said really bother me."

"Benny was an evil man," she said. "I hope he's rotting in hell. Good riddance. Randy knew what Benny did to all those women, and never tried to stop him."

She shuddered. "Actually, he aided him. How close we came to our own deaths because of someone's twisted sense of justice."

"I know. I try not to think about it." Kyle searched her face, hating the pain reflected in her eyes. "But it has a way of creeping up on me, especially where Randy is concerned."

"I don't like not knowing where Randy is," she said. "It's unnerving, knowing he's out there somewhere. What if he comes here?"

"He said he was heading to Mexico. That's probably where he'll go."

"I can't believe he was able to escape," she said, chewing her lip. She hugged herself, worry etched in her features.

"It's crazy," he said. "I thought for sure he was dead. I heard his skull crack the wall. Somehow, he crawled out of there and was able to get away. He was knocked out cold. The cops were on the scene in a matter of minutes. Rose Hill has so many places to hide though, and Randy knew the property. If anyone would know where to hole up for a while, he would."

"It's been two weeks," Beth said. "Who knows how far he got? I don't like knowing he's out there. I can barely sleep. I'm sorry, Kyle." She wrapped her arms around his neck, hugging him. "I can't imagine how you're feeling. How hurt you must be."

He didn't reply, seeking her comfort. Her softness. The horror of what had happened to them met them fresh in the morning and lay down to sleep with them in the evenings. Beth had trouble talking about it, but each day it was getting easier. He couldn't help but beat himself up for Beth's involvement. The investigation was still ongoing, spanning decades. If there were more victims, he hoped they could be put to rest.

He was glad he could shed some light on the disappearance of Karen Walton, pointing investigators to Benny's confession. They assured him they'd investigate it, but they had a lot of evidence to uncover. It would take time.

Frustrated, Kyle wondered where Randy could be hiding. Was he out there, watching them? Hopefully, he was far away from Pennsylvania. But how could he be sure? What if Randy came looking to finish off his witnesses? That thought kept him up at night, but he kept his fears to himself.

And then there was Benny. The Hampton family was still reeling over the events and their secret now set free. Anger and confusion suffused their conversations. Uncle Bill had taken it the hardest. True, he'd known Benny's diabolical side, but he was shocked over what his nephew had been capable of. It was going to take time for the truth to settle. Now the family had to decide on a funeral.

That evening, just as Kyle crawled into bed, Beth came running into their bedroom, Sammy against her shoulder.

"Kyle," Beth exclaimed. "They found him."

"Randy?"

"Yes. He was staying in a Florida motel under an alias. Someone recognized him from the news and reported it. He's being extradited back to Philadelphia. They said he was taken into custody without incident."

"Thank God."

Chapter Forty-Four

Kyle ended his shift at work. He was tired but restless as his mind grappled with the past. Despite Randy's betrayal, he missed his best friend. Words couldn't describe the bitter blow to his life. The last few weeks had taken a toll on him physically and emotionally. Despite Beth's best efforts, she could barely make a dent in his pain.

As Kyle walked toward the office, the setting sun blinded him. As he neared the parking area, a man stood in his path, watching him approach.

"Hey," Kyle said, skirting around his form.

"Hey," the man replied, following him. "Are you Kyle Hampton?"

"Yes." Kyle paused, turned, thinking it was a new employee.

The man's gaze penetrated Kyle, rooting him to the spot in an awkward moment.

"Can I help you with something?" There was something familiar about the guy.

"I'm Roy Hagen."

Kyle's breath left him.

"My...my brother Roy?"

"One and the same."

His brother stood before him, shocking him to his core. For a moment, he was speechless. Gawking. Absorbing Roy all at once. They had similar features, blond hair and blue eyes, though Roy was bulkier. He could see a bit of their mother in Roy's features. A pained expression lay in his eyes—a terrible uncertainty.

"I...I've been searching for you," Kyle finally said. He grabbed his brother in an awkward embrace, breaking away to stare at his face. "I couldn't find you. I didn't know which county you lived in. Is Hagen your last name? I was using mom's last name to search for you."

"Hagen was on my birth record. I don't know where the name came from, maybe my father, though no one ever claimed me. I just went with it."

"It's so good to see you," Kyle said. "How did you find me?"

"I heard about what happened at Rose Hill. It was all over the news. I wanted to make sure you were okay. I knew Randy was your friend, and I put two and two together. You weren't too hard to look up. I called your house and your wife told me where I could find you. I wasn't sure you wanted to see me, but I was in the area and decided to come anyway."

"Of course, I wanted to see you," Kyle said. "And here you are. I can't believe it. Do you have time to go somewhere, where we can sit and talk? There's a diner right down the road."

"Sure. I'll follow you in my car."

They parked in the café lot, went inside, and were seated.

Kyle sat down at the table, across from Roy. He had rehearsed so many times what he wanted to say to his brother, but now the words were stuck. It was hard not to stare.

After they ordered coffee and burgers, they both sat in silence.

"It's a little awkward," Kyle confessed. "I haven't seen you since we were teenagers. There's so much I want to know. I don't even know where to begin."

"Same." Roy shrugged.

"I suppose you heard the details about Benny and Randy?" Kyle paused as Roy nodded, then took a sip of coffee.

"I heard some of it," Roy said, putting down his cup. "Benny Hampton is dead. Not a shock where Benny was concerned. Sure, he was an oddball, a degenerate. But Randy?" He shifted against the chair. "Never would've figured. I knew him when I lived at Rose Hill. He seemed all right. He was a goofball. I wouldn't have pegged him for the kind of guy that would try to kill his best friend and his wife." He met Kyle's gaze. "Sorry."

"He's also a suspect in Karen Walton's death," Kyle replied, swallowing the lump in his throat. "Benny was holding her death over Randy's head. They discovered her body at Rose Hill. I guess it will take some time to figure out how she died. Benny said Randy had murdered her, but Benny was the last one to see her alive. He admitted that he had a role in her death. I guess the cops will have to figure it out. Did you know Karen?"

"Just from afar. She was older than I was, so I didn't see her like the other guys did. She was just another lost soul in the crowd."

"So awful she died," Kyle said. "I'd hoped Randy was innocent. It's hard to fathom that he'd kill her. He liked her so much and thought she was pregnant with his child."

"True," Roy replied. "Benny would seem a more likely suspect. When Benny lived at Rose Hill, he took liberties. Everyone knew how he was, but no one stopped him. He enjoyed terrorizing kids and screwing the girls. But in front of other adults, especially his uncle, he was on his best behavior. But Doctor Goodman got wind of Benny's activities. She began asking questions and someone spilled the beans."

"It was me," Kyle admitted. "I told Pop. I had no idea at the time that Benny was his son. I was afraid of him, not just for me, but for you and the other kids. Pop seemed troubled, but he did the right thing and had Benny sent to another facility. Life got better after Benny was gone. I could breathe again."

"Same," Roy said. "There were others bullies that took his place, but none quite as bad."

"You were so little back then," Kyle said, his words sinking in. "Skinny. Look at you now. You got really big, bigger than me, and you're my little brother. I almost didn't recognize you."

"I filled out." Roy grinned. "I like to eat." He paused, shaking his head. "So how was life after your adoption?"

"Different," Kyle said. "It took time adjusting. I felt like everyone knew I was adopted and was judging me. I tried really hard to fit in, but I still held on to that piece of Rose Hill to remind myself that I wasn't really one of them." He picked up his spoon and stirred his coffee. "Pop stopped donating his time at Rose Hill. I never questioned why. Now it makes sense. Benny was no longer there. I guess he thought he was protecting me by hiding the truth."

"Probably," Roy replied. "Scott Hampton adored you."

"Roy," Kyle said, searching his face. "I know this might be difficult to talk about. But...you were so afraid of Benny. I know he tormented you, used scare tactics. Did he ever touch you?" He paused.

Roy's blank stare spoke volumes.

"I'm sorry," Kyle said, backtracking. "I shouldn't have said anything. Of course, you don't want to talk about it. I'm sorry."

"No, he didn't." Roy cleared his throat. "But the girls, well, I have my suspicions, and I saw a few things. Of course, I was just a child and it didn't quite make sense, but it's in the past. I deal with it the only way I know how. Besides, he's dead now."

Kyle paused. "One of Benny's victims was Doctor Goodman. Do you remember her?"

"Yes, and my memories are less than perfect. I don't know why anyone would put that woman in charge over children. Once during a session, I had talked back to her and she taped my mouth shut. I had to sit on a chair, staring out the window for over an hour. When she ripped the tape off of my mouth, my lips bled. I refused to speak to her after that."

Kyle thought for a moment. No wonder Goodman was targeted by Benny. The doctor was cruel, and she'd been the one to officially send him to another facility. She was also a large part of the Hampton's adoption process.

"Doctor Goodman is an old woman," Kyle said. "She took it tough from Benny."

"I suppose," Roy agreed. "It doesn't surprise me that she survived. She's too mean to die."

"She only cared about her dog," Kyle said. "I guess Randy was going to keep it. His girlfriend had no clue as to what was going on." He wrung out his hands, leaning back. "So where have you been living? Married? Kids?"

"I'm divorced. I have two five-year-old sons, Blake and Stevie. Twins. I live in Philadelphia, and work on a construction crew."

"Wow," Kyle said, smiling. Having similar employment opened the conversation, and the mood lightened. Work, the city, and family. For the most part, Roy lived a mundane life. Much like himself, Kyle realized.

"Where did you go after you left Rose Hill?"

"I was placed in a group home in Ardmore," Roy said. "I stayed there till I was eighteen and saved up some cash. I worked part-time at a deli, then moved to Philadelphia. I worked odd jobs and then was hired by a construction company, been there ever since. The rest you know."

Kyle toyed with his fries, pushing them around on his plate.

"I feel awful the way things ended between us," Kyle confessed. "Mom died. You were so pissed off at me. I should've tried to reconnect, insisted Pop let me visit you. I'm sorry. I was your brother, and I failed you."

"Not a big deal," Roy replied, clearing his throat. "Can't blame you for high-tailing it out of there. I learned to survive with the best of them. I grew up and so did you. Don't blame yourself."

"Did you ever wonder who fathered us?"

"Sure," Roy said. "I'd like to meet the scumbag."

"I wondered if he knew he had children or maybe we're half-brothers."

"I thought about it," Roy said. "We can get a DNA test and find out. I wouldn't mind doing a bit of research on his whereabouts."

"You'd be willing to do that?" Kyle asked.

"Sure."

"He had to have taken advantage of mom's mental state," Kyle said. "I need to know how I came to be, even if I don't like the results."

"I'm fine with finding out," Roy said. "Let's start with the test."

Kyle breathed a sigh of relief. "I was told you got into a lot of trouble." Kyle changed the subject. "Did some violent things."

"That's an exaggeration," Roy said. "Especially if you got the information from Randy. I'm bipolar. I was going through some crazy mood swings, but I'm okay now. Meds keep it under control."

"That's it?"

"Yes. Did you think it was something worse?"

"I just didn't know. I thought it could be because of me."

"Don't flatter yourself," Roy said. "I mean, I missed you, but I was angry all on my own. Who wouldn't be? It was frustrating to see the injustices that went on. To live in hell at times. Then other times, Rose Hill was the greatest place to live. There was some great staff. I had friends there, learned a few things. Played baseball, bowled. I have my share of good and bad memories. I just wish I could remember Mom."

"Same," Kyle said. "I wish I could've spent more time with her. I do have a few pictures. I can make copies for you."

"I'd appreciate that. I don't have any."

"Even though I was adopted, I still felt alone," Kyle said. "I wanted Pop to adopt you, but he said Florence could only handle one kid. It was hard for a while, but then I moved on. I put Rose Hill behind me, but I never forgot about you, Roy. I want you to know that. Now, here you are. I'm grateful we found each other. I've missed you."

"I could've come to see you." Roy shrugged. "I knew where you lived. But like you, I just put the past behind me and moved forward. I didn't know if I wanted to stir things up again. But then I needed to make sure you were all right, and I thought, well, okay. Here we go."

"Thanks," Kyle replied. "I hope you can meet my wife. My daughter. I want to stay in touch. Are you okay with that?"

"Yes, I'd like that."

"Great! I know Beth would love to meet you. Pop would like to see you. He said so. I mean, you're my biological brother. We could meet up another day and visit him."

"I suppose," Roy said. "Maybe in time. Let's just keep it between us for now."

The flicker of hurt that crossed Roy's eyes spoke volumes. Kyle hated his brother's pain. He had so much to make up for and intended to do just that. He hoped in time to discover more about Roy's life at the asylum, but it was too soon. Hopefully, they had time. They continued talking and another hour slipped away. Kyle's phone rang. He knew without looking it was Beth, wondering where he was. Some things would never change. But after all he'd been through, he barely cared.

"Well, I'd better get going," Roy said, wiping his mouth with a napkin. "I've got an hour ride home, and traffic is lousy into the city, no matter what time of day."

Disappointed that the visit was ending, Kyle asked for the check. "My treat," he said, taking the note to the register as Roy left the tip. They met in the foyer and went out to the parking lot.

"I want to give you my number." Roy said. "Beth gave me yours."

"I'll add it to my contacts," Kyle said. Exchanging the information, he punched in the digits, added Roy's name to the list. He turned to find Roy shrewdly assessing him.

"It was great seeing you." Kyle reached out, shaking Roy's hand. "I'm so glad we talked. I wish…I wish I could go back in time. I wouldn't have left you. I would've listened. I feel bad for pushing you away. You were just a little kid, and I let you down. I hope you know how sorry I am." Then he clutched his brother in a bear hug, squeezing tight. Emotion rolled over him. Regret. Love. All the wasted years. They had barely skimmed the past, and certainly not the future. Awkwardly, they broke apart. "Keep in touch. I want to get together again soon. We've got so much to catch up on."

"Sure." Roy pulled a small paper bag from his pocket and handed it to Kyle. "Here, I kept this for you. I'll see you soon, Kyle."

As his brother disappeared into the shadows, Kyle tucked the package under his arm and unlocked his truck door. His emotions were soaring. His brother was alive. Roy didn't hate him. They still had a chance. All felt right in the world.

Just as Kyle opened the truck door, someone familiar moved behind him. In a split second, fear gripped him, terror striking his heart. A hand fell heavily upon his shoulder, squeezed. A face slid against his jaw, cheek against cheek. A soft snicker followed.

"If you twitch, you'll get stitched."

Kyle's blood ran cold at the gravelly words. He turned around, gawking at his brother, who wore a lopsided grin. Roy winked, saluted, and spun around on his heels.

"Remember that crazy game?" Roy called over his shoulder, then laughed. He opened his car door. "I still have nightmares."

"So do I," Kyle said, voice quavering.

As Roy's car disappeared down the road, Kyle stood and stared at the empty highway. He pulled the packet from his arm, opened the bag, and pulled out his old baseball glove. On the palm, his etched name was faded, but still noticeable.

In the lamplight, its years of use stood out in bold clarity.

He stood beneath the light for a long, long time.

A word about the author...

With a passion for writing, award-winning Tamera Lawrence likes to entertain readers with edgy thrillers and mysteries. Tamera draws on personal experiences to bring to life interesting characters set in today's complex world.

Thank you for purchasing
this publication of The Wild Rose Press, Inc.

For questions or more information
contact us at
info@thewildrosepress.com.

The Wild Rose Press, Inc.
www.thewildrosepress.com